THE *Mary Luck* TALES

WITCH'S CURSE

KATHERINE HALE STRINGFIELD

Published by
Martin Sisters Publishing Company
www.martinsisterspublishing.com
Martin Sisters Publishing ©2023

ISBN: 978-1-62553-116-2

Young Adult
Printed in the United States of America
Martin Sisters Publishing

For my little sister,
Anna Lynn Hale
I'll love and miss you forever.

CONTENTS

Acknowledgements

There are so many people that I want to thank. It has been a long journey but with help from people like Terra Stone, Dana Clifton, Regina Henry and many many others I have a book. Many thanks to my husband, Jamey Stringfield who patiently sat through read throughs and gave me honest advice. To my daughter Maddey who gave me tips on what a teenager would do, think, and say you are and always will be my inspiration. Also, I would like to thank the staff and student body (2010-to present) of Madison Southern High School for being my muse, critic and biggest cheerleaders. And a special thank you to my parents, Robert and Kay Hale for always being there for me and for raising me right. I love all of you.

PROLOGUE

It's been many years since I first saw fit to lead the once proud people of the Old World to Eastern Kentucky. They had been humbled, beaten, and broken when they set sail for America. Shunned by their beliefs and religion to the point of death, they left behind the only life they'd ever known. When they first arrived, the land was full of virgin forests abounding with riches unimaginable. They had left behind the barren highlands that offered only craggy cliffs and blood-soaked battlefields. To them, the Scots, this was a utopia.

At one time, they were my chosen people. They knew the old ways. They celebrated the feasts that paid homage to the gods who had created them. They knew the importance of the elements: earth, air, fire, and water. But along the way, with each new generation, a little was lost, and soon, the influx of the Romans and Saxons changed the beliefs and traditions. When the new religion finally took hold, I searched for another group.

I found what I needed to survive in the natives of the new world. It wasn't a new world to them, for they had always been there. It was their land, and they worshiped it, and it always gave back to them. These tribes were pure of heart and knew that balance in the way of the world was paramount. That is, of course, until temptation arrived in the form of Europeans. My once proud and pure people soon lost their way when shown worldly goods such as weapons that could kill from a distance and ways of smoking tobacco and cooking with spices from faraway lands. They began to covet these things and had wars that killed their own to obtain them.

I sent warnings of disease and failed crops, but they had lost their way and no longer sought the spirits' advice. So, I once again cast my eye to the druids and celts of old that had been forlorn to the mountains in Appalachia. Maybe they would once again regain my affection. There was a particular bloodline that had never forgotten the old ways. They were from the highlands and had seen their kin burned at the stake for their ways considered sorcery. But they persisted in honoring the sacred days of the year, and for that reason, I once again beheld them as my chosen people.

Who am I, you may ask? I have gone by many names in the past, Gaia, the eye in the sky, but for the sake of this story, let's call me Mother Nature, for I and I alone command the elements. I am the wind in your hair, the ground you walk on, the water within you, and the fire that warms you. Come along with me, and I'll tell you a story about a girl and her town and see if she will indeed be the savior or destroyer. Just know that there will be balance. When the scale tips too much, one way or the other. There will be a reckoning.

INTRODUCTION

Welcome to Mary Luck

Mary Luck, KY
June 1984

Ruby Lee Collins, newly turned thirteen, has long curly auburn hair. She's of average height and build, but nothing else about her is average. Her toned pale legs pump the pedals of her ten-speed bicycle as she swerves around mud holes and rocks that make up the road out of Shotgun Hollow. The heavenly-smelling honeysuckle wind around the hated kudzu that has taken over the side of her Papaw's hill.

Ruby Lee picks up speed as the road flattens just before the railroad tracks. She slows down to look both ways for a train, even though her acute hearing has told her there isn't one. But old habits die hard for a girl who has lived by the tracks her whole life.

Once on the paved road, she can let the bike coast and take a well-earned break. Since she has been cooped up for so long and hasn't even started on her tan, she takes a detour and rides through Crawdad Bottom. It was the first place she could ride her bike by herself, so she knew everyone, and if they were outside, they gave her a wave or nod.

The first house on the corner is a small five-room brick house, the most excellent house on the street by far. Beatrice Wells lives there alone, having been widowed for fifteen years now, her children gone and married with their own kids. Beatrice, or "Beechie" as she is better known, is famous for having the latest gossip.

Her house is the first one on the straight stretch after you cross the bridge into Mary Luck. If an ambulance goes through town, she's on the phone or, as Ruby's dad would call it, "the horn" before it reaches the Goble Curve. The first call goes to Kate Collins, Ruby Lee's mother, because Richard Collins, her daddy, is in the Rescue Squad and the volunteer fire department. It's well-known that if anything happens, Kate Collins knows what it is or can find out. Beechie isn't outside today, so she's probably inside, sitting by her window unit air conditioner, watching her story.

On up the lane, the houses look more neglected. Not to say these are bad people; they are just the less fortunate because of circumstances beyond their control. Things like mine closings, getting hurt at the mine, or Black Lung Disease caused by breathing too much coal dust. So the coal mines are the cause. It comes with the territory if you're born in the hills of Eastern Kentucky. There's the coal mine, moonshine, or moving down the line. Which is what most people choose to do.

They move somewhere north, like Michigan or Ohio, and work in a factory. These folks like to visit in the summer and bring their snotty kids who snub their noses at kids like Ruby Lee. However, time and again, these city kids end up loving Mary Luck and beg their parents to stay longer. That's what happened to Whitney Burkett and the Baldridge twins. But more about them later. Let's catch up with Ruby Lee before she leaves us eating her dust.

As Ruby Lee coasts by Mrs. Purdy's house, she's careful not to even glance at the front porch, where sitting in the sagging swing is the one and only behemoth herself. Having birthed eleven children, I suppose she has earned her massive girth.

The porch is rotted and sagging and has a clematis vine climbing the trellis on the side of the house while wind chimes made of pop cans rattle in the breeze. The shade from a weeping willow tree makes the derelict porch ominous. Factor in who the owner is, and you've got the makings of a storybook witch's house. This isn't far from the truth, either. It is said that Mrs. Purdy was the direct descendant of the notorious witch Baby Annie, who had lived in the deepest, darkest reaches of Rattlesnake Hollow in the late 1800s. Mrs. Purdy was said to read tea leaves and tarot cards and make tables walk at seances. Though Ruby Lee barely glances in her direction, Mrs. Purdy sees her, like calls to like.

Down the lane on the corner is an old rusted basketball hoop with no net that hangs from a light pole, dangling like a child's first loose tooth. Some mean ball games are played in the evenings when the weather is good. Now and then, they'll let a girl play. Ruby's big sister, Rosie, usually is one of those lucky few. She could shoot better than most of the boys, so that's probably why they don't let her play very often. They don't want to be shown up by a girl. No one is out today; it's way too hot. The weatherman said it could reach ninety degrees only in mid-June.

Moving on and picking up speed, Ruby Lee takes her hands off the handlebars, sits up straight, and lets her body create the balance needed to ride hands-free. She has only ridden this way for the past few months, so she does it now to ensure she hasn't forgotten how during her sickness. She quickly slips back into the stride and lets her body guide the way.

The small mining community of Mary Luck comes into view as she rounds the bend. It isn't much to look at these days, but at one time, around 1920, this was a bustling mining camp complete with a school, two company stores, and even a movie house. But by 1984, much of the town had gone to ruin. Take the 100 shotgun row houses that make up the streets of Mary Luck. About half of them are falling apart.

The first thing Ruby does is slam on her brakes and cause a skid mark in the gravel of the parking lot of Birdie's Grocery and Diner, locally known as The Nest. This draws a grimace from Shiny, leaning against the cinder block wall of Birdie's smoking a pipe. He fans away the dust with his free hand and mutters something like "Stupid heathen…." Ruby Lee pays him no mind. Seeing how he's the town drunk, nobody cares what he thinks or says. He's the equivalent of the local cur chased by kids on shows like "The Little Rascals."

Once inside The Nest, Ruby Lee makes a beeline to the back area designated for the "young'uns" to hang out to see if any new arcade games have arrived. Lucky for her, Space Invaders had been replaced by Galaga, her favorite. Ms. Pac-Man was still there and, of course, the Kiss Pinball machine.

That one would never go away. It was the favorite of Birdie's son Butchie who had been killed in a car wreck a few years back. Although Birdie had two more boys, Butchie had been her favorite. Some say that's what drove her to drink. She had her first bourbon the day Butchie died and every day after.

Everyone knows she keeps a flask under the counter, but if you're wise, you'll keep your opinions to yourself. You do not want to be on Birdie Daniel's bad side. She may be getting a little long in the tooth, but she's built like a Mac truck. There once was a rumor that she used to mud wrestle at a bar in Pike County. If truth be told, she beat their long-standing champ and used the prize money to build the luncheon counter. That's why no one has ever tried to rob the grocery or get out of line. Birdie won't stand for any foolishness.

When Ruby Lee gets to the checkout counter with her can of Pepsi and a Reese's Peanut Butter Cup, Birdie asks how she's feeling and if she has any pox scars. Ruby Lee shows her the still-healing sore on her shoulder and says she's feeling much better. Birdie tells her she has missed her, and that's the truth. Birdie enjoyed her talks with Ruby Lee.

The kid loved to hear stories about Mary Luck, and Birdie liked to reminisce. But some things were better left unsaid, like the ghost stories which Ruby Lee begged her to tell. However, today was a beautiful sunny summer day, and those dark thoughts were way back in the shadows of Birdie's mind.

Back on her bike, she heads to the park where her best friends Vera and Willie Joe are waiting. The park is almost brand new. The townspeople raised money and received grants to build it a few years ago. Before that, the kids had fashioned a makeshift baseball diamond out of scavenged junk.

Now, there is a regulation field complete with bleachers for fans. There is also a basketball court, a tennis court, and a track that circles the park. And, of course, there is a swing set, merry-go-round, and teeter-totters.

Ruby Lee parks her bike in the new bike rack and heads to the swings, where her friends anxiously await her. Vera hops off the swing and runs over to give her a hug.

Vera is a slight sort of frail girl, all knees and elbows, which all have a scab or bruise from riding her new skateboard. She has straight, light brown hair and brown eyes. Vera isn't the social butterfly that Ruby Lee is and doesn't have many friends. But she is fiercely loyal to those who know her, like Ruby and Willie.

Willie Joe, on the other hand, is the male counterpart to Ruby Lee. Intelligent, athletic, and the most popular boy in town. All the girls are in love with him. He has an athletic build and is tall for his age, nearly 5' 6", with wavy dark blonde hair with highlights from the sun. He already has a golden tan he will keep until October from mowing lawns. However, his most striking feature is his sparkling blue eyes. They are cerulean, and one can hardly tear away from them once he has caught your eye.

So, of course, Vera is in love with him. Ruby Lee, whom he secretly loves, constantly makes fun of him and calls him out on his bull crap whenever she can. Willie Joe responds with a punch to the shoulder, an Indian burn, or a frog to the forearm. Love licks, to be sure. But at age thirteen, those hints are lost on both of them.

Once the three friends have caught up, they walk to the school lunchroom. Mary Luck Grade School is a ten-room red brick building built in 1907 by the North East Coal Company when the town was established. There are eight classrooms, a library, and a principal's office. The floors are wooden and reek of the oil that they treat the wood with yearly. Everything in the school seems ancient to the kids of the 80s. All the books in the library are classics, so don't even think about looking for a Judy Blume or a Sweet Valley High book.

The gym and lunchroom were built around the same time as the school, so they also seem ancient. Until three years ago, the scoreboard had to be hand rolled to keep score. The PTA's endless bake sales and car washes purchased the new electric one.

Just like everything else in the mountains, if you wanted something, you had to work for it. Mary Luck is a forgotten place. One that people know is there but choose to ignore. There are dark secrets in the hollows and skeletons in nearly every closet.

Even though school is out, lunch is still served from noon to two o'clock, Monday through Friday, and it's free thanks to a government program.

Willie Joe races to the rusted lunchroom screen door and yanks it wide open, causing it to bang on the side of the wall, nearly ripping it off the hinges. He jumps in the front door and faces Edith Ward, the terror of the lunchroom.

Her hair net is pulled down on her broad forehead, creating a widow's peak. Her sweaty face and heaving chest stop Willie Joe in his tracks. In her right hand is the enormous greasy spoon she uses to pound the table and restore order whenever necessary, usually about a hundred times a day.

Willie Joe shrinks from her sneering face and immediately tries to apologize, but Edith doesn't have it. She points at Willie Joe with the greasy spoon and threatens to wear him out with it the next time he slams the screen door. After a full minute of glaring at all three kids, she tells them to get their grub. It's Friday, pizza and corn day; everyone's favorite.

The lunchroom is a square room with six fold-out tables lined up in a row. The stench of Clorox bleach permeates the air underneath the aroma of pizza. If Edith feels generous, she may fire up the popcorn machine and treat the kids. If Willie Joe hasn't put her in a mood.

Willie, Ruby, and Vera grab a plastic tray and get in line. The lunchroom is crowded today since it's pizza day. The kids from Miner Hollow are all here, eating what is probably their only meal for the day. Edith, as hard-hearted as she seems sometimes, always packs up all the leftovers for the holler kids to take home for the weekend. That's one of the best things about being from the mountains. They take care of their own. There are no starving children in Mary Luck, and never will be.

Willie Joe scarfs down his pizza in three bites and eyes Vera's plate that she's nibbling on. After a few torturous minutes, she slides her tray over to him, and he inhales the rest of her food, scooping up every last kernel of corn with his pizza crust. He chugs his chocolate milk, crumples up the paper carton, and shoots it in the garbage can, earning him another glare from Edith.

He takes a bow and glances at his adoring gaggle of fifth graders. Like most boys in Kentucky, he dreams of playing for the UK Wildcats someday. So, any opportunity to show off his skills to adoring fans, he always puts on a show. He has on his favorite UK t-shirt with his name on the back with the number four, the number of his idol, Kyle Macy.

Ruby Lee rolls her eyes at his antics and tells him to "give it up"! On the other hand, Vera gives him her brightest smile, gleaming with braces and rubber bands. They head to the park and find a shady area to relax and let their food settle while deciding what they want to do the rest of the day.

Let's leave them there for now and continue our tour through Mary Luck, where time stands firmly still in the 1920s. It's worth mentioning that there are two churches in Mary Luck: The Freewill Baptist Church and The First United Methodist Church. Which one you belong to isn't of much concern. What is essential, though, is that you go to one or the other.

Most residents go to the Baptist Church. It has had additions over the years, and they recently installed a baptistry so that they no longer have to baptize newly saved sinners in The Big Sandy River. If the weather was too cold, they had to wait till Spring, and sometimes those newly-saved sinners backslide before completing the process of being born again and washed in the blood of Jesus.

Brother Burkett had lost quite a few would-be parishioners that way. He believed you had to "dunk 'em fast before the devil could slip back in." Also, they have the only vacation bible school in town, a favorite of all the kids.

Once a month, they have a potluck dinner after church. Nothing like the food good Christian women from the mountains can produce. Edith's chicken and dumplings alone will make your knees buckle. Not to mention her cat-head biscuits.

As we leave the park behind, the shotgun row houses built by the coal company back in the '20s emerge from the scenery. They make up six blocks with an alley between the places that abut each other.

Main Street, or Front Street, as it is better known, abuts The Big Sandy River, while Mary Luck Avenue, or Back Street, better known, abuts the railroad tracks. The paved road circumnavigates all six blocks while three side roads divide them. The third block contains the post office/old company store, which is now used as a historical society.

The house that used to be a small hotel and saloon back when river travel was standard sits abandoned and forlorn. An eyesore for sure, with its glory days firmly behind it, *The Mary Luck Grand* now serves as the local "Haunted House." Complete with peeling paint, shutters that dangle askew, broken windows, and a porch that is warped from years of neglect. The structure seems to shrink further from the road than the row houses. If you know when to turn your head as you go by - which most folks do even though they are barely aware they are doing it- it's almost as if it isn't there, like a flicker in your peripheral vision.

On down the block, you have the "Other" store. Ally-Fair Wells owns and runs this store, considered by Birdie Daniels as her competition. This couldn't be further from the truth. Wells' Grocery and Sundries is little more than a defunct two-pump gas station.

This is a Northeast Coal Company leftover. Once upon a time, it served as a filling station for the company bigwigs to gas up their Tin Lizzies. Nowadays, it sells candy, cigarettes, and, if you know who to ask, beer and 'shine out the back door on Sundays. Compliments of Ally's cousin, Lester Wells.

Ally-Fair inherited the store from her daddy after he "went to be with the Lord" in the '60s. Ally, who once was fair, has shriveled to nothing because of a broken heart. Her one true love, Jessup "Jessie" McCoy, went MIA in the French countryside during WWII. The two were to be wed when he came home, but that day never came.

Without a body to prove he was dead, Ally-Fair never gave up hope that one day he would return. After a few years, the McCoys had Jessie declared legally dead, had a memorial service, and buried an empty coffin, but Ally would never accept that.

More than a few men pursued her, but she refused them all. She settled into her spinsterhood by age twenty-three and still wears the diamond chip promise ring given to her by her sweetheart. She has become the local "Miss Havisham" from *Great Expectations*. Wearing her loneliness as Miss Havisham wore her decaying wedding dress to show the world that her love hadn't faded and that she was still in mourning for her lost love.

As she is known around town, Miss Ally sits behind the counter reading The TV Guide and nibbling on a pack of Nabs. Her once chestnut brown hair, now gone almost entirely white, is twisted up in a severe bun that lets not even the smallest tendril escape. With her tortoiseshell reading glasses perched on the end of her shapely nose, she has an owlish look about her.

But try as she may to hide her beauty, it still shines through in her light green eyes, rimmed with dark sooty lashes. It has been whispered for years that it is almost a sin that such beauty be wasted on someone who doesn't appreciate what the Lord has given her.

Across the street from the grocery is the town post office. The building was originally the movie theater erected by the coal company in the '20s. So did the town when the mines dried up in the early '40s. The coal company left and took the funds to run the theater and all the other modern conveniences the miners had grown accustomed to, such as the adjoining soda shop, swimming pool, and catalog store. Without money to operate those vices of entertainment, the buildings sat empty and slowly rotted.

After WWII, when the country was again viable, the town repaired itself by converting the theater into the Post Office. Today, only the bottom front room of the two-story building is used. The other rooms are piled with old furniture, records, and files from the mining offices.

Edgar Wilcox's wife Patsy is the Post Mistress and has keys to the building; once a week, when Patsy is at her prayer meeting at Lucy McKenzie's house, Edgar and his cronies, AKA. The Yarn Spinners get together and tell tales. Some are made up, but some are based on facts.

The Yarn Spinners have lived in Mary Luck their whole lives and pride themselves on knowing everything that has ever happened in their town. However, unbeknownst to them, they have three spies in their midst.

In the early winter this year, our favorite Trio was riding their bikes in the alley when Vera's bike threw its chain. Never one to pass up an opportunity to play the hero, Willie Joe promptly jumped off his bike and propped Vera's bike upside down to put the chain back on.

Vera is thrilled to see Willie Joe come to her aid and sees this as a sign that he likes her. Willie, however, is trying to impress Ruby Lee with his mechanical abilities, which he fails at miserably. Ruby Lee, the son her daddy never had, pushes Willie aside and slips the chain back on. His face reddens with embarrassment, but he is in awe of her. Is there nothing this girl isn't great at?

While the chain is being replaced by Ruby Lee, Vera loses interest. She wanders over to the post office and peers into the back window, where the glow of a pot-bellied stove lights the faces of the old men. The window is open, and she hears the conversation going on inside. This isn't the usual tall tales the old men usually tell; this is serious and a little scary.

She motions the other two over and places her index finger over her lips, shushing them. They hunker down and join Vera under the window.

There are five men gathered around the stove, sitting on cane-backed chairs. Wilson McKenzie, Ruby Lee's Pappaw, Delano Slone, Matthew Honeycutt, Vera's uncle, Edgar Wilcox, and Claude Wells,

Willie Joe's Pappaw. All the kids in town know these men because of the tales they tell most evenings at the park just before dark. Those stories used to give the kids nightmares when they were little, but now they are a joke.

But tonight is something different. It seems to be serious, maybe even genuine. The men sound older and wiser. No chuckles or winking eyes going on now. The Trio is enthralled, barely noticing when the streetlight comes on. The buzz of the sodium arc kicks into high gear, the universal cue for all kids to head inside. But the lure of the story being told is worth the lecture they will all surely get for being out after dark.

The decision to leave is taken out of their hands by the sudden sneezing attack that afflicts Vera since she's allergic to everything. She tries hard to stifle the sound, but in her haste to escape, she kicks a glass bottle that shatters on the road. The talking inside stops, and the kids dash to their bikes and take off down the alley.

When out of earshot, they all look at each other with wide eyes and start talking simultaneously.

"What was that story?"

"Who were they talking about?"

"Do you think it was a true story?"

"I bet they meet there every Thursday." Ruby Lee says.

"Why do you think that?" asks Vera.

"Because tonight is Mammaw's weekly prayer meeting, and Pappaw was there. I wondered where he went while Mammaw had all her friends at the house. Guess now I know." Ruby stated.

"We should come back next week and sneak inside to hear better." Plotted Willie Joe.

"How are we supposed to get in, genius?" asked Ruby Lee

"We can get in; the door is unlocked until eight so people can get their mail. We can go upstairs and sit in the loft. The area over the back is open, and we will just have to be quiet and stay hidden." Vera says with a smug look.

Willie Joe beams at her and gives her a high five.

Ruby Lee seems to mull this plan over and then asks, "What are we gonna tell our parents?"

"That's easy," says Willie Joe

"Vera, tell your folks you're studying at Ruby's house and Ruby, you say you're at Vera's, and I'll say I have basketball practice or something, no big deal."

And so, on the last Thursday of every month after that, our Trio began eavesdropping on the town elders to hear stories about things that happened before they were born. The first story they heard was from Ruby Lee's Pappaw. They had listened to a very watered-down version of the story years before called "The Green Lady." In that version, a lady hit by a train was decapitated and walked around on foggy nights looking for her head. That had scared them when they were eight, but now it was just something to joke about, like Snipe hunting.

The next day at school, The Trio were dying to ask their teacher about the story they heard bits and pieces of the night before. Mr. Music was born and raised in Mary Luck, as was the aficionado on everything about their town. He told his students stories about his childhood and what it was like to grow up during the 1940s. He remembers what it was like before TV was invented. This fact was mind-blowing to the kids of the 80s.

Ruby could usually get Mr. Music talking, and he'd spend hours telling tales. Mary Luck Grade School only had eight rooms, so there was only one teacher per grade. So, no changing classes or having a locker. These kids stored their things in the 'cloakroom,' so they had little to nothing in common with the kids they saw on

TV shows like *Growing Pains* and *Who's the Boss.* He showed them how to make a Window Rattler from an old wooden thread spool on Halloween. His stories were the best.

By the following Thursday's meeting, the Trio had devised their plan, and everything went off without a hitch. It was very fortuitous how they happened upon this group of men. Almost like the hand of fate was involved. The knowledge they were about to glean from these yarns spun by the town elders would prove invaluable in the coming months.

PART ONE

THE FIRST TALE

The Green Lady

January 1984

When Ruby's Pappaw, Wilson McKenzie, started to talk that Thursday night, his voice took on a note of seriousness they had rarely heard before.

As the old men filed into the storeroom, the eavesdroppers inched closer to the loft's edge. Their excitement was palpable. They waited with bated breath as the yarn spinners sat in cane-backed chairs facing the roaring pot-bellied stove. With no prompting, Wilson McKenzie spat tobacco juice in the old coffee can and began his tale.

"Happened back in '33. I worked at the train depot when the poor wretch came in that terrible night. She was great with children but looked half-starved to death. Her cheeks were hollowed, and she had dark circles under her eyes. Even her hair looked hungry, all limp and dull. A woman in her condition should've been glowing with health, but she was anything but."

"She shuffled into the station with a thread-bare carpet bag that looked like it was from another century. Her coat was patched and too light for the frosty night. She wore no gloves, and her hands were red and chafed. A wool scarf was tied around her head as she didn't have a hat. She sat on the wooden bench, and I saw that both her shoes had holes in the bottom. She and I were the only ones at the station that evening. The other passengers had walked over to the Company store to get a bite to eat or just stretch their legs."

"There was a layover while we waited for the exchange train to take the passengers to Ashland. We talked a bit. Said she was a widow on her way to stay with family until the babe was born. Said she used all her money to buy the ticket, even sold her wedding ring."

"I knew she had to be starved, so I convinced her to let me buy her dinner. I called the store, had Birdie fix her something, and put it on my tab. I'll never forgive myself for that. They say, 'no good deed goes unpunished,' and that has never been truer."

"I watched her leave, following the directions I gave her. That was the last time I saw her alive." Wilson paused, dabbed his eyes, and honked his nose in his linen hankie. Ruby Lee had never seen this act of compassion in her Pap. It was shocking and unsettling to her and the others. They sat there in the dark, silent and somber. Having collected himself, Pap continued his story.

"I heard it from Birdie later that the poor woman gobbled up the two hamburgers and fried taters as if she hadn't eaten in months. Said she was drooling by the time the food was ready. She repeatedly thanked Birdie for the food and the extra she packed up. She gathered her stuff when the train horn blew and left the store."

"I can only guess what happened next, seeing as there were no witnesses, but I think this is as close to the truth as anyone can get. There were two tracks back in those days, one for the holding train and one for the passing train. The rails were controlled by a switch that moved them to allow for passing. The poor lady was walking along the tracks when the switch changed and caused her foot to become trapped between the rails."

"I can't imagine the horror of being trapped while a locomotive was bearing down on me. Burt Lemasters, the engineer on the train, said he didn't see her until he was right up on her. It looked like she was hunched over, trying to protect her unborn child. Burt never drove another train after that night and said he could never get her face out of his mind. The sheer look of terror. He jerked the brake, for all it was worth, and tried to stop, but it was a wasted effort. By the time the train reached the depot, it was over. Everyone from the store heard the train's screech and the dying woman's screams."

"There were better than twenty people on the tracks that night. Old Doc Morgan used a butcher's knife to cut out the baby and save it, but it had been too long. The poor thing was blue when he got him out. As for the lady trying to save the baby, she got her head sliced clean off. They's a heavy fog that night; we looked 'till dawn; it wasn't until late the next evening that we found her head. An animal had got at it before we did. Both eyes and part of the jaw had been eaten, and what meat was left had turned green. Worst sight you ever did see. It ain't never left my memory as much as I wish it would."

"We never did find out who she was. I didn't think to ask her name, so I put a call into Ashland in case her folks came looking for her. No one ever did. I wondered if she would meet a man and was ashamed to say so, seeing as she wasn't married. I guess we will never know. We all pitched in, had her a funeral, and buried her and the babe in my family cemetery. We marked the grave with a wooden cross and put the name Mrs. Greene on it."

With little comment, the story ended on a very somber note. The eavesdroppers waited till the men left before barely breathing. They were all in shock. How did something like that happen and not be common knowledge? Finally, hearing a story told the way it was intended changed them. All three matured in the thirty minutes it took to listen to a horrific story. Let no one ever say there isn't power in the spoken word.

The kids headed out to their bikes, each lost in their thoughts.

"So, we meet back here next time?" asked Willie Joe

"You better believe it! I can't wait to hear what else has happened that we don't know about." Ruby Lee said excitedly.

"Sounds good to me," Vera added.

The girls headed back to their houses right across the tracks from each other, and Willie Joe headed to his house down in River Side Addition. "Be careful y'all," he shouted before singing Duran Duran's "The Reflex" as he rode away in the moonlight. The girls snickered at his off-tune singing and started home.

They weren't used to being out this late, so they pedaled a little faster than usual; the railroad tracks followed them the whole way. With the story fresh in their minds, the once familiar setting now took on an ominous feeling. Nearly eight o'clock and right on time, the train could be heard miles away, echoing off the mountains. The trill of steel wheels rolling on rails and the first of three horn blasts, once a comforting sound, became dark and scary. A harbinger of what was to come.

When Vera reached her driveway, she paused by the streetlight to take up her post. Ruby still had to go down the lane and across the tracks into Shotgun Hollow by herself, so Vera held vigil till she saw Ruby Lee flash the front porch light off and on. Vera shivered while she waited. The wind blew and whistled as it went through the trees. Snow was coming. She could smell it in the air. Thoughts of sleigh riding and bonfires went through her mind, and then, for no reason at all, she became frightened. As if the wind had reached down her back and traced an icy finger along her spine.

Ruby Lee's House

Ruby Lee Collins flicks the light switch on and off three times to signal Vera that she has made it home safe and sound. Ruby, the middle child of the three Collins daughters, learned the hard way that if she were to get any attention at all, she must excel at everything she does. Lucky for her, she is bright, athletic, and has an irresistible personality.

She is usually the family entertainment when the power has gone out, or the TV antenna gets blown down by a storm. When that happens, it takes most of the menfolk from the 'holler' to make the trek to the top of the mountain to fix the blasted antenna. Though cable is now available in the mountains, the days when there were only three channels and PBS isn't that far behind them.

Those days, Ruby Lee would do her skits borrowed from The Carol Burnett Show. These would leave her mom and sisters rolling with laughter. She secretly looked forward to the nights when the TV was out so she could show off her skills. Sometimes she would showcase her singing abilities by performing song after song from *Annie* or *Grease*.

Ruby Lee idolizes her big sister Rosie. She is fifteen and in high school. Therefore the role model Ruby Lee looks up to. She is Ruby's protector, mentor, and antagonist. For example, they loved to watch wrestling on Saturday evenings on TBS, one of the best things getting cable brought to their world. Tommy 'Wildfire' Rich was their favorite. So Rosie, acting as a coach, had Ruby Lee wrestle the only other person in the holler that was her age, Johnny Ray Thompson.

That poor kid got his butt whipped every time, too. Ruby Lee almost choked him out with the sleeper hold she had mastered. After Johnny Lee had had enough or his momma came down and called for him, Rosie would take the swings off the swing set and have Ruby practice gymnastics so she could be the next Mary Lou Retton.

That Ruby Lee hadn't broken her neck yet was a miracle. From back handsprings off the picnic table to flips off the swing set, there wasn't much Ruby Lee was afraid to try at her sister's goading.

The youngest Collins' sister is Ruthie Jean. A sickly child that suffers from asthma and is allergic to almost everything. She is the pet of Rosie and Ruby and therefore is protected by them. She gets to have her own room at the Collins' household, a three-bedroom, 2 1/2 bath ranch with an upstairs, because of her constant sickness that included bouts of whooping cough, bronchitis, and sneezing fits.

At least, that was Rosie's excuse for giving up her room. Truth be known, it was because she was scared to sleep in her room alone after watching 'Salem's Lot. That movie scared the crap out of both Ruby and Rosie. They had nightmares for months after watching it. The scene with the kid vampire scratching on the window, asking to be let in, is something that never left her mind. That there is a graveyard behind her house didn't help either.

The family patriarch is Richard Collins. 6 '4 "with broad shoulders makes him a force to be reckoned with and, with three daughters, he had to be. No boy was gonna mess with his daughters.

Richard has strawberry red hair, which earned him the nickname "Big Red" because of his stature and booming voice. He works as a train engineer for the railroad. He sometimes gets to come through Mary Luck, and when he does, he lays on the horn from one end of town to the other so that his girls know it's him.

Kate Collins is the family matriarch. Do not make a mistake and think she's meek and mild because of her small stature; she's a fireball. Mrs. Collins is a stay-at-home mom but has a mini beauty shop made by closing in the carport. She cuts hair, gives perms, and colors hair. This is just in her spare time, though. Her girls always come first. She has a homemade supper on the table by five o'clock Monday through Friday.

As Richard walks in, the tv is turned off, and everyone sits down to eat. Usually, one extra kid is at the table, but no one is ever denied a meal at the Collins' home. Kate is in the PTA, co-sponsor of the cheerleading team, and a member of the Community Development League and the historical society. The Collins family is part of the backbone that supports Mary Luck. Like in most small towns, the people that make up the community keep it running.

But, with all this goodness and Mayberry-esc feeling I've painted for you, there is assuredly a dark side. With good, there is always wrong; you must have both so that there is a balance in life. Too much of one or the other, and the natural order of life is thrown off-kilter.

That's what is happening in Mary Luck in 1984. A darkness is falling, and though she doesn't know it yet, Ruby Lee is about to set in motion a turn of events that will bring to life long-dead secrets and a curse that has waited one hundred years to be exacted.

Snow Storm

February 1984

Snow began to fall on February 1, 1984, and didn't stop for two days. By the end of the storm, there were twenty-eight inches of snow with some drifts as much as six feet. School was canceled for the foreseeable future, and the kids were all elated to have fun-filled days of sleigh riding and bonfires. Most adults who still had to go to work put chains on their tires and used their four-wheel drive if they were lucky enough to have it.

This storm was a doozy, though. There was a lot of snow, and the temperature was negative ten degrees. This meant that some people were going to freeze to death. The town decided years ago that when the weather got that bad, they would allow some less fortunate families to come to the school and stay until the weather improved.

The fire department went around town and checked on the elderly. There were still people who lived in the shacks in the holler that didn't have electricity. If the people wouldn't leave, they'd give them blankets, wood for a fire, and food to see them through. Just another way that the people of Mary Luck cared for their own. At the school, cots and pallets were made up in the classrooms. Edith would cook chili and soups for anyone needing a hot meal. Someone would usually bring a guitar or banjo, and Pickin' and Grinnin' would follow.

It had warmed up a bit before it started snowing, so the first precipitation fell as freezing rain. Two inches of ice covered everything, and soon, all the power lines were down, and trees crossed nearly every road. Without electricity, there were a lot more people at risk of freezing. The school was heated by a coal-fed boiler, so everyone who relied on electricity for their heat had to come and stay at the school. This included Ruby, Willie, and Vera's families. Every chainsaw and lantern in town was put to use. Edith and most of the women in town gathered together all the food they had to make a big kettle of vegetable beef soup cooked over an open fire.

The kids in town took to the hills to go sleigh riding. Junior Wells donated an inner tube from one of his coal trucks, and it was inflated to an enormous size, big enough to hold ten kids. A bonfire was started, and when night fell, even some parents joined in, and a jar of moonshine was passed around amongst them to keep warm. Miraculously, no one got out of line; only one scuffle between two brothers, Timmy, and Donnie Slone, fighting over whose turn it was to pack the sled back up the hill.

Ruby, Willie, and Vera had taken a break from sledding and sat close to the fire, each lost in thought as their eyes watched the dancing flames. Ruby seemed transfixed and thought she saw a face in the embers. It was fleeting, but she saw it. There was a full moon that night, and with all the snow, even at midnight, it was as light out as dusk. She went for a walk and looked at the trees laden with snow. Heavy wet snow was her favorite kind because it morphed the trees, making the familiar scenery into an alien landscape. Surrounded by the weight of the snow on trees, it felt like she was inside a soundproof room. The voices below sounded muffled and flat.

Ruby saw a flash of movement from the corner of her eye and heard a rustle of branches. She walked on in search of the source, thinking it was probably a rabbit or squirrel. This far away, the snow was unmarred by footprints or sled tracks. She enjoyed being the first steps on the virgin snow, almost like walking on the moon.

She thought about lying down and making a snow angel, but then she saw her. A little girl in a red coat. She called to her, but she darted behind a tree. Ruby didn't recognize her even though she looked about ten years old. The only thing that proved that she had been there was the tree branch bobbing up and down where the girl's coat had brushed against it.

When Ruby got to the spot she had seen her, she was nowhere to be found. Feeling puzzled, she wondered where she could've gone since there wasn't anywhere else to go except uphill. Suddenly, for no reason at all, Ruby got spooked. All at once, she felt too alone. She could no longer hear the shouts of the kids down below.

That's when she noticed hers were the only footprints in the snow. The girl's prints should've been there but weren't. Ruby turned on her heel and ran as fast as she could. The comfort she had felt surrounded by the snow-laden trees only moments before now seemed smothering.

Ruby thought she was going the wrong way for a second because the trees seemed to go on forever like a hall of mirrors. She looked down, kept her eyes on her footprints, and ran toward the voices and the fire in the distance. By the time Ruby reached her friends, she was out of breath. Vera caught her as she went to her knees.

"What's wrong, Ruby Lee?" Vera asked with concern in her voice.

"I don't know. I got spooked. I thought I saw a little girl, but when I went to look for her, she wasn't there." Ruby stated, feeling a little silly for being scared. "It was probably somebody's cousin or something 'cause I didn't know her."

"Well, you looked like you'd seen a ghost," said Vera

"Maybe I did," Ruby stated matter-of-factly.

That night at the school, Ruby woke up and went into the hallway to get water from the fountain. When she came back in, she saw someone at the window. It was the girl in the red coat. She raised her hand and waved, and Ruby waved back. She really didn't overthink about it being half asleep. But suddenly, she sat up straight. She trembled all over. How was that girl outside waving to her? They were on the second floor!

Scared stiff, Ruby lay back down and snuggled up to Vera. She didn't find sleep again till dawn. In the light of day, she convinced herself that she had just imagined seeing the girl or she was dreaming. There was no way the girl could've been outside the window. Unless she was a ghost.

THE SECOND TALE

The Drowning of Rebecca Jo Wells

It was a windy, wintry day. The trio were snug in their hiding spot and grateful that heat rose from the pot-bellied stove.

Ruby had had a dream the night before about being in a dark and desolate cemetery that wasn't hers. The only thing Ruby could see amidst the darkness was a faint glow from the sliver of the moon. It shined down on a tombstone that read "Baby Annie."

Ruby awoke with a jolt of adrenaline straight into her heart, making her gasp for air. There were goosebumps all over her body. She laid back down, shaking, and pulled her covers over her head. She couldn't figure out why she would dream about Baby Annie. Sure, she was the local boogeyman, but Ruby didn't believe in witches.

After our trio heard the true story of the Green Lady, they were chomping at the bit to listen to more. So, snuggled out of sight, the kids got ready to hear another tale, and The Yarn Spinners did not disappoint.

Tonight's tale is from Claude Wells, Willie Joe's Papaw. He's reticent tonight, melancholy in his mannerisms. His gnarled hands slowly whittle a cedar piece. He isn't making anything out of it; he likes the feel of his Case knife as it shaves the wood into curly shavings that pile by his feet.

When he finally speaks, the other men stop talking and take their seats, always in the same order.

"I'm going to talk about Rebecca Jo tonight. There are things no one knows about that awful day. I know I have never talked to any of you about it, even though we were all friends then like we are now."

"The death of my sister tore my family to pieces. My mother was suicidal, my father wouldn't eat, and I was guilty. If only I hadn't left her, she would still be here. That's a burden I've been carrying since '37.

I was just fifteen, and, like the rest of our pals, I loved to play in the snow. I had a toboggan sled bought from the company store. It was a cherished possession, and I'm sure all of you took a ride on it sometime in our childhood."

There were nods amongst all the men sitting there. They had happy memories on their faces. But when Claude began again, the somber mood resumed.

"Rebecca Jo had the most startling blue eyes, the same as Willie Joe's are now. He doesn't know it, but he was named for her too. I doubt he even knows he had a great-aunt. My family never talked about Rebecca after she died. I think they thought the pain would go away if they didn't talk about what happened, but that only made me miss her more. I felt like they were forgetting her, so I made sure to think about her enough for all of us. If only I hadn't forgotten my damn gloves, she might still be here."

"Now, Claude, you can't blame yourself for Rebecca's drowning. It was an accident. The ice was thin, and you couldn't have known she'd skated down there." Edgar nodded in sympathy.

"That's where you're wrong, Ed! What I'm about to tell you is what really happened that day. It's been over fifty years, but I remember it like it was yesterday. The memory chills my blood and makes me shiver to think about it. There were things about that day I could never make sense of."

"For instance, I know I had those blasted gloves in my pocket when I left the house! It was a bitterly cold day. It had been in the teens for over a week. I never would've left the house without them."

"But when we got to Mary Luck Pond, my gloves were not in my pocket. I figured they'd fallen out on the way, so I backtracked, thinking they had to be close. Rebecca was already putting her skates on, so I told her to stay at the end, where we always skated. I even told her I thought the side by the bank was probably thin because it was at the deep end and usually froze solid last. She promised me she'd stay where I told her. Those were the last words I ever spoke to her."

Claude's voice had shrunk to barely a whisper, and tears were glistening in his eyes. With the pain of loss and tragedy written on his face, he seemed to age in front of everyone.

Willie Joe was unusually quiet and wouldn't look the girls in the eye. He was trying his best to hold back tears of his own. Seeing his Papaw like this was getting to him, and rightfully so.

Claude collected himself and picked up his tale where he left off. "So, feeling okay to leave Rebecca for what I thought would be just a few minutes, I headed back towards my house. I walked slowly so that I wouldn't miss my gloves."

"I didn't find them till I got home, in my bedroom. Mommy was cleaning up dishes from lunch and asked why I was back. I told her I'd forgotten my gloves, and she said she hadn't seen them. I went to my room and searched. I found one under my bed and one in the closet."

"This struck me as very odd. I didn't keep my outdoor stuff in my room. I thought Rebecca was pulling a prank on me. She knew I kept my room tidy. That had to be it. But why hide my gloves? She knew that if I didn't go skating, neither could she."

"I got a sick feeling deep in my gut. I didn't know why, but I felt that something horrible was about to happen. I couldn't have imagined anything worse than what I found at the pond."

"I ran back so fast I was panting like a dog; I bent over at the waist and tried to take in what I saw. Rebecca was nowhere to be seen, and there was a hole in the ice. I ran toward it and fell to my knees to look inside. A few bubbles were still rising as I looked for her. I saw her red scarf and followed it with my eyes under the ice."

"She was directly under me. I beat the ice with my hands. Her eyes were wide open, and her mouth set in a scream. I saw her kick one last time and then noticed a hand around her ankle."

"I know that sounds impossible, but I swear to you, I saw that. I jumped back, scared to death, and took off running like the devil was on my ass."

"Someone later told me that I was screaming like a banshee and brought people running just by my hysterics. I kept saying, "Somebody's got Rebecca under the ice!""

"Delmer Honeycutt was the first to get to me, and he shook me right hard and then slapped me across the face. I stopped screaming, but I could only get out that Rebecca had fallen through the ice."

"Mamaw Bluebird came to me then. She wrapped me in a quilt and held me tight. Sometimes a woman's bosom is the only thing in the world that can comfort a child, and I think if it hadn't been for her, I might have ended up raving in the loony bin!"

"By the time I calmed down, half the town was at the pond. Mommy was out of her mind. Her cries are something I'll never forget as long as I live. No parent should ever have to bury a child."

"Daddy tried his best to comfort her, but she was just beyond help at this point. When his eyes fell on me, they came with a look of pure hatred. He left Mommy and headed toward me, yelling as he came, 'Where were you when your sister was drowning?' he grabbed me by my shirt and twisted it around my neck, lifting me off the ground as he shook me".

"I was so scared it's a thousand wonders I didn't piss myself.

Somebody pulled Daddy off me, but he fought to get free to get at me again. I bawled and felt like life as I knew it was over. And it was. "

"Daddy apologized later, but his heart wasn't in it. I know he always blamed me, just as I blamed myself."

Willie Joe's Pappaw blew his nose on his handkerchief and wiped his eyes. His lifelong friends struggled to keep it together. They had all attended Rebecca Jo's funeral and knew her death had ended her family. After about five minutes, Claude continued his story.

"You fellers are probably the only reason I made it through my childhood. Without your friendship…. well, you know. Anyway, the part you don't know about Rebecca's death is how she died."

"My sister didn't accidentally drown. It was murder, sure, as I'm sitting here. As I said, when I got to Rebecca, she tried her best to kick to the surface. I saw what looked like a gnarled hand, a woman's hand, clamped tight around her ankle. I beat at the ice, trying to save her. I've never been so scared in all my life. I know this sounds like I made it up. It's unbelievable." Claude visibly shivered as his memory cloaked him in chills.

"Sheriff Hale came to the house the next day and asked me some questions. I was so nervous that I barely got out the story. After I finished, he asked me about what I was yelling."

"I had put that out of my mind, but when he asked me that question, I froze. I saw that hand in my mind. The Sheriff just stared at me, waiting for me to answer him. My dad came up behind me and pinched my neck, and said, 'Answer the sheriff, boy.' I told him that when I reached the pond and reached for Rebecca, I saw a hand around her ankle. That someone was down there with her."

"This was the first time my daddy had heard me say this. He didn't take it well at all. Flat out called me a liar, saying I was trying to lay the blame on someone else. He grabbed the strap from the nail on the wall and whooped the fire out of me right before the

Sheriff. Daddy might have beaten me to death if he hadn't been there. Sheriff Hale had to stay his hand and tell him I'd had enough."

"I cried my eyes out for days, but not for the whoopin' I deserved, but for the loss of my beautiful sister. We were really close. That's odd for a big brother to say about his sister, but she was my best friend."

Claude paused a minute and looked into the fire; you knew he was seeing Rebecca in his mind.

"I never told another soul since then about that hand until just now. The only reason I'm a telling you fellers is that now I have proof."

"The coroner didn't do a full autopsy on Rebecca, seeing how it was a cut-and-dried case of accidental drowning, but he was still obligated to examine her and file a report. After Mommy and Daddy passed away, I packed their belongings and stored them in my attic."

"A couple of months ago, while putting away the Christmas stuff, I glanced back at the steamer trunk I had inherited from my grandmother. Laying on top was a picture of Rebecca. I had never seen it before in my life. It was a picture of her ice skating on that damn pond. She was standing in the exact spot she drowned. I have stared and stared at that picture. I could tell she was holding something in her hand. I blinked several times to clear my old eyes, and sure enough, she had my gloves in her hand. I couldn't believe it!"

"I can't make sense of it. Who would've taken that picture? She had the same thing she had on the day she died. I nearly had a heart attack right then and there. I broke out in a cold sweat and had to sit down. As I sat there, stunned beyond belief, I saw an envelope on the floor, one of those big yeller ones with the round tab and string you wrap around it to keep it closed. I'd never seen it before either, so I picked it up, read the front, and I'll be damned if it wasn't an autopsy report from the coroner, Jonas Wheeler. I opened it and read the cover of the document. It was for Rebecca. Again, I got woozy. It took me a minute to right myself to read it. I have it here in my pocket. I'll read what Doc Wheeler said."

An Autopsy Report for Rebecca Jo Wells, Age 10:
Cause of Death: Accidental drowning?
Remarks: Water in the lungs. Strange marks on the right ankle look human. Five clear indentations are indicative of a hand. Looks like claw marks.

Claude's hand shook as he carefully folded the report and put it in his pocket. No one spoke. It was a lot to take in. The eavesdroppers were spellbound. Willie Joe was pale and didn't even try to hide the tears on his cheeks.

Finally, Edgar spoke up. "What in the Sam Hill is going on around here, Claude? That was one hell of a story. And, for the record, I believe every word. Y'all know they's e magic in these mountains. Something has started to stir, and I don't like it. Not nary a bit!" The eavesdroppers perked up at the word magic and looked at each other in wonder.

The fire had long since burned out, and so had the story. The men gathered their chairs and struggled to understand what they'd just heard. The last one to leave was Claude. He glanced back as he was shutting the door, and a ray of moonlight lit his face so that his eyes gleamed, and it looked as though they locked on to Willie Joe.

Willie tensed and squeezed Ruby Lee's hand that he didn't even remember holding. He promptly let go, much to her regret. She liked the feeling of his hand in hers. That was new.

She quickly stood up and started down the stairs. She would not fall prey to Willie Joe's charms and become one of his sappy-eyed followers. Vera liked him, not her. Right?

However, as Ruby lies awake in her bed late that night, she

replays when she realizes she is holding Willie Joe's hand. She got a fluttering in her belly that made her cheeks flush. Her last thought as she drifted off to sleep was his cerulean eyes.

The Spring Equinox

March 1984

A warm spell descended upon Mary Luck the first week of March. Known as a False Spring, the old timers warned that although the red buds were budding out and the crocuses were blooming, you should wait until Easter Sunday to plant your garden and Mother's Day to set out any flowers. The Spring run-off down the mountains was swelling the banks of the Big Sandy River and threatening to flood the lowlands. Mother Nature saw fit to cleanse the land every few years. Wash away the old to make room for the new. Spring is, after all, the season of rebirth.

THE THIRD TALE

Late For Dinner

The trio got there early and set up the loft to be ready when the story started. Vera had brought her Andy Gibb sleeping bag since it was old, out of style, and not anything she cared about. They had all brought Cokes and candy, Sprees and Reese's cups for the girls, a Whatchamacallit, and Big League Chew for Willie Joe. For these kids, this beats going to the movies.

The men filed in one by one. Matthew was first, so he started the fire in the pot-bellied stove even though it was a warm 70 degrees. However, the sun would soon be down behind the mountains, and as the breeze filtered out of the hills with the scent of honeysuckle, there would soon be a chill in the air. Older people tended to get cold easier than young'uns did, and with the tales they'd been telling, the air wasn't the only thing that left a chill in their bones, young and old alike.

When the Yarn Spinners had finished shootin' the breeze and got themselves situated. Edgar's pipe lit, Claude's cedar stick primed for whittling, Wilson's wad of Beechnut securely tucked deep in his jaw, and last, Del's final honk on his handkerchief, Matthew sat down, leaned his chair back on two legs, as was his custom and began his story. It was comforting that no one had to ask who was up next. It was as though they all just knew—an unspoken truth.

"Well, boys, I have a tale I've never told before. I see how that seems to be how we've been doing things of late. I think you're right, Claude: things seem spooky right now. Just little things from day to day. Nothing big, just strange dreams, misplacing my keys or watch, only to find them someplace odd. It dawned on me the other day that this year marks 100 years since the demise of Baby Annie. I'm not sure if there's a time limit on curses, but it chills me just a little to think that maybe that old hag isn't through with this town yet. But that's for another day. The older men gave one another meaningful glances, and Matthew began after a few quiet seconds.

"It was 1934, and I was a young feller of only twenty-four. I had just married a few years before and had John Michael already two years old, with Marissa nearly ready to debut. I worked over at John's Creek when North East Coal mined a vein of coal on the other side of Jockey Holler. I'd take the ferry across the Big Sandy and hitch a ride up to the mine with anybody passing by in a wagon. I was sure glad to have that job seeing as how this was during The Hoover Days when most people were scraping to stay alive.

Mary Ellen was not happy that I had to work underground, but she dealt with it so we could eat. Before Van Lear cut me loose, I was training to be an inspector and was nearly ready to take the necessary tests when the big wigs up North pulled the plug on us and closed the mine. I can't tell you how relieved I was to find another job that fast. I had three mouths to feed, with another one on the way."

The men all nodded in agreement. Their shared experience left no need for an explanation. Wilson snorted and spat on the floor, mumbling something about Hoover. Matthew began again.

"I usually went to work about 5:00 in the morning and got home about 6:00 that evening. I went in at dawn and got home at dusk. You've all worked that shift, so you know. I don't have to tell you how awful it was. But I was a young man, happily married and a proud daddy. I was still a fortunate man, job be damned!"

"It was early April, and it started like any other. I ate my breakfast of biscuits and gravy and drank my coffee. Mary Ellen, great with child, still managed to send me off with my belly full and a kiss on my lips. God almighty, she was a good-looking woman! God rest her soul."

"About an hour before quittin' time, I had to take a whiz. We had a place off to the side in an unused crosscut to which we all took our business. I was zipping up my pants when the roof got to workin', and I heard the first rumble. Now you all know that a mine makes noises all the time. But, as I said, I wasn't used to being so far below. I ran down that crosscut like my hair was on fire, only to be laughed at by some older men. They told me I was being a danged fool and that I still had work to do. So, I grabbed my pickaxe and returned to the seam I was working on."

"Before I got three steps, the entire roof crumbled. I reached for Buddy Webb, who got covered up, and I was holding his hand as he drew his last breath. He died with a scream on his lips. I was close to the shaft elevator, and as I ran for it, the roof started comin' in on me. I got hit on the head pretty hard, taking me to my knees. I heard the shaft elevator go up with the lucky few who got out. The roof settled down, and though I wasn't badly hurt, I couldn't move. I could hear the cries of the dying men. Soon, fire damp filled the mine. The air tasted stale, and I was struggling to breathe."

"I ain't ashamed to say that I cried, thinking I'd never see my wife and son and our unborn child. I closed my eyes and imagined them in my head. I saw myself walking up the lane and waving to Mary Ellen as she washed dishes and looked out the kitchen window. I went to the well, drew a bucket to drink, and then washed my face and hands to look like myself. I went out back to the smokehouse to take off my coveralls. I could smell the pork chops and potatoes frying in rendered fat. I heard little John singing, 'Jesus loves me.' I saw all this in my head because I was sure this would be my last thoughts on this earth."

I passed out after that, and for how long, I didn't know. The next thing I knew, hands pulled me by my shoulders, and I got my first breath of fresh air. Brothers, I can't describe how sweet that air tasted in my lungs. I decided, then and there, that I would never go back underground for any reason!"

Matthew stopped for a minute to collect himself and let his words soak in so that his next revelation would have the maximum effect. These men were seasoned storytellers; if they knew anything, it was how to keep their audience on the edge of their seats.

For the first time all night, Matthew sat his chair down on four legs and bent over with his elbows on his knees, hands clasped. As he leaned in, so did the others, the eavesdroppers included.

"I remember when that collapse happened; we lost a lot of good men that day." Stated Claude.

"Well, here's what you don't know. By the time I got home, it was well past dark. Jimmy Derossett and Perry Castle drove me home. We parked at the bottom of the hill, and with me between them, with their arms holding me up, we staggered the rest of the way up to the house. I had never been so happy to see that little house or the beautiful woman and child on the porch. I didn't get a hero's welcome, though."

Mary Ellen started hollerin' and cussin' me, saying words I didn't know she knew. I couldn't believe it. Here I almost died, and she's mad I was late for supper! It wasn't until she saw me in the light that she believed I wasn't drunk. I stopped her cussing by kissing her. The other men told her the whole story of the mine collapse while I sat on the porch hugging little John. She hadn't heard the news since we lived so far up the holler."

"I went inside and stripped off my clothes as I walked, swearing I would never wear them again. Burn them, Mary Ellen. I got no use for them!!"

"After I cleaned up, ate, and had a few shots of Shine, I asked her why she was so mad at me for being late. She knew I'd never step out on her!"

"She looked me in the eye and told me something I've never been able to explain. She said that she was standing at the sink washing up some dishes at my usual getting home time. She said she saw me walking up the lane. I waved to her and headed back to the well to clean myself up."

"That's when she took the cornbread out of the oven so that it would be good and hot. Next, she flipped the taters again so they'd be good and crisp the way I liked them. She had pork chops already on the table. She poured me some milk and got Johnny set up in his highchair. They were waiting for me to say the blessing, and while they waited, the baby was singing Jesus Loves Me or trying, anyway. I asked her what time this happened, and she said 6:00 sharp. Said I was right on time."

"I told her there was no way that could have been me. I couldn't move in that mine. Then it hit me. That was about the time I imagined coming home. Everything she described was what I imagined from the food on the table. I envisioned my favorite meal, and that's what she fixed. It was odd for us to have pork chops. Those were lean times, you know, but she said that it was a special occasion, and I asked her what it was, and she said our anniversary."

"I can tell you, fellers. I was one lucky son of a gun that day. The good Lord sure was looking out for me. It still haunts me to this day. I can hear those pitiful cries for help, and I remember feeling the life slip out of Buddy Webb's hand as I held it. Mary Ellen said that for years I would wake her up screaming in my sleep. And one night, she woke up to find me out of bed, standing in the front yard, staring up at the moon. Said my eyes were open, but I was sound asleep. That's the only time, to my knowledge, that I ever went sleepwalking."

"I could never shake the notion that I died for a few minutes and that Mary Ellen saw my ghost that day. It's the only way I can explain what she saw. The older men sat mulling over Matt's story, and after about five minutes, Claude spoke up. "Del, I think you and Matt got the right of it. You somehow managed to send your spirit to your wife for a final farewell, but God had some more use for you and spared your life. I don't think any of us here are surprised that you were able to do that. You loved Mary Ellen more than any husband I have ever witnessed; furthermore, this town is cursed or blessed. Either way, things happen here that don't happen in other places. I'm unsure if that's a good or bad thing…. it just is.

Matt spoke up as it seemed time to leave and said, "I have one more thing to add to my tale. I've kept this to myself all these years. I didn't even tell Mary Ellen. I left it out until you'd heard my tale to make sure you would believe me, and I think you did." Nods went around the room. "Well, that day in the mine, as I returned from doing my business, I saw Buddy Webb standing and facing the wall. I asked him if he was okay, and when he turned to me, his eyes rolled back in his head. I thought Buddy was having some fit, and as I reached over to him, he broke into the evilest smile, threw back his head, and cawed like a witch. He told me to run for my life. But it wasn't his voice; it was a woman's."

"Then he took his pickaxe and started digging into the roof and a bunch of stack rock. You know, the thin rock that's hard to keep solid. I didn't stay around to see the first rocks fall but fall, they did. Buddy caused that cave-in. The only thing is, that wasn't Buddy."

"It took me a little while to figure it out, but as I lay there trapped, it came to me where I was. We were mining the land taken from Baby Annie. My hand to God, she took over poor old Buddy, and she was the one that killed those men. I'm unsure why God spared me, but I can never get his face or that voice out of my mind." Matthew hung his head as if wearied. The other men digested this little nugget and came to the same conclusion. It had been Baby Annie. She was behind everything wrong that happened in this town.

This last revelation ended things for the night, and as the older men shuffled out, the trio gathered up their things and barely spoke until they got outside. Once on their bikes, Willie Joe was the first to break the silence. "What in the heck do y'all think is wrong with this town? I always thought the stories we all grew up hearing were just bullshit. Didn't you?" the girls both nodded yes.

Vera said, "I used to get scared by those stories when we were little, then they seemed silly. Now I'm scared for real."

"Me too!" said Ruby Lee. "But I've always thought this town was spooky. Maybe it's because I live by a graveyard. Sometimes when I'm outside on the swing, I see things out of the corner of my eye, or I think I hear voices. Giggles and singing. It always freaks me out."

Willie Joe shivers and says, "Stop talking about this shit. It's almost dark, and I have to ride home by myself. And I'm not ashamed to admit that I get scared, too. After these stories, we'd be stupid not to be scared!"

The trio parted ways at The Nest and rode their bikes as fast as possible to get home before dark. Not so that they'd make their curfew but to be inside when darkness fell completely. That's when other things came out. It was their time.

THE FOURTH TALE

The Wake That Awoke

Beltane,
May 1, 1984

Ruby Lee's 13th birthday party was a big deal for her. She was finally going to be a teenager! Her mom and dad got her a ten-speed bike, and she couldn't have loved anything more. That evening, all twelve classmates came to her house for a party. She had a Baskin Robbin's pralines and cream ice cream cake, her dad grilled hotdogs, and her mom made homemade chili sauce using Edith Ward's recipe. She also made coleslaw so that they could have slaw dogs, Ruby's favorite.

After all the eats, they played badminton, horseshoes, and then a game of tag. Tired and thirsty, they gathered around the picnic table and guzzled down Kool-Aid. It was getting dark, so Ruby's dad lit the bonfire so they could sit around it and listen to music and tell stories. When the fire went out, the boys had to go home.

As Ruby stared into the weakening flames, she got a feeling of oneness. Beltane was the fire festival celebrated by her ancestors, and having been born on that day and blessed with beautiful red locks, she was the living embodiment of fire. The flickering of the flames entranced her. So much so Vera had to shake her to get her attention. When she focused on Vera's eyes, she briefly saw something dark lurking in her best friend, hiding behind the innocent facade. Ruby jerked away from the hand on her shoulder, suddenly afraid of her touch. It was a knee-jerk reaction. The two girls stared briefly at each other, and then the spell broke.

That night, Ruby couldn't shake the feeling that something was wrong with Vera. But the next day, Vera was her usual self, and with the May Day festivities happening, Ruby forgot about the weird feeling she had had the night before and instead enjoyed the day of fun.

As April gave way to May and the village of Mary Luck prepared for the annual Beltane festival, Ruby was incredibly excited as her sister Rosie was the May Queen. All the children would dress in their Easter finery and provide the procession as the May Queen rode through the streets in a horse-drawn wagon decorated in spring flowers.

All over town, people decorated their houses with spring flowers. After the procession finished, the children gathered around the MayPole and, through a rhythmic dance, wrapped the pole with beautiful ribbons. This festival rarely takes place nowadays, but in 1984, the tradition was alive and well.

The founding families were of English/Scottish descent, and their traditions came with them. There were still enough of these families to insist the practice remained. So on the eve of Beltane, The Yarn Spinners are gathered around preparing for another tale of yesteryear. The trio is also in place, eagerly awaiting yet another dark story.

This evening's story was coming from Edgar Wilcox, Vera's uncle. Edgar was a retired coal miner out of necessity but a banjo player by choice. He was famous in the area for his pickin' and grinnin'. Tonight, though, his usual good nature was severe and sad, which made it all the more eerie.

"Well, I guess it's my turn for a spooky tale, and I got one. I think it was 1932 when I first fell in love. The May Day festival brought back all the memories I had forgotten. In '32 , I was about twelve years old, and we had gotten a new teacher. Boy, was she ever a beauty. She had long black hair that was so dark it sometimes looked blue."

Her name was Mrs. Adrienne Philips. It was love at first sight. You fellers probably don't remember seeing her as you'uns had already gone to High School. But I was smitten from the first look. She started right after Christmas. It was her first job. She was so different from the other teachers we all had growing up. She dressed nicely and smelled so good. The other teachers always sneered at her behind her back. They were so jealous they looked for any excuse to embarrass her."

So, as the plot thickened, Edgar paused to light his pipe. The eavesdroppers were entranced. They hadn't even heard a watered-down version of this story. They inched just a little closer to the loft's edge so they could listen to it better. The looks that they gave each other said that this was getting good. So, with ears perked up and their attention completely surrendered, they settled in for an evening tale.

Puffing hard on his pipe, Edgar got going. "I know you all remember ole Miss Fitch. The old spinster who looked like a crone and should have had the name Witch instead of Fitch." All the men nodded in agreement. "Well, anyway, she hated Mrs. Phillips from the get-go. She gave her hell any chance she got. I saw her make her cry once, and it took all I had not to say something to her, but I was just a boy, and I'd heard all the stories about Miss Fitch -she was a great-granddaughter of the witch Baby Annie."

"Even though she was already dead by then, rumor has it that her ghost haunted the town because of a curse she put on it due to some imagined slight she thought the townspeople had done to her. I'm a grown man now and don't put much stock in curses, but I was a scared boy back then, so I kept my mouth shut."

"It was the May-day festival weekend that my world turned upside down. I'd stayed after school to clean the chalkboard and bang out the erasers for Mrs. Philips. I did anything she asked me to and offered to help almost daily. The day before the festival, I was helping Mrs. Phillips like I always did."

"She was standing on a ladder hangin' up paper flowers. I had been handing them to her, and she was tacking them up. I can still see her sweet smile." Edgar says with a dreamy look on his face. With that expression, you could still see the love-struck boy hiding beneath the surface. "As I was handing her flowers, I heard my mother calling for me outside. I looked out the window and didn't see her, but I kept hearing her, and so did Mrs. Phillips."

"It was strange for Momma to walk down to the school, holler for me, and not come inside. So I headed downstairs and out to the playground but couldn't find her. Puzzled, I went back inside and heard a loud thump from upstairs. I took off running and went up those steps three at a time.

When I reached the classroom, the lights were off, and though it wasn't dark outside, storm clouds were hovering overhead. My eyes took a moment to focus, and that's when I saw Mrs. Phillips lying on the floor."

"She looked dead. I was so upset that I didn't see the other person in the room until I was almost on top of her. It was a true hag. I'd never seen a picture of Baby Annie, but God as my witness; it was her. Her hair was a wild, tangled mess. She was completely white-headed, had bulging black eyes, had gnarled-up claw-like hands, and wore nothing more than rags. She was leaning over Mrs. Philips, mumbling some words I'd never heard before."

"At first, I thought she was there to help until she turned those eyes on me. I froze and stood there with my mouth hanging open, catching flies. She turned to me and said, 'Get away, boy, before

I have you for supper.' Then she cackled when she saw the look on my face. I finally moved my legs and ran to the house without stopping once."

"I was breathless and panting, and it took five minutes for me to calm down enough to get my words out. Finally, I could only say that Mrs. Phillips fell off the ladder and was hurt badly. Daddy took off after Doc Wells and Momma grabbed Versie Owens off her porch next door, and they ran down to the school. I almost tried to stop them because I hadn't told them about the witch I had seen. But my mind felt scrambled, and I knew they'd never believe me. The more I thought about it, the less real it seemed."

"Daddy had Doc Wells in our wagon, and they flew by the house lickety-split. That's when I went back down to the schoolhouse. I didn't go inside; I was too afraid. Doc Wells and my dad came out with the saddest faces. Then I knew that my beautiful teacher was dead. I couldn't believe it. We had just been talking, and now she was gone."

"Her Husband was a mine inspector, and he was on his way. I couldn't imagine being him and having to face life without her. To say the man was distraught doesn't even come close to describing his pain. They had to tear her out of his arms. I have never to this day seen a man so destroyed."

"Eventually, the women could start preparing her for the wake. Word had spread fast, and every woman in town had either brought food or was helping to set up the viewing room. Even though the couple had only lived in Mary Luck for five months, the whole town pitched in to help Mr. Philips in his time of need."

"Both of the Phillips' were from Virginia, and there was no way that their folks could get there before the funeral. Wasn't any embalming in those days. Most folks wouldn't have used that method if it had been around. Daddy always said it was unnatural."

"Richard Hackworth made her coffin; his wife Barbara made a nice pillow and batting. They laid Mrs. Philips on her dining room table at her home. Fresh flowers were everywhere, and she was covered with a white netting to keep away bugs and mice."

"The first night of the wake, nearly everybody in town showed up to pay their respects. Everyone agreed that since the funeral would fall on May Day, they would name her the May Queen, pull her coffin through the town, and let the procession go to the church."

"And so, the next day, the saddest May Queen procession in town history took Mrs. Phillips to the church. As Reverend Burkett began his sermon, an all-out gully washer emerged from the sky. It rained cats and dogs. The creeks were all flooded, and it rained for two hours. It was the damnedest thing I ever saw. With all the rain, there was no way they could bury her. The grave had three feet of water, so they kept her at the church and held another wake for her."

"I managed to be able to stay the night at the church since all the men were out tending to the flood damage. My mother was there, so that's why I got to stay. At about 3:00 a.m., almost everyone was asleep except for a few women and me. I was sitting on the front pew when I saw her hand twitch. At first, I thought I was seeing things, but it startled me and awakened me. I sat real still and didn't take my eyes off her. That's when I saw her whole hand slide down. I jumped up and ran to my mother, and she told me to calm down and that sometimes corpses twitched like that."

"I wasn't convinced, so I walked back up to the coffin and stared at her, and I saw her chest move as she inhaled and then exhaled. I went to screaming and a hollerin' and woke everybody up. Then, all of a sudden, Mrs. Phillips sat straight up in that coffin. It was pure chaos. People were running out the door and praying on their knees. Norsie Wells flat passed out, and I just about pissed my britches. But the most hysterical person was Mrs. Philips."

"She was crying and tearing at that netting. Her husband dragged her out of that coffin, carried her to a pew, and sat her down. She was so upset she almost passed out, and if Versie hadn't had her smelling salts out already, having just brought Norsie around, she probably would have. She said that she could hear everything that was going on but couldn't move or speak, and the fact that if it hadn't rained, she'd have been buried alive set her into hysterics all over again. Before it started to rain, she'd made peace with God and prayed that she wouldn't last long in the grave."

"Doc Wells showed up and examined her and couldn't believe he had pronounced her dead when she was in a deep coma. Mr. Philips was irate and started cussing out ole Doc Wells and threatened him with a lawsuit, and I don't know what all. But Reverend Burkett calmed him by reminding him that the miracle to have her back was more important than anything."

"I have kept the secret of seeing the old crone to myself all these years, but I figured it was my turn since we all seem to be spilling our guts. Mrs. Philips finished the school year, but she and her husband moved back to Virginia. Before she left, I asked her if she remembered seeing an older woman the day she fell. She said she had dreamed that, but she must have been there if I had seen her too. She asked me if I knew her, and I just shook my head no and left it at that. I didn't see any use in telling her who I'd seen, seeing as how she was leaving in a few weeks."

"It took me a while, but I think I pieced together what happened. I believe Miss Fitch summoned the witch. She was the one that lured me away using my mother's voice. When I was gone, the hag knocked her off her ladder and then put a spell on her that paralyzed her. But what she wasn't counting on was the rain. Also, Mrs. Philips was the May Queen. That storm was sent by Mother Nature herself to save her. Spring is about renewal and life. She wasn't going to let her May Queen die."

"I probably sound like a superstitious fool, but I know what I saw that day, and it was Baby Annie—conjured up by her great-grand-daughter because of jealousy. Oddly enough, though, I heard about two years later that Mrs. Phillips died in a car crash. I guess it was just her time to go, or else Baby Annie felt cheated and had one more trick up her sleeve."

Wilson spoke for the first time that evening, saying, "I remember when that happened. I wasn't at the wake, but I remember the storm. And Mrs. Phillips was a looker." he said cheekily. "And if you say you saw that filthy hag, Ed, I believe ye. We've all heard the story about her curse, and, like you fellers, I always thought it was just a bunch of nonsense. But I've noticed a pattern as we tell these stories."

"I think I know what you mean, Wilson." Stated Claude. "Every time something bad happens in this town, she's the source. We've all fallen prey to her in some shape or fashion. All of us except you, Delano." All eyes turn to Del, and he looks up sheepishly and says, "Well, it ain't been my turn yet. You won't stop flappin' your gums long enough for me to get a word in edgewise." He crosses his arms across his chest and then breaks up into laughter. They all follow suit, and for the first time in months, the yarn spinners smile. The hidden trio upstairs must cover their mouths with their hands to stifle their giggles.

When the men are gone, the trio looks at each other, and Willie Joe says, ", Wow." The girls just mentioned Baby Annie. Even in 1984, the kids knew all about her. She had been the local boogeyman since time out of mind.

That night, as the kids rode their bikes home, once they were alone, they each had a moment of pure terror at the thought of running into Baby Annie. She was their worst nightmare. With all the newly found knowledge about Mary Luck and the near certainty that witches were real, none of our trio will sleep well for a while. But, being resilient at thirteen, they will be ready when the time comes.

THE FIFTH TALE

June 1984

Ruby Lee came down with Chicken Pox on the first day of Summer break. Rosie and Ruthie were getting over it, and they were the ones to drag that sickness in. Ruby was fit to be tied that she had gotten it after all her bragging that she never got sick. But Ruby was most upset about maybe missing the latest tale by the Yarn Spinners! Luckily, her Mammaw was keeping her sequestered at her house so she could nurse her back to health and not infect the kids that her mom babysat in the summer. Mammaw couldn't have her prayer meeting, so Paps couldn't sneak off and have his yarn spinning.

After two agonizing weeks of scratching and lying around with nothing to do but watch game shows and Westerns with Mam and Pap, no MTV at their house. Ruby Lee championed getting out of the house and seeing her friends. She had already missed two World premiere videos on MTV, and she didn't think she could miss out on anything else. Dang it!

Tonight would be the fifth story the trio would hear from the Yarn Spinners. They were betting Delano would tell a story since he hadn't told one yet. The trio were giddy as they climbed the ladder to hide in the stifling loft. They'd played all day at the park and ridden their bikes all over town, and now they were about to hear another spooky tale. Willie Joe was brown as a biscuit, and his hair had bleached out in the sun to make it blond. This combo made his eyes sparkle and made Ruby Lee start to see what Vera had always seen. Ruby Lee tried to avoid his eyes so he wouldn't see the blush that crept up her cheeks.

Unfortunately, Vera saw this exchange, and she instantly felt a gut punch. The thoughts of Ruby Lee and Willie Joe being a couple made her want to puke! She was smart enough to see that what she had always admired about her best friend was the same thing that Willie Joe saw. This thought did not make her feel better.

However, she was happy to have this time with Willie Joe, so she pushed those awful thoughts to the back of her mind and settled in the loft beside her crush. The trio got situated, and the first of the Yarn Spinners showed up in less than five minutes. Claude was setting the chairs up, and because of the heat, he didn't light the pot-bellied stove, much to the trio's relief. The other four men arrived, and after some small talk and pipe lighting, the story was ready to be told.

As they had suspected, Delano was the storyteller that night. Del was a quiet man, mild-mannered and kind. He was known to have a pocket full of candies and handed them to all the town kids. He always wore bib overalls with a UK t-shirt underneath that stretched taut across his considerable belly.

Del began his tale without being prompted. "Back in about 1922, when I was about ten years old, I saw something that has haunted me my whole life. Back then, I lived in the river bottom, and amongst our little neighborhood of maybe twenty houses lived Petunia Purdy."

"Now, I know that we all know her and have probably had dealings with her in the past, but back then, she was maybe nineteen and had four kids already. When her husband ran off on her, she was pretty needy. So, to make a little money, she took to fortune-telling. Everyone knew she was a great-granddaughter of Baby Annie, so she made quite a bit of money."

"As a kid and naturally curious, I couldn't resist seeing what happened during these seances and palm readings. Well, fellers, I got more than I bargained for. I waited till one night when quite a few people were at her house and took a wooden crate to stand on so I could peep in the window."

"That night, several folks that we know were there. I won't name names, but trust me; there were a few surprises. As the sun set, I sneaked into the backyard and set up my crate. I heard Mrs. Purdy's voice, and I peeped in the window. The people there were all sitting around her kitchen table and holding hands. Mrs. Purdy was in a kind of trance, I guess. She threw her head back and was moaning and carrying on. Then the big show began."

"As I watched, I saw her table rise off the floor and rock back and forth. My hand to God, that table was walking. I was afraid so fell off my crate and twisted my ankle to where I knew I couldn't run. She leaned out the window and started hollering at me."

"I was crying about my ankle and the fact that she had turned from the window and ran out the back door. She grabbed me by the scruff of my neck and dragged me to the back porch. The first thing she did was check my ankle. That surprised me because I thought she would put a spell or curse on me. But she went into the house after telling me not to move."

"When she came back, she had a kind of poultice made up and put it on my ankle wrapped in a dish towel. I was still suspicious of her and had tears running down my face. I started apologizing as soon as I could catch my breath! But she silenced me with a look. You all have seen that look. She could stop a train with that glare."

"Anyway, she got right up in my face and said, 'Look here, son, you ain't to be going home and tell what you saw here tonight or who was here. Do you understand me? This here is my livelihood, and people pay as long as nobody knows they come here. I got mouths to feed, and since that no account piece of dog shit husband of mine left, it's all on me to provide for me and mine."

"I ain't got no book learnin' and no skills to speak of except my fortune telling. But if you were to go around town telling people so and so was here and that got back to the church folk, why nobody would come."

"So, Delano, if you don't want me to curse you with a spell that will make your pecker fall off, you'll keep your trap shut. Occasionally, I may need you to do something for me. Nothing bad, well, not too bad. She chuckled after she said that, and my blood turned cold. I noticed then that she was missing some teeth and her that young. She had a hard life, but damn boys, she looked rough even back then. No wonder her husband left."

Claude spat in the old coffee can and said, "I don't blame you for being scared. I wouldn't have crossed old Purdy back then. Hell, I wouldn't cross her now. I always thought that fortune-telling stuff was malarkey, but the older I get, and the more I see, I think maybe there is more to it than I thought."

Del situated himself back in his seat and started again. "Well, Claude, hang on to your hat 'cause what happened next will make you a believer. At least, I hope it does, or you'll think I'm loony and haul me off to Eastern State. But anyhow, I didn't hear from Mrs. Purdy again till about July. I was walking past her house, and she hollered at me to come over to the porch where she was sitting on her swing."

"My heart was in my throat, beating about a mile a minute, but I knew better than to ignore her. I sucked in a deep breath and opened her gate. I made my way up to her porch, which was already sagging, but not like it is today. She said, "Quit dragging your feet, boy! I see you run by here every day. Be quick now. I know you don't want anyone to see you here. Sit down on that milk crate, and let me talk to ye.""

"Fellers, it was one of the scariest moments of my young life 'cause I knew I owed her for peeping in the window and for her not tellin' on me. But I was mighty fearful of what the price would be. I found out soon enough. "Now, since we made our bargain, you owe me.... let's say, a 'Favor.'"

"I shut my eyes and tried to say the Lord's Prayer in my mind, but she grabbed my chin and said, 'Open your eyes, you scared little mouse. Here's what I need you to do. Tonight, after everybody at your house is asleep, you sneak up to the graveyard. When it strikes midnight, fill this here Mason Jar with dirt from the grave of one of your kin. Don't matter which one, but it has to be at midnight. Not a minute before or after. Be quick cause you can only get it while the clock strikes twelve! Don't ask me any questions; just do what I say, and don't tell a soul. Bring that here and put it by the smokehouse out back. Then get your Peeping Tom butt back to your house. Now go!' She tried to smile, but those missing teeth ruined her face. She had never looked scarier."

"Did you fellers ever hear the story of Saw Blade?" nods of agreement went around the room, with Matthew mimicking a shiver. "That story always scared me to death as a wee one. "

"Well, wait'll you hear this. My Pappaw told me the story when I was a boy. He meant only to scare me a little to make me go to bed, but it did more than that to me. I was terrified! The way old Pap told it was that Sawblade, so named because he always won the log-cutting contest at the May-day festival every year. He won using a saw he fashioned himself, and they said he honed it to a razor-sharp edge. So, because of that skill, he was named Sawblade."

"His given name was George Crider. Pap said that at one time, they'd been friends. They drank a little 'shine together now and then. But tragedy struck when Sawblade's eighteen-month-old son died of the Thrush. He and his wife were devastated. It was so bad that his wife Mary drank a whole bottle of Laudanum and died in bed."

"Now that drove old Saw Blade into the depths of despair. And understandably so. He was so drunk he couldn't even stand up at her funeral. But no one could blame him, so some men held him under each arm, laid him in the back of a wagon, and drove him home. For about six weeks, no one saw him. Some ladies from the church tried to call on him, but he never answered the door. The only proof he was still alive was that the food they brought was gone the next time they came by. Empty baskets or plates set out on the porch.

Finally, he was seen in town one day. He was staggering, knee-walking drunk down Front Street. He was hollerin' and cussin' every breath. He drew a lot of attention from the people that saw him. He hadn't shaved since his wife died. His hair was a tangled mess, and you could smell him before you saw him."

"His clothes were the same ones he wore at the funeral, and it looked like he hadn't bathed in a month of Sundays. Well, that about did it for the folks of the day, so a group of men dragged him back home and tried to get him to straighten up. But he refused and became violent. He punched one man in the face, breaking his nose, and that was the end of help from the town. They all washed their hands of him."

"The next time someone saw him was when Opal Powers died. The gravediggers went up to ready the plot, and there he was. Laid out on his wife's grave, an empty 'shine jug lying by his side. But the crazy thing was that he was stark naked. And when one man came over and nudged him with his boot, checking to see if he was alive, he came to and started raving about a wild cat as big as a collie dog."

"He had a bite on his leg crusted with blood and some drool. It looked infected and painful. The men tried to calm him, but he was beyond reason. He took off up the mountain, and no one has seen him since."

"At least not in human form. Pap said that after the story got out, people started claiming to see a wild man with hair all over his body and fangs for teeth. These stories came from many young'uns out sneaking whiskey on Miner's Ridge. So not a very reliable source."

"But the next person to see him was Reverend Lucius Greer. He was hunting near Collins Peak, near where they buried Mary Crider. It was early in the morning, just before dawn. The Rev was sitting up in a tree waiting for the sun to rise, and when it did, he caught a glimpse of Saw Blade. He had a human face covered in gray and white hair. He crouched down, his head bowed, staring at his wife's grave."

"A deer came out of the brush. It was a doe, and as soon as it spotted Saw Blade, it took off running, and Sawblade threw back his head and gave out a hellish cry that was half human, half cat. The Rev said he started praying, and when he opened his eyes next, the sun was coming up, and Sawblade was gone. He said sometimes it seemed unbelievable even to him."

"He was a man of God, so who would challenge that? Pap was a good teller of tales, and he said that he thought he'd seen old Sawblade one snowy night. The moon was full, and with the snow, everything looked bright. He was coming down the lane to his house and looked up and saw what he thought was a man, but he walked in a crouch, and then he heard a screech and then a howl that sounded so lonesome. He said he shivered and took off running to the house."

"Now, I believed every word of what my Pap told me. So when Purdy said I had to go up on the graveyard at midnight, I almost soiled my britches. But I couldn't tell Purdy no. I didn't want any curse on me or my pecker. So that night, I laid in bed worried sick, almost to the point of needing to puke. I borrowed my daddy's pocket watch and bowie knife and set out with my Mason jar. Thankfully, the moon was out, and the night was clear, so I had plenty of light.

I took the pasture path and then went up the side of the mountain with the rocky cliffs. I made my way over the Kudzu and was finally at the top. The graveyard was not nearly as full as it is now."

"I found my Great Aunt Bessie's grave and settled to wait. I had come a little early so as not to miss the witching hour. That would've been bad. I waited ten minutes, so I started whistling to pass the time. A screech owl swooped down from an oak tree and snatched up a field mouse and liked to have given me a heart attack. Damn, owls sound like a woman screaming. He returned to his nest for his meal, so I got up and moved."

"This was my family cemetery, so I knew any grave here would work for Purdy. I pulled out my pocket watch and saw I only had two minutes left. I turned left, and that's when I heard someone walking in the woods. I told myself it was probably a rabbit or squirrel and went on. I was so jumpy. Everything was scaring me. I looked at the watch and saw I only had seconds. I ran to the nearest grave and fell to my knees."

"Midnight was here. I used my knife to loosen the soil and started scooping up dirt when I heard something behind me. Frozen in place, I turned my head slightly, and that's when I saw it. It was Sawblade, my hand to God; it was him!"

"He looked a hundred years old! His hair was gray and silver, and it covered his entire body. His hands had claws, and his teeth were long, sharp, and pointy. He smelled like a cat, you know that ammonia smell cats have. Well, he smelled like that, but worse."

"For whatever reason, I glanced up and saw what I had done; I was digging dirt from Mary Crider's grave. I just knew that my life was over. I started quivering and bawling and saying I was sorry. He looked at me and glared and said, 'Leave.' But it sounded very gravelly. Like someone who hadn't talked in a long time; real scratchy like."

"He didn't have to tell me twice. I grabbed my jar and descended the mountain as fast as possible. I was eat up with briar cuts and had burrs in my hair. When I got to Purdy's, it was just about 12:15, and I could see people moving around inside. I had no desire to peep in the window. I returned to the smokehouse and sat that jar of dirt on the steps."

"When I turned to leave, Mrs. Purdy was right behind me. I guess my face was pale and horror-stricken 'cause she grabbed my chin and said, "What did you see, boy?" I couldn't speak, so she leaned down, sniffed my neck, looked up wide-eyed, and asked me, "You saw him, didn't ye!""

"I knew who she was talking about, so I nodded and bawled like a big baby. She shook me by my shoulders and told me to calm down. She made me sit down on the steps where I'd left the graveyard dirt, then she pulled up an old wooden grate and sat down in front of me. Then she told me a story."

"I reckon they're less than five people that have seen Saw Blade in his cat form. Me being one of them. I have never told anybody what she told me that night. Had I not just witnessed Sawblade myself, I'd not have believed her."

"So, she tells me that a werecat had bitten Sawblade. She said that back in the 1880s, a band of Scottish Travelers would come through the mountains. They had wares to sell: tinctures and charms and such. They'd pitch their tents just outside of town, and people would go and trade. These were the gypsies smuggling her great-grandmother out of Scotland when they burned her mother for being a witch."

"She said the old gypsy king had been born with the Were curse. He would walk the earth in cat form every full moon, and any human bitten by him would suffer the same curse. I asked her how she knew, and she said her mother told her. The gypsy king came and found her , Baby Annie, and asked her to help find the man he bit and help him remove the curse before the next full moon so that he wouldn't become a werecat. They needed the power of a full-blooded witch for the spell to work. And since they had saved her life, she owed them this deed."

"Purdy said someone that Baby Annie refused to help, saying that Sawblade got what he deserved. She hated everyone in town for what she saw as slights against her. The gypsy king warned her that she would pay a steep price if she didn't help him. It wasn't long after she lost her property and her life."

"Now, I don't know much more about all that, but I do know what I saw, and I'm pretty sure it's a miracle I ain't prowling the hills in cat form every full moon. This story is something I've never told a soul. I hope you all don't think I'm crazier than a bed bug, but it's the truth."

"I had to sit outside for thirty minutes to pick all the burrs and stickers off my clothes. When I finally could lie in bed, I prayed to God for forgiveness and thanked him for sparing my life. I never knew what Purdy did with that dirt, but she never asked me to do anything else, thank the good Lord. So, that's my story. It changed me when I saw that man creature. I believe in things we can't explain. I think we all do."

The trio sat in shock! A man-cat creature! Here in Mary Luck. Holy Shit!! Willie Joe whispers, "Maybe we can get a picture of it, and they'll put us on *That's Incredible!*"

"No way," smirks Ruby Lee. "You're too chicken to go up on the graveyard. I bet he wouldn't even go in the daytime, right Vera?" Vera smiles and agrees with Ruby Lee. Willie Joe doesn't like this one bit. "Whatever! I'm not a chicken but I can't sneak out at night. My dad grounded me last time and said if I did it again, I'd get grounded longer and the belt too. I can't risk it, girls, sorry!"

What the girls, or no one outside Willie Joe's house, knew was that ever since they laid off his daddy from the mines, he'd gotten mean. This change occurred in the late winter after close to six months since the layoff. His prized possession, his little red Dodge, was repossessed. This humiliation made him start drinking again.

He'd been sober for ten years, but when they hauled off the truck, he went to Uncle Ed's Liquor Store and bought a fifth of Wild Turkey. From that day on, he woke up and drank until he passed out, and heaven help the fool who woke him up. The slightest infraction by one of his children or wife earned them a drunken slap to whichever part of their body was closest.

The worst was when his little sister Cindy dropped her bowl of cereal on his foot, and he smacked her in the face so hard it knocked her baby tooth out. She was only six, so Willie Joe lit into him and told him he ought to be ashamed. His defense won him the beating of his life. He got a punch to the face that blacked his eye and bloodied his nose, then his father took off his belt and striped his back from top to bottom.

All the while, his mother and sisters were squalling for him to stop. His mom finally took the broom to him and cracked him in the head. He turned loose of Willie Joe, and he lit out of the house and ran to his tree house, where he cried his heart out.

It wasn't the beating that hurt him the most; it was the loss of his father and his once-happy family. When he saw his father pull out of the driveway, he went to the house to check on everybody. His mom gathered him to her and smothered him with kisses. His Pappaw was right. Sometimes all you need to feel better is the comfort of a mother's embrace.

Nobody knew about the decline of the Wells family. His mother made sure she put on a brave face when she was out in public. She kept Willie Joe home from school so he wouldn't have to explain his bruises. He was afraid of his friends, especially Ruby, ever discovering that his father had become a drunken family abuser. So, he shoved all that angst deep inside himself and acted like everything was hunky dory. If Ruby only knew, she never would have teased him.

"Excuses, excuses. I knew you'd find a way out of it. But, if you'll come to my house tomorrow at about one and watch me and Vera work my Ouija board and then go up on the graveyard and have a séance, we may let you live this down. Maybe we can bring back Saw Blade while we're at it!"

"That's never going to happen 'cause that stupid Ouija board is a load of horseshit, as are seances. How dumb do you think I am? You all have probably rigged up something to cheat with and try to scare me. Because I got scared when I watched *Halloween* when I was ten, you girls think I'm a big scaredy cat."

"So, piss on it. I'll be at your house tomorrow, Ruby Lee, and show you how brave I can be." Ruby Lee was at the turnoff to Shotgun Hollow. She puts on her brakes and skids a little in the gravel. Her long auburn hair falls beautifully down her back as she whips her head around. Willie Joe's heart melts a little, but he never shows it. He keeps the scowl on his face while he looks up at her until she breaks into a smile, and he can't help but smile back. "see ya later, alligator," says Ruby Lee.

"After a while, crocodile," returns Willie Joe.

He stands on his bike pedals and uses his legs to climb the hill. Vera has witnessed this exchange in her usual quiet manner. Every time they argue, they look at each other, and it's a different look than it used to be. But Vera fears that it's love. And if that's true, her heart will never be the same.

Vera's House

Vera goes to her room, pulls out her diary from between the mattress and box springs of her bed, and writes the happenings of the day, which always end up being about Willie Joe. He looked so cute today in his cutoff jean shorts and sleeveless Panama Jack t-shirt! The shirt was blue and matched his eyes perfectly. He looks like a surfer with his brown skin and sun-bleached hair. If only he would look at her like he looks at Ruby Lee. There is some hope in sight, though. The brothers from Catlettsburg are here for the rest of the summer, so maybe Ruby would like one of them. Vera had learned a poem from her cousin and was dying to secretly give it to Willie Joe. It goes like this:

> *I had a heart, and it was true*
> *But now it's gone from me to you*
> *Take care of it as I have done*
> *For you have two, and I have none*
> *When I die, if you're not there*
> *I'll sign your name on the golden stair*
> *And just to prove my love is true*
> *I'd go to Hell to be with you*

Ruby Lee admitted in the Spring that if Chris Wells was still cute, she would ask him to the Sadie Hawkins Dance. He was cute last summer. Hopefully, he'd gotten cuter. With Ruby out of the way, maybe by the grace of God, Willie Joe would finally look at her. Then she would give him the poem.

Vera closed her diary and returned it to her hiding place. She turned on the radio, and her favorite song was playing, *Stuck on You*, by Lionel Richie. Vera drifted off to sleep with thoughts of

Willie Joe's beautiful blue eyes! Little did she know, but this would be her last wonderful dream for a long time.

The Out of Towners

Every summer, an influx of kids comes to Mary Luck. When the coal mines dried up, many folks moved up north to find factory jobs. But the call of the mountains always brought them back. Most folks had beautiful memories of growing up rural. And you can't get much more rural than Mary Luck.

It was a two-hour drive to any mall. There wasn't a swimming pool or arcade, but the need for those things disappeared once you played in the mountains. Exploring caves, hiking, and, of course, ghost stories.

Superstition abounded everywhere. The kids even had a nickname for Sally Evans, who had a superstition for everything. They called her Superstitious Sally; she knew it but didn't mind. She trusted her omens of death and always knew when she was about to have company or, more importantly, when someone would die. They all could laugh at her if they wanted. She'd get the last laugh. She'd live to be one hundred.

The kids brought to town by their parents were always in culture shock. They grew up in a world of suburbs, malls, and theaters with more than one screen. Here in Mary Luck; it seemed you were cut off from the real world, and it usually took those kids about a week to come around. But once they did, they learned to love the mountains and appreciate the beauty and heritage they belonged to by blood.

The first to arrive in the summer of 1984 was the Baldridge twins, Josh and Josie. The brown-haired, brown-eyed pair shared the same lips and nose, but that was where the similarities ended. Josh was tall and lanky, and Josie was fine-boned and petite. They got in the second week of June and planned to stay until August. The twins are from Lexington, and they stay with their grandparents, Mabel and Clarence Baldridge, who were both born and raised in Mary Luck. Their parents, Connor and Stephanie, are going on a missionary trip to Guam and be gone for two months.

The twins are thrilled to have the entire summer to hang out with their friends, Willie, Ruby, and Vera. They love all the scary stories and want to learn how to work the Ouija board. They were spellbound, watching Ruby and Vera work it back at Christmas. The fact that it was banned by the church made it even more enticing. However, being native to Mary Luck through the blood of their kin made them a part of the curse, too.

The twins met up with the trio at the park the first day they arrived. Hugs and high fives went around the group, then the girls began discussing the latest *Sweet Valley High* book, so Josh and Willie went to the basketball court to shoot some hoops.

When the group was back together and sitting at the picnic table in the shade, Josie told them about her new hobby. Back in the early Spring, she had bought a deck of Tarot cards, and she wanted to tell everyone's fortune. This announcement was met with squeals of delight from the girls, but Willie, Joe, and Josh just rolled their eyes. They started making plans for the rest of the summer when suddenly three people showed up, which changed everything.

Tammy Turner, the biggest tale packer in town, came over to the group with two fresh faces. George and Hughey Webb. They were thirteen and twelve, respectively. They were from Fairview, KY, which wasn't much bigger than Mary Luck, but it was only five miles from Ashland and twenty miles from Huntington, WV, so they considered themselves city kids. These boys hadn't been to town to stay in the summer for at least three years, so they didn't remember anyone. That's where Tammy came into the fold.

The Webb boy's grandparents are Boyd and Virginia Webb. They are the parents of the boy's Father, Stephen, who married Sylvia Daniels from Olive Hill. However, their relationship is on the rocks, so they dump the kids off on his parents so that they can try to salvage their marriage. Tammy introduced the boys to the group and filled us in on the sordid details, which made both boys blush at their sandy blond hairline. Vera and Ruby had enough sense to not make eye contact and change the subject.

"Hey Tammy, I heard that Whitney Burkett is due here any day now. She's supposed to spend the entire summer this year." Ruby informs her.

"Oh, I know all about it. I talked to Whitney's Mamaw yesterday. Whi t will be here tomorrow. She's already promised to stay with me all night. We've been pen pals for over a year now, ya know." Tammy says this last bit and tosses her frizzy brown hair over her shoulder. "See y'all later. Come on, boys, let's go get a Coke or something. Try to find something to do in this shit hole place."

Ruby Lee gives her the finger when she turns her back while Vera sticks her tongue out at her.

Willie snickers, and so do the twins.

"What a bitch that one is!" States Josh.

"Tell me about it. We have to put up with Tammy every day at school, too. No escape from Tammy the Terror," says Willie.

Vera pushes the rewind button on her boombox, and soon Def Leppard fills the air with *Rock of Ages*. Then, to their utter surprise, Whitney Burkett waltzes into the park. Her newly permed blonde hair, shiny with mousse and hair spray, is perfectly coiffed in a stylish bob. She is by far the wealthiest of all the kids, but she isn't a show-off, anymore that is.

When she first came for a week in the summer, she snubbed all the kids and soon became an outcast. Her constant bragging about having two Ataris and her own private phone line in her bedroom soon wore thin with the kids of Mary Luck. They were used to poverty; it was around them every day. So, to have someone flaunt their wealth and sneer at those less fortunate, the others weren't having it.

The turning point for Whitney was when she got called fat. Whitney wasn't obese, but she was a little chunky. Especially compared to Ruby and Vera, who were thin as a rail. Out of pure boredom and the fact that her grandpa was the church preacher, Whitney came to bible school at the Freewill Baptist Church. Bible School was an event that all the kids in Mary Luck and the surrounding towns looked forward to every year.

Whitney turned her nose up to anyone who approached her. At recess on the first day of Bible School, Whitney stood by the baseball field fence in her e-Spirit outfit and pristine white Keds chewing gum and blowing bubbles. That's when she heard some boys talking about her. To make things worse, it was Tommy Harris, the only cute boy her age in town, according to Whitney. She'd heard him say, "Man, it's a shame that rich bitch is such a fat ass. If she was skinny, I'd ask her out and maybe even ask her to 'g o with me.' I bet she'd buy me anything I wanted. I hear she has two Atari's and every game made. But even with all those perks, I could never like her unless she dropped about fifty pounds."

Tommy hadn't seen Whitney standing by the fence, but when he saw her and saw the look of hurt and pain on her face knowing she'd heard every word he said, he cracked up and snickered and said, "Hey fat ass, lose a few hundred pounds and grow some tits instead of a gut and maybe then I'll consider going out with you."

"She should be so flattered. Tommy, you need to look at that beak you call a nose and rein in the insults. You're nothing but a big fat bully!" Shouted Ruby Lee from the bleachers.

Tommy threw his bat down, came over to the fence, and yelled, "What's it any of your business, Red? I bet she's snubbed you, too. She doesn't even appreciate you sticking up for her."

"Yes, I do!" Whitney speaks up for the first time.

"I know I'm a big girl, but I have feelings too, ya know?"

Whitney moved to stand by Ruby in the bleachers and threw an arm around her shoulders.

Tommy guffaws and says, "Go drink some Tab and run some laps, fatso!"

"Ass Hole!" shouts Ruby at his back as he takes centerfield.

Whitney giggles at that, and she turns to Ruby and tells her, "Thank you for doing that. I know I've been a snob to you and all the other kids. I'm really sorry. I'm not good at making friends. But I'd like to try with you."

"Sure, Whitney, my name is Ruby Lee, and this is Vera and Willie Joe. We ain't rich, but we know how to have fun. I said something because he used to Go With my sister Rosie and when she broke up with him because he picked his nose all the time, he said some awful things about her. He thinks he's the cock of the walk, so I thought I'd take a shot and bring him down a peg or two."

"Well, whatever the reason, I'm grateful to you."

"Cool! Now tell us all about where you live." Asks Ruby.

And from that day on, Whitney was part of the gang.

Ruby was the first to jump up to hug Whitney, followed closely by Vera and Josie. The boys hung back, and each gave her a high five when the hugging was over. Anything more than that would've been too personal for the guys. The music had switched to Bryan Adams', 'Run to You, courtesy of Vera's mix tape and boombox.

Whitney had gotten taller, and this caused her to slim down, so she was no longer the chubby girl. Her confidence seemed to be better, too. Ruby was happy for her. Whitney had really blossomed and became a great friend to them.

"So, what's up with you and Tammy being Pen Pals?"

"Do what? She wrote to me, and I sent her a Christmas card. And that was it."

"Well, she told us you and her were best friends and that you would stay all night with her on your first night here." Stated Ruby.

"That liar. I never said that. I was hoping to hang out with you all. The only thing is, Tammy's granny lives next door to my Pap, so I'm sort of forced to be friends with her. And I will, but I don't have to like it. She makes me so mad the way she lies about everything," says Whitney as she pulls a pack of Hubba Bubba from her pocket and hands it around to the group.

"Hopefully, the Webb boys will keep her busy. I feel sorry for them." Points out Ruby as she blows a bubble, then another one inside the first. She holds it there and tries for three, but it bursts and smears over her face.

"Aw man Ruby, that's nasty. I mean, "Gag me with a spoon!" laughs Whitney.

Whitney had a VCR and had watched "Valley Girl" about a hundred times. She loved to quote the movie any chance she got. This thrilled Ruby and Vera. They saw Whitney as worldly. She was fourteen and going to high school in the Fall. At their age, one year older meant more. Ruby had just turned thirteen, and Vera wouldn't be until July.

"Vera has something to tell you," says Ruby

Vera looks at Ruby with a puzzled expression, then says, "Oh, yeah, my dad is gonna let us have a slumber party in his new garage before he puts anything in it. It should be finished by this weekend. It has electricity too, so we can put my stereo in there. It'll be great."

"Totally! Like, I can't wait." Adds Whitney. She blows an enormous bubble and says,

"Hey, I just had a great idea! Let me ask first, but it will be a surprise if I can. You'll, like, totally flip out!"

"My mom is taking us to the Lake Pool tomorrow if you want to go. We've got plenty of room in her car." Says Ruby.

"Who all's going?" asks Whitney

"Me, Vera, Willie, my sisters, and you, if you can go."

"Cool, I'll ask, but I'm sure I can go. Have you all seen Sixteen Candles yet?"

"Yes, yes! It was so awesome. Jake Ryan is so gorgeous." Says Ruby. She gets a dreamy look on her face and giggles. The other girls laugh at her.

"Take it easy, Ruby, he's taken. I saw it in Bop magazine." Says Josie.

Josie takes on an air of seriousness and asks, "I need to tell you all something. I got the tarot cards, so when we first got in this morning, I did a reading for my Gran, and it was different from anything I've ever seen."

"What do mean?" asks Ruby

"Sometimes the death card shows up, but it's not always a bad thing, but this time it was. If my reading was right, death would be on the way. I'm scared. It really freaked me out."

Ruby puts her arm around her shoulder, tries to console her, and says. "Look, maybe you just read it wrong or something."

"No way! I even checked the book that I learned from. I didn't tell Gran anything; I didn't want her to worry."

"Ok, there might be someone who can help. Ruby turns to Vera. "Have you seen Superstitious Sally lately? "

"Every day of my life. She's always out on her swing, and I ask her for the weather report. She told me it would rain today even though there ain't a cloud in the sky. But she told me that the wind was blowing and turning the leaves on the trees belly up, which meant rain. Guess we'll see."

"Why do you ask?"

"I was just thinking maybe we should visit her and see if her omens show any signs of death. Y'all have got to meet Super Sally anyhow. She has these concrete ponds by her porch filled with huge goldfish. You can dip your feet in them, and the fish will nibble your toes and tickle your feet. She's so fun to talk to; she always has a superstition about everything. The funny thing is, she's almost always right about her predictions."

"Sounds good to me," says Whitney. "Lead the way, my darlings!"

Superstitious Sally's House

Super Sally's house sits upon a grassy knoll that gives her a bird's-eye view of the bridge that spans the Big Sandy River and the road into Mary Luck. A five-room white house with gingerbread trim in baby blue. It looked like something out of a fairy tale. It reminded Ruby Lee of where Little Red Riding Hood's grandma would have lived.

As the kids approach the house, Sally is on her front porch swing with a glass of lemonade. On the side table sits a pitcher of said lemonade with six glasses of ice beginning to melt.

"Come on up here young'uns, and quench your thirst. It's hot today, but rain is coming, and it smells like it's gonna be a gully washer," Sally says while she gazes at the sky, puts her nose in the air, and takes a deep breath.

The twins and Whitney exchange a look of bewilderment, but the trio takes it in stride. "How does she know that?" Whitney mumbles under their breath.

"She watches for signs or omens and can tell you the weather any day of the year," says Vera. "I'm sure there was a sign that told her we were coming too."

"It's about time y'all got here. My nose had been itching since noon, and I knew someone would visit me today. I saw you're coming up the road, and I say to myself, 'Sally, them kids is coming to visit with you.' So, I went in and got some glasses and fetched ye some lemonade out of the Frigidaire. Now be careful on that walkway, and don't step on no cracks lest ye break your Momma's back!"

Willie Joe stopped mid-stride and placed his foot between the cracks, which was hard, seeing as cracks were everywhere."

Ruby Lee got to the porch first. She went over and hugged Sally around the neck and placed a sweet peck on her cheek.

"Miss Sally, these are some of my new friends, Whit…." Sally shushed her with an upheld hand.

"I know exactly who these children are. These two here are Baldridge's. I can tell by that foxy up turn to your noses, and this one here is a Burkett." Sally proclaims.

"How do you know I'm a Burkett?" asks Whitney

"Well, I could tell by your eyes, my dear. The Burkett's all have eyes that color hazel. Take that and your dimpled chin, which some believe is the marking of the devil's hoof print, and there's no denying your lineage."

"Wow, Miss Sally, you should've been a detective!" Whitney says with the slightest hint of sarcasm.

Miss Sally retorts, "That sass is all your grandma, though. Her being a Flannery from up on the Ridge."

Whitney turns red and tries to apologize, having realized her rudeness, but Sally says, "No need to say sorry. You can't help your genes. You can pick your friends, but you can't pick your family. So, choose them wisely." Sally warns.

"What brings y'all to my doorstep on this fine summer day?" asks Sally.

"We were wondering if you'd seen any omens lately that said something bad was gonna happen?" asks Vera as she sits beside Sally on the swing.

"Why on earth would you want to know something like that?" Asks Sally.

Josie speaks up for the first time and explains, "Miss Sally, I got some Tarot cards a while back, and I'm still learning how to read them, but whenever I try to do a reading for my Gran, it's always showing death and bad luck. Ever since we got here, all my readings have been like that."

"Well, child, I never put much stock in those cards. I depend on the portents of nature to tell me when evil is afoot. The last time I saw your Gran, she looked healthy enough so I wouldn't get upset. However, I heard a rooster crowing at midnight last week, and then last night, a dog was howling at the moon even though it was just a sliver waxed. If it howls two more nights in a row, that's a sure sign that someone will die."

Sally takes a minute to ponder, then says, "I thought I saw a butterfly out after dark the other night, but it could've been a miller or moth. But if it was a butterfly, that means death is lurking around. Have you had any dreams about babies being born?"

"Not that I can remember." Says Josie.

"Have any birds flown in the house?" asks Sally.

"It probably wouldn't hurt to hang a horseshoe over the front door, like I have here. Make sure you always enter and exit by the same door. The same goes for getting in and out of bed. To do otherwise invites bad luck. If you see a calico cat, pet it if you can, as this breed is surprisingly lucky. But do not kill any ladybugs. That is terribly unlucky. Don't walk under any ladders or open any umbrellas in the house, and whatever you do, do not break any mirrors. Breaking a mirror will bring you seven years of bad luck." Miss Sally says this last while pointing her finger at Josie and fixing her with a piercing look.

"Yes, ma'am! Thank you for the good advice."

"How did you know we were going to visit?" asks Josh.

"Besides my nose itching to beat the band, I dropped my dish towel while getting my biscuits out of the oven this morning. Then I dropped my fork as I brought my plate to the sink because I was swatting at a bee. The signs were all there, and here you are, so I think you can see I was right." Miss Sally says proudly while placing her arms over her considerable bosom. "And, I have another word of advice. If you start having bad dreams, do not tell anyone what you dreamed of before you've had your breakfast, or it will come true. "

"I'll definitely remember that. I've had some doozies here lately, and I'd not want to see them come true." Ruby says with a shiver. "Sugar, hang you a horseshoe in your bedroom and keep your Bible by your bed; those nightmares will stop," Sally says as she pats Ruby on the knee and gives her a wink.

"One other thing, I don't mean to scare you, but a picture on my wall fell today for no reason whatsoever. I was just sitting on the couch watching the PTL, and it just dropped to the floor, and the frame broke."

The kids just stared at her and waited for her to continue. "Why is that so scary?" asked Willie Joe

"For goodness sakes, ain't your folks taught you nothing? When a picture falls, it means that a catastrophe is upon us. And since the frame broke, it will be terrible."

"What kind of catastrophe?"

"Any catastrophe is bad. But it says to me it will be brought on by natural causes. Like a severe thunderstorm with lightning or a flash flood. My good friend Ethel Landry from Van Lear told me once that a picture fell in her house one morning, and that night, lightning struck her barn outside and burnt it to the ground while it poured the rain."

"What signs have you seen today about the weather?" asks Josh

"Well, let me see. I first noticed the leaves flipping up and showing their belly when the wind blew. Next, I stepped on an anthill when I went out to feed my chickens. I saw old Bessie, my cat, chewing on some grass. So, with all those signs, it's gonna rain, and if my nose tells me right, it will be bad. I can smell the rain that has lightning. You can giggle all you want, but mark my words; there will be light in the sky tonight."

"Ruby, go in the house and grab six acorns off my kitchen table," Sally directs.

When Ruby returns, Sally tells them, "Y'all put this acorn on your window sill, and lightning won't strike in your room. Acorns are lucky, so pack one in your pocket if you need extra luck. Finish up your lemonade, and then be on your way. It's almost time for my story."

The kids drain their drinks and tell her thank you. Vera gathers the

glasses and takes them inside, and when she returns, they're ready to go.

Vera then tells the girls as they walk down the lane that her daddy has made the garage ready for their sleepover. They make plans to meet up at her house at seven. Josh and Willie act hurt that they're not invited.

Josh then tells Willie he could come and stay the night at his house, and they can do manly things. "Okay, sounds good to me," Willie says. "I'll bring some Atari games, and we can try to beat the high score."

"Cool, man. It'll be nice to have a guy to play against. Playing with girls is like taking candy from a baby!" "I bet you can't beat my high score on Pac-Man, boys. I'm the best one at my school." States Whitney.

"I just bet you are. You'll have to prove it with no one to back you up on that," teases Willie Joe.

"Any time, any place, dork face!" Whitney says as she dodges a punch to her arm.

Giggles erupt from all of them as they stroll home. It's almost supper time, so one by one, they drift away and go their separate ways.

The Slumber Party

Ruby is the first to arrive at Vera's. She has brought her hot pink and purple sleeping bag, her Duran Duran sleep shirt, and her Ouija Board. Her mom has sent snacks too. Doritos, Oreos, Rice Krispy Treats, and a two-liter of Pepsi. Vera's mom makes microwave popcorn, Totino's pizzas, Lays potato chips, and French onion dip.

The girls set up Vera's stereo and tune in to Q95, where Footloose plays. They squeal in delight and boogie. As shy as Vera is, you'd never know she was such an excellent dancer. Ruby hopes she will show off for Whitney and Josie and finally let someone besides her see how great she is.

Vera is one of the funniest people she knows, but sadly, she's so quiet that hardly anyone has ever seen that side of her. Ruby knows that because of her braces, Vera rarely smiles in public, and she has begged for a year now to get contacts so she won't have to wear glasses with Coke bottles for lenses. Ruby also knows that Vera has a massive crush on Willie Joe. She tries to deny it, but it is painfully apparent anytime he's around. She retreats into her shell even further and admires him from afar. If only she would talk to him more; maybe he would notice and see her as more than a friend.

Just as the end of the song gets close and the girls are singing their hearts out, a hard knock on the window scares the crap out of them, and they yelp! They run to the window to see who is spying on them and are relieved to know that it is only Toby and Timmy, Vera's little brothers. "Y'all git out of here!" Vera yells as she flings open the door and chases after them. "Daddy told you two to stay away from here. If you come back , Ruby will whoop the tar out of you." The boys have been scared to death of Ruby ever since she put Toby in Figure Four and Timmy in the Sleeper Hold.

A car horn blows, and the girls turn to see Whitney and Josie get out of Whitney's Papaw's Cadillac. They each have a sleeping bag, a bag of snacks, and make-up bags. Vera's dad shows up with a portable TV and tells them to hop in the truck, and he will rent them a VCR and some movies. This is going to be the best slumber party ever!

All four girls pile in the truck's bed and hold on tight. Vera's daddy's truck is loud, and he revs the engine and makes them squeal with delight as they fly down the road. None of them care that the wind is messing up their hair or that the truck bed is filthy. This will probably be their last summer to be this carefree. It didn't have to be said. They all knew it. Their unspoken awareness of this is what makes this time so unique. It would be gone in a flash, and they acknowledged it by not pointing it out.

When they arrive at Super Star Video, the girls rush inside to see if *A Nightmare on Elm Street* is in, but all the copies are already rented. "Damn!" says Whitney, then she quickly covers her mouth with her hand when she realizes that Vera's dad is standing right behind her. The girls all giggle, and her dad rolls his eyes and goes to the counter to fill out the paperwork to rent the VCR.

The girls are browsing the "teen rom/com" section when Whitney spies with her little eye the best movie she has ever seen, *Little Darlings*!

"Oh, my God!" Whitney squeals. "We have to get this one. Have any of you ever seen this?" All three girls shake their heads, no, and this makes Whitney almost lose her mind. "You guys are gonna flip out! Matt Dillon is such a dreamboat. He is totally gorgeous in this movie."

"Okay Okay, , calm down. Dad will let us rent at least three, maybe four, movies." Vera states. "Ruby, go see what horror movies they have." She looks at the meager selection and decides on *Slumber Party Massacre* and *Prom Night*. She was torn between *Phantasm* and *Creepshow*. She'd let the others choose while she looked at the older movies. *The town that dreaded Sundown* looked super creepy, but there wouldn't be one cute boy in that one. She could tell by the cover.

Then she saw it. The movie haunted her nightmares for years and still made her nervous just to think about that little boy scratching at her window. *'Salem's Lot* scared the crap out of her. It was a made-for-TV movie, but it was horrific for her. Ruby quickly hid the cover of the film so that no one else would see it. She didn't think she could handle vampires tonight.

Another squeal. This time it was Josie. She gushed, "Have you all seen *The Outsiders?*" Whitney had, but Vera and Ruby had not. "Oh, you guys, this movie has every cute boy in the world in it. Rob Lowe, C. Thomas Howell, Patrick Swayze, and Leif Garrett." That last name did it for Vera. She loved Leif Garrett; she had the record *"I Was Made for Dancing"* and played it every day in sixth grade. Ruby loved Shaun Cassidy and Andy Gibb. *Shadow Dancing* was her all-time favorite, but Leif Garrett was dreamy, too.

Vera grabbed all four of the movies and handed them to the clerk, so her dad wouldn't see that they were rated R. The clerk returned with the videos already bagged and gave them to Vera with a wink. She blushed and giggled like only a 13-year-old girl can. Ear-splitting and off-key.

Her dad rolled his eyes for the hundredth time since they arrived and hefted up the VCR. His wallet was twenty-five dollars lighter. He shrugged to the clerk and said. "Ah, Hell, they're only young once. If I can make my little girl smile, it's worth every penny." The childless, unmarried clerk shrugged and said, "Good for you, man;

I hope you have some booze to make it through the night." Virgil Wilcox smiled, shot the clerk with a finger gun, and said, "You're damn straight right there, my friend!"

As he opened the door with his considerable backside, the bell on top rang out, causing the clerk to shiver. He hated that damn bell. It sounded to him like work.

The girls were all seated in the truck bed, and they sped the five miles back to Mary Luck as if on wings. After crossing the bridge, the temperature seemed to drop. The fog from the river lay close to the road and hid anything that might crawl by night. That thought made Ruby shiver. After hearing all the stories from the Yarn Spinners, she knew this town had a dark history. Though she didn't know it yet, she soon discovered how haunted Mary Luck was. It reminded her of the introduction from *Tales of the Darkside*.

"Man lives in the sunlit world of what he believes to be reality. But... There is, unseen by most, an underworld, a place that is just as real but not as brightly lit... a Darkside.

To Ruby, that described Mary Luck to a tee.

Back at Vera's, the girls all changed into their PJs and headed to the garage to watch movies and talk about boys. Who could ask for more? They decided on *The Outsiders* to watch first, saving the scary movies for closer to midnight. The girls curled up in their sleeping bags and ate snacks while gushing over Soda Pop Curtis and Pony Boy. And, of course, Leif Garrett. Even though he is a real dirtbag in the movie, he is still so cute. Matt Dillon stole the show for Whitney. She couldn't wait to show them *Little Darlings*.

After hearing Johnny's letter to Pony Boy after the movie and all the snot noses, and tears had been wiped away, the girls filed out of the garage and headed to Vera's house for a pee break. Unbeknownst to them, Willie Joe and Josh had sneaked out of Josh's Mammaw's house. They'd been hiding in the ditch across the road from the garage. When the girls left, they high-tailed it over and hid inside the garage.

Willie Joe exclaimed, "I think I've died and woke up inside a Pepto Bismol bottle. Have you ever seen so much pink before, Josh?"

"No way, man, this place smells like a perfume counter at Lazarus. Girls can be so strange sometimes. Let's hurry and hide before they get back. Grab that bag of Doritos too!" Willie Joe scoops up the bag, and they find a place to crouch behind Vera's dad's Craftsman Tool Chest that stood five feet tall and would do just fine. The boys were chowing down when he heard them giggle.

"Here they come. Be quiet now. We will wait until they start their movie, and then we can jump out and scare the pants off them. Do you still have your pillowcase?"

asks Willie Joe.

"Sure do. I cut the holes out just like you said."

"Man, this is gonna be so fine. Wish we had a camera to show everyone how scared they were."

"Yeah, that would be so cool," Willie says wistfully.

"Shush, they're here."

"Like totally, Vera, your Dad is so funny. You're lucky to have a dad who would do all this for you. My dad barely speaks to me. He just hands me money and tells me to go buy something," states Whitney.

"Wow! Wish my dad would do that. I have to work like a dog to get a penny out of him," says Ruby Lee.

"I'd go without the money just to spend time with my dad. Y'all don't know how good you got it," says Whitney with a sniffle.

The other girls look at the floor, and Josie says, "Let's watch your movie, Whitney."

She shakes off her sadness, puts on a cheerful face, and hurriedly puts *'Little Darlin's'* in the VCR.

When the boys hear what Whitney says, they almost decide not to scare the girls, but their adolescence kicks in, and they put their plan into action. They wait until about fifteen minutes into the movie, and then they place their pillowcase masks over their head. On the count of three, they jumped up from behind the tool chest and yelled, "Surprise!!"

The girl's shriek is so loud the boys cover their ears. They are so afraid that they just stand there clutching onto one another. Willie Joe runs over toward Ruby Lee, and she hauls off and slugs him right in the nose. Willie Joe grabs his nose as blood spreads on the white pillowcase.

He jerks the mask off and says, "Shit! Ruby Lee, I think you broke my nose!" At the same time, Josh has grabbed Whitney, and she deftly kicks him in the balls. He falls to the floor with a groan and a girlish squeal. Whitney jerks his mask off and immediately laughs.

"Serves you right, asshole! You don't mess with us and not pay the price!" Vera sees the light come on in the house and knows her dad has heard them screaming and that he will be there any second with a shotgun.

"Y'all hide. Daddy's coming!" says Vera worriedly. The boys slowly move back to their hiding place. Wille Joe is holding his nose, and Josh is still weak-kneed and has to crawl. Safely hidden, they look at each other and just shake their heads.

Vera's Dad busts in the door wearing his long handles and a wife beater. A fresh stain on the front where he must have spilled his beer trying to get up fast out of his Lazy Boy. His hair is every which way, and his eyes are bloodshot. "What in the Sam Hill is going on in here?" he yells.

"Nothing Daddy, I just saw a gigantic spider, and we were all yelling 'cause we couldn't catch it and kill it. It got away, though, so we're fine. I'm sorry we scared you." She says this last so sweetly that it's a wonder she didn't get a cavity.

"Alright, you girls, have fun. I'll be up for a while if you need a spider killer. Come and get me." He says this last with a considerable slur followed by a hiccup burp.

When the door closes behind him, Ruby runs to where Willie and Josh are writhing in pain.

"What the Hell? Willie, what did you expect we would do? I mean, duh. You scared the crap out of us." Ruby says this while standing with her hands on her hips, glaring at them.

"Well, I didn't think you'd break my damn nose."

"Oh, I'm sure it's not broken. Here let me see."

"No! Don't touch it." Willie says as he swats Ruby's hand away from his face.

"Quit being such a baby! It's already stopped bleeding. I didn't feel it snap when I punched you, so let me see it."

Ruby tilts his head back and runs her finger over the bridge of his nose. "It's not broken," Ruby pronounces with an air of authority.

"How would you know? You ain't no doctor." Says Willie whiningly.

"No, but I broke Eugene Webb's nose in the fourth grade when he spit that big phlegm g lobber on me. Have you forgotten that?" Ruby replies.

"Oh, yeah. I guess I forgot about that. It's stopped throbbing, but I'll still have a big fat nose for a few days. The worst part is telling people I got hit by a girl!" Willie says as he hangs his head in shame.

"When they find out who did it, they'll think you look better than you should." Says Ruby as she smirks and then breaks into giggles.

Whitney approaches Josh and says, "I'm not gonna come over there and check out your injury. Your raisin-sized balls are your problem!" Josh blushes to his hairline and flips her the bird. She gives it right back and tosses her hair over her shoulder as she turns on her heel and giggles with all the girls.

"When did you two creeps sneak in?" asks Josie

"When y'all went to pee. We haven't been here that long. All your deep, dark secrets are safe." Willie says this while placing his hand over his heart. "Why don't y'all sneak out with us?"

"And do what?" asks Josie.

"My daddy would kill me if he caught us," Vera says while nervously wringing her hands. Willie walks over, places his hands on her shoulders, and looks her in the eyes. Vera stands stalk still and instantly becomes complacent. It's as if Willie has hypnotized her.

"Vera, from the looks of your daddy, he's had more than a six-pack tonight. My guess is that he's already passed out in his chair. Just keep a movie on. He will think y'all are in here safe and sound. I promise it'll be fine." He says this last with a squeeze of her shoulders. When he lets go, Vera seems dazed, but Willie hardly notices.

"Where is there to go? It's just Mary Luck." States Whitney. "Yeah, but it's dark outside. Makes everything a little scary." Josh said with a gleam in his eye while wiggling his eyebrows.

"Spare me, boys. I'm not easily spooked. I don't believe in ghosts," states Whitney.

"You should be," says Willie. "If you knew all the stories that we did, you'd be scared. Mary Luck ain't the sweet little town you think it is."

"What are you talking about? Surely you don't believe all those silly stories those old men tell at the park? They are so not true!" Whitney says.

"Well, we just know some terrifying shit that happened here."

Willie retorts and starts to say more when Ruby jumps in and says, "You're right, Whitney, those tales are kid's stuff." Ruby glares at Willie Joe.

He catches her meaning and backtracks, and says, "I know where we could go unless you girls are chicken."

"And where would that be?" asks Whitney.

"We could sneak up to the window at Mrs. Purdy's house."

"Be a Peeping Tom at an old lady's house. Gee, how cool is that?" Whitney says sarcastically.

"Yeah, but Mrs. Purdy is a relative of the witch, Baby Annie. And she was one bad Mamma Jamma! And Mrs. Purdy knows how to do seances and make tables walk." He says proudly.

Ruby Lee takes over the conversation since Willie Joe can't shut his mouth. Before the summer kids arrived, the trio had decided not to share their secret. They wanted the Yarn Spinners to be something only they could hear. It was exceptional, and they wanted to keep it just for themselves. Willie Joe wanted to be a show-off; if he didn't watch it, he would spill the beans.

"I think we should do it. What do y'all think?" says Ruby.

"I'm in," says Whitney and Josie simultaneously. They all turn to look at Vera, and she seems hesitant. Willie Joe walks over to her and puts his arm around her shoulders, and she blushes pitifully. "Come on, Vera. It'll be fun. And I promise you we won't get caught, and if we do, I'll take all the blame."

"Okay, okay, let's do it! Let me go first and peep in the window to ensure my daddy's asleep."

The kids all leave the garage and take off to the back of Vera's house. They crouch in the darkness and cover their mouths to stifle their giggles. None of the girls had ever sneaked out of their house before. For them, this was really being a rebel.

When Vera came around the corner, she motioned them to follow her. Safely away from her house, she says that her daddy was indeed passed out.

Willie Joe says, "Told ya. My dad drinks a lot these days, and I can always tell when he's about to pass out." He says this with a hint of sadness but quickly recovers and shrugs it off. Boys are like that at their age and can't show too much emotion, especially in front of a bunch of girls. Gotta keep up the macho act or be labeled a sissy.

Vera's house is in the River Bottom, or the Bottom as it is locally called. Her house is by far the newest and most excellent in the area. Though it is only a three-bedroom ranch with one and a half baths, it is a palace compared to the houses in the back row. That's where the poorest of the poor lived. Tar-paper shacks, some still with an outhouse. Those families have more kids than they can feed and live hand to mouth. If not for school lunches, they would probably starve.

The kids run behind the row of trailers behind Vera's house and come out on the Lane where Mrs. Purdy lived. They decide to go around the back of the Hackworth's and Music's house to hide under the chestnut trees behind her house.

"Do you all still have your lucky acorn with you?" asks Willie. The girls all shake their heads no, seeing as they are in their PJs that do not have pockets. "Uh oh. That's not good." Vera gives a jolt, and Willie quickly says. "Just kidding, just kidding."

"So, what's the plan? Are we gonna play ding dong ditch or what?" asks Whitney.

"I'm not gonna do it. I know it sounds stupid, but I don't want to risk having a curse put on me. My cards are still not coming out right, so I'm staying here." Josie says this last as she firmly plants her tiny feet in the grass and crosses her arms over her chest.

Josh rolls his eyes at his twin and says, "I'll do it. I'm not scared of some old hillbilly witch." He takes off before anyone can stop him. They all make themselves as small as possible under the tree.

Josh slows his approach as his bravery wavers when he gets to the steps leading up to Mrs. Purdy's back porch. There were Mason jars everywhere. They all have things floating in them. And they stink to high heaven. Josh gathers his courage and goes up the three steps, and once there, the smell gets worse. He has to pull his shirt over his nose to breathe.

He suddenly wants to get as far away from there as possible, but he can't look chicken in front of his friends. He'd never live it down. With his head down, he reaches out to knock on the door, but instead of hitting wood, his hand is roughly grabbed, and he is yanked nose to nose with Mrs. Purdy. She says hatefully, "What do you think you're doing here, boy? I don't like people sneaking around my place." Josh is shaking all over and has lost the ability to speak. His fright is palpable. He is fighting the urge to piss himself. "Now, you and that passel of young'uns over there under my trees, get your asses off my property. Don't you fools know I know everything that goes on around me? Now git or be got!"

Under the tree, the girls have to forcibly hold Josie down to keep her from going to help Josh. When Purdy talks about them, they shrink back and hold their breath to see what will happen next. Finally, they see Josh flung off the porch. He quickly finds his feet and runs toward his friends but doesn't even stop to see them; he hurdles the back fence and takes off toward Vera's.

When the kids catch up to him, he is bent over at the waste gasping for air. Josie runs to him and throws her arms around him. He pushes her off and says he needs a minute. They all gather around him and exchange glances of concern.

Willie speaks up first, "Hey man, you okay?" "No! I'm pretty fucking far from okay, okay. That woman really is a witch. She knew we were there even before I knocked. She grabbed my shirt and pulled me almost off my feet. Her breath would gag a maggot. Oh God! It was terrible." Josh hangs his head and doesn't mind that they can all see his tears. He accepts Josie's hug, and then, one by one, the others gather around and have a group hug. They had all been scared, Josh obviously being the worst.

Ruby Lee had a weird feeling when she was there. It was like she had been there before. She felt drawn to the house and Mrs. Purdy. She had always feared her, but now she felt an odd familiarity. She wasn't what you'd call scared. It was more like curiosity.

The boys came in and voraciously inhaled the girls' snacks at Vera's. Vera said they could stay and watch a movie if they promised not to do any more surprise scares. They agreed, and Ruby Lee put in *Slumber Party Massacre*. This slasher flick paled in comparison to the shock they'd just had. It was more comical than scary. They made fun of the bad acting and fake blood. But it was fun for them to be breaking the rules. It was harmless fun.

When the movie was over, it was after one in the morning. The boys gathered their masks and said goodbye, and then Willie Joe said, "Y'all sleep tight, don't let the bedbugs bite or let old Purdy getcha! She just lives right over there." He points to the river. "Yeah, but you must walk by the graveyard in the dark. Better be sure to whistle." Ruby says with a wink. Willie always whistles by the graveyard, even in the daylight. Try as he might to act tough. Ruby knows he's always been afraid. He shrugs off her warning and says, "After tonight, nothing can scare me." "Famous last words." says Whitney.

The boys shut the door on that last remark and wait until they are out of sight, then break into a dead run. They get to Josh's and dive in the open bedroom window. They jump in the bed and pull the covers up to their chin even though it's easily eighty degrees. Neither speaks lest they admit their fright. In five minutes, they are fast asleep.

Later that night, at about four a.m., the first streak of lightning lights up the sky, followed by a deep thunderous rumble that shakes the foundation of many of the houses in Mary Luck. Super Sally is awakened but simply rolls over and goes back to sleep. She can sleep soundly with all the protection she has around her home. The thunder wakes the trio, and they smile. Super Sally sure nailed this one.

The storm that night would bring with it omens and portents of evil. Now that was the harbinger of what was to come. A dark pall fell on the town, and it would be long before it would find its way back to the light. Things would never be the same once the wheel of fate had been spun.

At The Pool,
The Next Day

The morning after the slumber party, Ruby's mom picked the girls up and took them to the Jenny Wiley State Park lake pool. After the late-night thunderstorm, there were trees down everywhere. One tree, in particular, had been struck by lightning and had a burned streak that peeled the bark like a banana. It started at the top and went to the roots on the ground. It was a beautiful maple tree that turned the brightest red come fall. Ruby hoped it wasn't dead. She loved sitting under it when the leaves turned. It seemed to make everything glow when the sun shined down on it. It was like being in another world where everything was rosy.

The pool was only seven miles away, so the girls piled into the back of Kate's Jeep Wagoneer. They left the hatch window open to let the cool wind in. Though it had rained hard for about two hours, the sun quickly evaporated it, making it steamy. It was mid-July, and when the humidity was this high, and there wasn't a breath of air to be had, the best thing to do was get in some kind of water -a pond, lake, river, or, if you were lucky enough, a pool.

Bette Davis's Eyes came on the radio, and the girls all squealed, so Kate turned up the radio as they sang along with Kim Carnes. It was close to 10:30 when they got there, so there should still be an excellent place to lay out. Kate told them they were not, under any circumstances, to leave the pool. No riding around with any boys and no walking down to the paddle boats or over to the skylift. Ruby assured her they'd behave, then turned around and rolled her eyes. Her mother hollered out the window, "I saw that!" Ruby took off with her friends, not daring to look back. She wasn't like Lot's wife. She'd never be a pillar of salt.

Inside, they paid their admission and rushed down the steps to find a suitable spot. They looked longingly at the pump house, but it was off-limits to anyone not in high school. Ruby and Vera couldn't wait to be able to lay out there. All the cute boys and cool girls hung out there. As these thoughts ran through Ruby's mind, she spotted Tammy Turner and Teresa Spears.

Tammy caught her eye, waved, and said, "Sorry, girls, high school only. Whit, you can join us to get away from the kids."

Thankfully, Whitney replied, "Nah, I'm fine, but y'all have fun."

"Oh, I definitely will. Beau is working, so I can look at him all day." Tammy sits up and sticks out her chest to make her A-cup boobs look more prominent. Ruby can't help herself. She snickers and has to run away before she bursts into full-blown laughter.

One thing Ruby had learned the hard way was not to get on Tammy's wrong side. Sure, she was as scrawny as all get out, but she could make up a tale so fast it'd make your head spin. Lying came so quickly to her that you never knew when she was telling the truth. And she was the prank call queen. If she put in the time, she could tie up your phone line all day. This would then involve the parents, and nobody ever wanted that!

The other girls catch up with her and lay out their beach towels.

Ruby picked a spot so that they would face Beau's lifeguard chair. Every girl in the place, especially Ruby, had a massive crush on him. He stole her heart the day she and Willie Joe were almost thrown out of the pool for chicken fighting.

A new lifeguard had blown his whistle, motioned them out of the pool, and scolded them for horse-playing. That's when Beau swooped in like *The Greatest American Hero*. He told the new guy to lay off. They were just kids having fun, and besides, Red and Willie were the reigning champs. He tousled her hair and gave her a wink, and Ruby's heart was won.

He always teased her and called her Red. Usually, she hated being called that, but not when Beau said it. He was in college now, so she was thrilled he was home for the summer and still a lifeguard. Beau looked like a bronzed god. His coppery tan, blond hair that lay in a perfect feathered style, aqua blue eyes, dimpled cheeks, and brilliant white-toothed smile made him every girl's dream guy. It never crossed Ruby's mind that Willie Joe had the looks to be a future Beau. One day soon, Beau just might have a rival.

At about 11:00, the high school girls rolled in. These cool chicks that Ruby and Vera admired and wanted to be just like. They were all so pretty and tan. Wearing their bikini tops with cut-off Levis', they oozed confidence and superiority. When they made their way past all the ogling eyes of every boy and man there, they pulled up short when they saw Tammy and Teresa.

Ruby sat up and told the others, "Oh man, this is gonna be good." They had a front-row view of the destruction of one Tammy Turner.

"Just what in the hell do you think you two are doing? The pump house is for seniors only." Said the blond in the red Body Glove bikini.

Tammy sat up quickly, "We're in high school too, come on up, ladies, and hang out with us."

"Um, I don't think so, little girl. You need to move your ass off our place. Maybe you didn't hear me the first time. It's seniors only!" said the blonde.

"Oh, yeah, but we thought we could all hang out. I'm gonna be a freshman, so it'd be so cool to be seen with y'all."

"I don't think so. We pick who gets to lay out up here, so beat it!" The blond was losing patience, but Tammy just wouldn't quit.

"Please let us stay up here. I will do anything you say."

"You will? Then get your skinny asses off our fucking pump house! NOW!!" the blond screamed this last part, and everyone turned to see the commotion. Just then, Beau came up the back stairs and asked the blond what was happening. She filled him in, so he blew his whistle in Tammy's face and told her to move it or be banned.

That might be the highlight of the summer for them. To see Tammy put in her place was sublime. They were seen walking to the upper deck and using the phone, presumably telling her mom to come to get them. They went out to the steps and waited to be rescued.

"Oh my God, that was so awesome!" Says Whitney while grinning ear-to-ear.

"That has to be one of the greatest things I've ever seen!" says Ruby.

"You got that right!" chimed in Josie.

Ruby noticed Vera wasn't saying much and realized she felt sorry for her.

"Vera, what's wrong?" asked Ruby.

"I don't know. I think maybe that was a little too mean."

"Really? After all the times she has picked on you, how can you not enjoy this moment?"

"I know she's a bully, and she probably got what she deserved, but she was humiliated in front of everybody here. I just think that they went too far. And besides, she's one of us, Ruby. She's from Mary Luck. You know that we all stick together on this side of town. No matter what!"

This last statement made Ruby ashamed. It was true. If you were from Mary Luck, you stuck together. Anyone not from there made fun of them. Mary Luck had been called the armpit of Prestonsburg for years and years. We were a close-knit town, clannish and proud of our own traditions. We took care of our own. It was an unspoken code they all lived by. To go against it was you trying to out-grow your raisin'.

"Well, you're a better person than me. She's done nothing to me personally, and I can still enjoy seeing her put in her place." Says Whitney as she smirks, then giggles. "I bet she won't show her face for a week."

"That's my Vera, the sweetest girl I know." Ruby puts her arm around her.

The girls reapplied their Hawaiian Tropic oil and put zinc oxide on their noses. Vera turns up the radio and hears The J. Giles Band singing *Centerfold*. It was the perfect teenage summer day. Sadly, it would be one of their last. Their innocence was about to be stolen by a witch that died over one-hundred years ago.

Opening the Door

Ruby Lee's house,
12:45 p.m., July 26, 1984:

Ruby and Vera were on the back porch swing looking through the new Bop magazine Ruby had gotten that day. The centerfold was Duran Duran, Ruby's favorite. She couldn't wait to hang it up on her wall with all the others she had collected. John Taylor was so gorgeous. She went to bed every night, staring into his eyes.

The girls had their thermoses of sweet tea ready for their hike. Ruby had brought her Ouija board and set it up on the picnic table. Ruthie, Ruby's little sister, was thankfully around the hill at Nancy Beth's house. She loved her, but man, could she be a pest -always wanting us to play Barbies with her like Vera and Ruby wanted to play with dolls. They're way too old for that, like totally.

The sound of gravel alerts the girls to the arrival of Willie Joe right on time. Give that boy a gold star. He puts the kickstand down on his bike and turns to go out back. Ruby Lee's mom comes out the door with Jack, the kid she babysits, on her hip. "Hey there, Willie Joe, want a cold drink? I got sweet tea, Kool-Aid, or Tang."

"Thank you, Mrs. Collins. I'd love some sweet tea. Yours is always the best."

"Why thank you, Willie Joe. The girls are out back. Go ahead out there, and I'll bring it to you."

Willie Joe blushes a little. He's always thought Ruby's mom was so pretty. He heads to the back porch and finds his best friends gawking over Duran Duran. Girls can be so silly. They need to listen to some legitimate rock' n' roll like Quiet Riot and Kiss, not that sissy pop music. Gag! If he has to hear *The Reflex* on the radio or MTV one more time, he might throw up! But for now, he needs to prove he's not a chicken.

"So, What's a happenin' hot stuff?" Willie Joe tries his best to imitate Dong from Sixteen Candles, and he fails miserably, but it garners giggles from the girls and a radiant smile from Ruby Lee. "Mission accomplished," he thinks.

He deftly jumps up on the porch, wiggles between the girls, throws his arms around them and squeezes. The girls squeal and push him out of the swing. "you're too big to sit three in a swing! Sit on Mommy's lawn chair, goofball," Ruby kids. About that time, Mrs. Collins comes out and hands Willie Joe a thermos with Holly Hobby. Willie Joe looks at it, and she says, "Sorry, it's the only one left. Take it or leave it?"

"It's fine, Mrs. Collins. I'm sure your tea would be great in anything." As Willie says this, Ruby and Vera are standing behind her with their index finger in their mouth, mimicking throwing up and mouthing, "Gag me with a spoon"!

When she went back into the house, Ruby Lee pounced. "Geez, Willie Joe, you're such a suck-up! Gag!"

"It's a gift! I can't help I'm awesome!"

"Oh, my god, you are so full of yourself!"

"It's confidence, not conceit. There's a difference Ruby Lee."

"Shew, fight about it later. Let's get to playing. Let's start with the Ouija board," stated Vera.

"I don't know how to play that stupid thing!" whined Willie Joe.

"It's easy. Just ask a question, put your fingers lightly on the planchette, and watch it spell out the answer," Vera explained.

"Okay, let's do it," Willie Joe said with an eye roll.

Instead of the picnic table, they put the board on the round table for small gatherings. They took their seats and placed their fingers on the indicator. Ruby Lee asked the first question. "Does any spirit want to talk?" the indicator started to slide, and her heart went to her throat. Ruby had felt nothing like the jolt that went through her. The board answered yes, so Vera asked who it was. The answer was immediate: Annie.

Willie Joe was not buying this and told the girls they were pushing the indicator. They swore they weren't, but convincing someone without proof is complicated. The next question was, "Are you a friendly spirit or an evil spirit?" it immediately spelled out BAD!

Willie Joe jumped up and said this was 'pure bullshit' he wasn't falling for their tricks. "Next, you'll be telling me this spirit is Baby Annie! How dumb do you think I am?"

Ruby Lee started to speak, but Vera silenced her with a hand motion.

"We don't think you're stupid. I'm a little spooked. I've never seen the board work that good." Vera said.

"Me either," said Ruby Lee. "I have an idea. Why don't we go up to the graveyard and have a séance? There's no way we can fake that!"

"Okay, but I gotta be home soon, so let's go now," said Willie Joe.

"Don't forget Holly Hobby," teased Ruby Lee. Willie Joe tried to snatch it from her, but Ruby Lee put it behind her back, and they did this back-and-forth dance until finally Ruby gave in and let him have it. This little display of flirting did not escape Vera's ever-watchful eye.

Finally, they started up the path to the top of the hill. Ruby's house sat at the head of the holler inside a U-shape with mountains on three sides. All three kids knew this area well after playing there their whole lives. By the time they reach the top, they head to the giant silver maple tree for shade. It was hot outside, and there wasn't a breath of air. The sky was cloudless, but the humidity hung in the air like a greasy dish rag.

The trio drank some of their sweet tea and decided to do their séance under the tree in the shade. That is until they saw the enormous mounds of red fire ants. They all jumped up and shook off their clothes, and ran to the area of the hill that had a round depression in the ground. It wasn't huge, but they could easily sit around it and hold hands.

"So now what?" Willie Joe was losing patience, so the girls plopped down and told him to do the same. Once he did, they told him to hold their hands and close his eyes. He did, with some reluctance.

Once they calmed down, Vera said, "We would like to speak to Junior Bates, the boy who had drowned in the pond that claimed the life of Rebecca Joe. If you're with us, give us a sign?" After about thirty seconds of silence and nothing going on, Willie Joe dropped their hands and said it was too hot and he was going home.

Ruby Lee grabbed Willie Joe's hand with pride on the line and took over the séance. "You have to believe, Willie Joe. After all our stories, how can you think this is bullshit? Give it a chance. Just clear your mind and concentrate on my voice. Close your eyes, both of you."

"Now, with clear minds and pure hearts, we ask that any spirit that wants to come back come back and give us a sign." Suddenly, there was a breeze. You could hear it moving through the trees as it made them sway. By the time it reached them, they were entranced by the singing they heard, though it was barely audible.

They opened their eyes and stared at each other. They felt connected, as though an electrical charge was linking their hands. Every hair on their arms was standing up. When the breeze hit them like a rush of arctic air, chill bumps joined the raised hairs on their bodies. They dropped their hands and felt unplugged.

They all turned their heads toward the singing coming around the cow path from the adjacent hillside. They could make out three small shapes as they moved through the thick foliage. When they reached the clearing and were visible, it was hard to put the wrongness of what they saw into words.

At first glance, they looked like three small children. They were about five or six years old and dressed in old-fashioned clothes. The one in the back was pulling a little red wagon. But the one in the front was the one that garnered the most fear. He had carrot-red hair, not the pretty auburn like Ruby Lee's. His hair was kind of long to his shoulders. But when he spoke, the fear of God went through all three of our trio.

He was maybe fifteen feet away, and he stopped and pointed at them and said, "THERE THEY ARE!" The trio stood with mouths agape and just stared for what felt like hours when in all actuality, it was more like mere seconds.

Willie Joe was the first to come alive. He dropped their hands and took off without looking back. It took the girls about five more seconds to take off running, too. Vera stopped before they started down the hill and said, "Wait, let's see who they are?"

Ruby Lee nodded, and Vera said, "Hey! Who are you?"

The redhead turned around, sneered, and said, "You'll find out soon enough." He threw back his head, and a demonic snarl echoed down the hollow. For a moment, his eyes locked with Ruby Lee's, and a jolt of fear struck her heart, and she ran faster than she ever had before.

When they reached Ruby's house, they tore through the back-door, bawling their eyes out. They scared Kate Collins half to death. Anger replaced her fear when the girls told her what had happened.

She said, "That's what you get for messing with the devil. Ruby

Lee, take that Ouija board to the burn barrel, and I don't want to hear of you doing any séances anymore. You hear me?"

Ruby crumples to the floor, "But mommy, don't you believe us? I'm scared to death. And I swear we ain't making this up!"

"Oh, I believe you alright! You just shouldn't be messing with stuff that you can't understand! Some things shouldn't be spoken of. Ever! Do as I say, and don't give me any lip. Your daddy will be home soon, and I must get supper. Now GO! And Vera Sue, you take yourself back across the tracks."

The girls stood there, trying to absorb what they'd heard. Being separated from each other was the last thing they wanted, but the look on Kate's face told them not even to dare ask to stay all night with each other.

Ruby and Vera went out on the back porch and grabbed the Ouija board. To Ruby, it felt like it was hot, and a slight vibration came from it, and she dropped it and jumped back as if it had bitten her. Vera gave a little yelp and hugged Ruby.

"I can't touch it, Vera; you must get it."

"I ain't touching that thing!"

"Use that towel and grab it. If we don't, Mommy will come out here and wear us both out. Please!"

"Okay, but you owe me."

Vera picked up the dish towel, threw it on top of the Ouija board, quickly picked it up with two fingers, and held it out in front of her as if it were a poisonous snake.

At the burn barrel, she tossed it in, and it fell to the bottom and settled on the ashes. The girls gave it one last look and turned stunned faces to one another. Their faces had suddenly aged in the last few minutes; the childhood innocence that once clung to them had faded like a soft breeze.

Once something life-altering happens, like seeing the impossible, you can't ever see the world the same way. The trio would never be the same.

"I'd better get home before your Mom jumps down our throats again."

"Yeah, Daddy will be here soon. I sure hope she doesn't tell him."

"Lord, no!"

"Be careful. I'll watch you as you go and make sure you reach the door."

"Thanks, Ruby Lee. But you're the one that needs to be careful. They were right behind your house."

"Thanks for the reminder! I won't sleep a wink tonight. I wonder how Willie Joe is. He got out of there quickly. I'd give him hell over being such a scaredy-cat if this weren't so scary. I hope he's okay."

"Ah, he'll be fine. You know Willie, always a cool cat."

They both giggled and snickered, and the panic was over just like that. It's funny how quickly kids can bounce back. They believe with their entire being that they are invincible. In their innocence, they naively think that good will always triumph over evil. And why wouldn't they? They learned in Sunday School about David and Goliath, Jonah and the Whale, and the resurrection of Jesus Christ.

The A-Team always gets the bad guys in their world, and the Duke boys outsmart Roscoe and Boss Hogg. To them, this episode in their life, although scary as crap, will ultimately work out to their advantage. That is their belief, and that may be their superpower. Their never wavering faith will help. If only this were a TV show. But real life rarely turns out that way.

The trio are at a period in their lives where they are on the precipice of adulthood. The crux of that change will turn their bodies into vessels of chemical imbalance. As they wipe the pixie dust of childhood from their eyes, they will see the world differently. No more Santa Claus, Tooth Fairy, or Easter Bunny; they've left that behind.

That night, Willie Joe sleeps with his Snoopy night light that he dug out of his closet. He would die if anyone knew this shameful fact, but he couldn't sleep in the dark. He puts his headphones on and listens to his Journey cassette. As *Faithfully* plays softly in his ears, his mind keeps replaying the moment those kids come out of the path.

The awfulness just rolled off them like a scene from *The Exorcist!* Praise Jesus. They didn't speak with a demon voice. That would have done him in! It was bad enough with his little kid's voice. The way they pointed at Ruby Lee made him want to protect her, but his fear overtook him. He was in fight-or-flight mode, and the flight won out.

He'd never ridden his bike so fast. He flew into his house, ran upstairs to his room, snatched his Bible from underneath his bed, and clutched it to his heart. He covered his head with his blanket because spooks couldn't get you if the blanket were over your head. Right?

Vera hugged Ruby and reluctantly began the short walk to her house. When she got to the tracks, Vera glanced back to ensure Ruby was still watching. Ruby was waving at her. Vera waved back, and although she hated being apart from Ruby, she had never been so glad to leave that holler and get as far away from that graveyard as possible. Vera didn't think she'd ever be able to go up there again.

She still couldn't believe it, not really. And she was shocked by her moment of bravery. She wasn't sure what had come over her, and made her try to talk to those creatures. That wasn't like her, but she liked this new side of herself. Maybe someday soon, she could even outdo Ruby at something.

Too bad Willie Joe didn't get to witness her new self. Vera suddenly had a moment of truth. If she could do it once, she could do it again. She stood a little taller and had a bounce in her step by the time she got home.

Vera's House: 2.0

When Vera got home, her Mother was folding laundry and watching *Guiding Light*. She walked in, kissed her on the cheek, and flopped down in the plaid armchair reserved for her daddy. With a suspicious look on her face, her momma looked her over.

"What's got you so giddy? Some boy kiss you or something?"

Vera immediately blushed from head to toe and yelled out, "No way, momma! Shew, yuck!"

"Don't you lie to me, girl? I can't remember the last time you smiled like that. It must be a boy,"

"No, momma! Can't I smile and be happy for no reason? It is Summer, and I'm a kid, you know,"

"Don't be getting snippy, Missy! I guess you're allowed to be happy for no reason. It just isn't like you, is all. Now go wash up and get ready for supper. You're making me miss my story."

Vera rolls her eyes at her Mother and dashes down the hallway just in case the eyes in the back of her momma's head are watching.

She washes her hands, and when she looks in the mirror, she notices that her zits have cleared up and her braces seem to be doing their job. The gap between her front teeth looks smaller.

She goes to her room and turns on the radio, and lo and behold, *Jessie's Girl* is playing, and she's only missed the opening bars. Singing along with Rick Springfield, she boogies in front of her full-length mirror and notices another startling fact: her mosquito-bite-sized boobs have rounded out. She might even have something to put in her A-cup bra in her drawer since Christmas.

Life was suddenly looking up. She glances out her window at Ruby's house, and a smirk comes across her face. She's startled that she would feel this way about her best friend. As she watches, the sun slips behind the mountain and illuminates the landscape of trees and tombstones in dark orange and yellow.

She sees a flicker of movement, and suddenly, the day's events return to her. Fear returns in full force, and she can't believe she'd just blown it off and been dancing and singing when creatures were on the loose. An urgency floods her, and she runs to the kitchen and calls Ruby.

Richard Collins answers, and he gruffly says, "Hello."

Vera almost hangs up, but her fear makes her ask to speak to Ruby in a small, sweet voice.

"Can I speak to Ruby Lee, please?"

Richard says, "Nope."

Vera knows he's a man of few words, so she doesn't ask why.

"Okay, thank you."

Mr. Collins hangs up with not so much as a goodbye.

Vera's daddy is laid back in his Lazy Boy, drinking Stroh's and watching *Cheers*.

Though Virgil Wilcox has nothing in common with the cast besides his love for beer, he watches it religiously.

As Vera passes by the living room, her daddy asks her to get him another "cold one." She back peddles, heads to the fridge, and pulls one of the remaining beers from the plastic rings. That would be Daddy's fifth beer: One more, and he'll be ready for bed. Her daddy loves beer but only allows himself six in one sitting. When she returns with the beer, a commercial for Alka Seltzer is on.

"Plop, Plop fizz, fizz. Oh, what a relief it is," sings Virgil as he woozily giggles and takes the beer from his daughter.

"I might need some of that in the morning, Buggie." That is his pet name for his daughter, which she loves and hates simultaneously.

"Wanna open it for me, Bug? You can lick the tab and see if you like beer."

Vera grabs the round tab and drags it back. . She puts it to her tongue and grimaces as the beer taste hits her senses.

"Gross, daddy! How can you drink that stuff? It's terrible."

"Thank God you think that. Maybe you won't inherit the family habit."

"No way. That was awful."

"That's my girl. Give me a goodnight kiss, and then get to bed."

Vera leans over her daddy and kisses him on the cheek, and he grabs her nose and pretends he stole it off her face. She rolls her eyes and tells him she's too old for that dumb trick. A little bit of the light in his eyes dims as he puts on a sad face and pretends to cry. She giggles, and all's right with the world.

Cheers is back on, so Vera heads to bed. She pulls the window shade down, turns her stereo on low, and jumps under the safety of her covers. She pulls the old quilt under her chin and turns to the window. The scary events of the day flood her mind, but she evens that out with her newfound confidence. She sleeps with thoughts of Willie Joe looking at her like he looks at Ruby.

Ruby Lee's House: 2.0

When Ruby leaves the burn barrel, she high steps it to the house and her Mother's safety. Even though she's madder than a wet hen, she knows she can do nothing to make her Mother not love her. That unwavering assurance is an embrace in and of itself.

When she walks in, her mom takes cornbread out of the oven, and that heavenly scent lifts her spirits just a little. She goes to the sink and starts washing the dishes. Kate Collins is a fabulous cook but the messiest one known to man. Her daily chore is to either clean or put away the supper dishes. Ruby catches her Mother's eye and starts to say something, but she stops her by saying, "Not a Word!"

Ruby casts her green eyes down but peers through her lashes to check her Mother's face. She doesn't seem upset, so maybe she won't get another tongue-lashing. Her Mother jumps back as she tries not to get burned by the popping grease she is using to fry taters. She has tiny scars up and down her arms from years of frying almost everything they eat.

Tonight's meal is fried chicken, fried potatoes, and mustard greens with bacon and cornbread. Too bad Vera will miss out. This meal is her favorite. Since Vera's mom got a microwave, she has almost quit "real" cooking. She's really into microwavable meals. She says it simplifies her life since she's a part-time working mom helping at the post office with her mother-in-law, Patsy Wilcox.

Ruby's mom says she gives that job about six weeks, and then one of the women will tear the other's hair out. They have a famous love/hate relationship. Beechie Wells wanted to bet on how long the job would last, but Kate told her she was taking it too far. Beechie stuck to her gossip, and there sure was enough of that to go around. I reckon they fought on the first day.

After supper, Kate fixes a fresh Coca-Cola over ice in her favorite tea glass with daisies. She goes to the front porch swing, smokes a Salem Light, and sheds the stress of her day. In her hand, she has a crossword puzzle book that she has almost finished when she hears giggling.

She glances into the house through the bay window and sees all three of her girls doing their chores. Not my girls, she thinks. She hears a rustling in the bushes about that time, then more giggles. Kate feels chilled to the bone. What Ruby told her happened that day is haunting her every thought.

Ruby was telling the truth. She saw it in her daughter's eyes. Kate knows there are things about Ruby's birth that she told no one. Now, she'll have to do the unthinkable and face a woman she has avoided for 13 years: Mrs. Petunia Purdy.

Kate Pays a Visit to Mrs. Purdy

On the day Ruby was born, her Mother was nine months, one week pregnant. It was a boiling spring that year. It was going on 90 degrees by that evening. Kate skipped the May Day Festival and opted for a trip through the Bottom, hoping a good walk would help speed up her labor.

She'd been having mild contractions all day, but nothing came of it even though it was the night of the full moon. Wise Women of the mountains said that was when a baby would surely come. Throw in the fact that it was Beltane, too, and you have the makings of a unique birth. Ruby Lee did not disappoint.

As Kate reached the end of the first lane, she was in front of Mrs. Purdy's house when she doubled over in pain. She staggered to the grassy area and went to her knees. She left a trail of amniotic fluid from where her water had broken. Mrs. Purdy was on her porch swing. She moved faster than anyone would've ever thought possible. She hauled Kate up and practically carried her inside.

Once on the bed, Mrs. Purdy reached under Kate's sundress and tore off her underwear. Kate was screaming in pain, asking her to call Richard. Mrs. Purdy said there was no time. The baby was crowning. She told Kate to bite down on the old leather strap she kept on a nail and push when she said.

Out of her mind with pain, Kate began pushing. Two pushes and the baby came bursting into the world but did not return her Mother's screams. When Purdy held the baby up, it was silent and faceless. The look of horror on Kate's face prompted Purdy to tell her, "It's a caul. This baby is special."

She deftly removed the membranous piece of flesh from the baby's face. She held its nose, blew breath in its mouth, and smacked its bottom. With an ear-splitting cry, Ruby Lee arrived and was placed on her Mother's chest while Purdy massaged Kate's stomach to expel the afterbirth—a clean birth with little blood or tearing. There had to be something special about this baby.

A few neighbors had gathered in the yard to see what all the hollerin' was about. Beechie Wells entered the door when Purdy said who was inside. She came to Kate's side and hollered back to Versie Mullins to call Richard Collins and have him over here pronto, and if he was down at the festival, somebody ride down there and fetch him. Beechie started ordering everyone to do her bidding.

"Purdy, I need a clean towel or blanket to wrap this child in so it doesn't freeze to death!"

"Now calm down, Beechie, it's hotter than July 4. That baby isn't going to get cold. Besides, I brought this child into the world. I reckon I got enough sense to swaddle it, seeing as I had eleven young'uns of my own. Now get out of here and bark your orders from the road!"

"Well, I never!" Beechie said with a huff as she stomped out of the house close to being a shack. The floor bowed as she walked onto the porch, making the pop-can wind chimes tinkle.

"And you never will," Purdy threw back at her as Beechie went through the screen door that she was sure to let slam hard enough to knock over some bottles of herbs on the mantle. Lord only knows what was in those bottles, so it was a good thing they didn't break. It might've had some graveyard dirt in one of them from a very long time ago.

When they were alone again, Mrs. Purdy sat in the rocking

chair beside the bed. Kate looked at her straight and told her how grateful she was to her.

"Mrs. Purdy, I can't thank you enough for delivering Ruby Lee. You surely saved us both. And that thing on her face. I would've never known how to remove it. What did you say it was again?"

"It was a caul. I'll tell you, I've never delivered a babe with one, but when I was small, my little brother came early and had a caul. If it hadn't been for the Granny Witch delivering him, he surely would've died. So that's how I knew what to do. It's a common practice amongst people in my line of work." Mrs. Purdy gave Kate a poignant look that said everything there was to say.

"I need to tell you about the caul, though. This child will have the gift of sight and could develop other abilities since her birth is on Beltane. The worlds are thinner at this time of the year, and magic can seep through the veil when Mother Nature sees fit to bless someone. I believe we will see great things from this one."

"I have no idea what you're talking about. I'm a Methodist. But if you say so, I'll take you at your word."

"It doesn't matter your beliefs; seeing is believing. Mark my words, Kate Collins, when this child is close to becoming a woman, she will show signs of her gifts. If I'm still here when the time comes, bring her to me."

"Yes, ma'am. I will."

This returned to Kate as she crossed the tracks and headed to the Bottom.

Walking up the lane toward Mrs. Purdy's house, she whispered a prayer asking the Lord to protect her child. She didn't know if she could bring Ruby Lee to Mrs. Purdy. She slowed as the ramshackle of a home came into view. Keeping her eyes on the road, she watched as her Aigner sandals smacked the pavement and her traitorous feet carried her onward. She knew in her gut that this was the right thing to do, but her heart was breaking simultaneously.

At last, Kate was at the gate, and Mrs. Purdy called her from the front porch swing.

"Come in, little Katy. I won't bite you."

"Why, child, you look pale as a ghost!" Mrs. Purdy chuckled at her pun. She knew why Kate had come to her. Mrs. Purdy had not forgotten to keep up with the Beltane child. She was coming into her gifts.

Kate reached the porch and sat down on the first step. She lit up a Salem Light and looked Purdy in the face.

"You were right. Ruby Lee has her gifts, just like you said she would. She hasn't got her period yet, but I know it's coming any day. I need your help. She's got herself in a fix. She had a séance and conjured up those three little boys. You know which ones I'm talking about. I'm scared. I've never told her anything about her birth. So, it's my fault this happened. I should have warned her. I couldn't truly believe what you told me was true. I'm a fool, I guess."

"Well, child, now you know, and I hope you will bring her to me so I can teach her how to use what she's given."

"I will, I promise. Tomorrow evening okay with you?"

"That'll be fine. But I don't want you here with her. You go home and come back later. I've never known a child born the way she was, like a beltane with a caul. That's truly special. I wouldn't be surprised if she couldn't raise the spirits in the whole town!"

"Oh, God, no!" prayed Kate.

"I'm just funnin' you. Don't get all het up now."

"Well, begging your pardon, that wasn't funny to me at all. I'll have Ruby Lee over here by six. Richard will be at the rescue squad meeting. I'd rather he not know about this. You know he isn't from Mary Luck: Raised differently and has no tolerance for spirits. He'd never allow her to be over here. So, let's be careful." Kate said, with her head down to hide her shame.

"I won't tell nobody. And I don't get much company these days, anyway. She'll be fine."

Kate decided not to tell Ruby Lee until the next day where she would be going. She wanted to let her have one more night of innocence.

That night, with the veil lifted over Mary Luck because of the séance and the power of Ruby Lee, several town's folks will get some visitors.

PART TWO

Sightings

We've got a long way to go, and a short time to get there
I'm east bound, just watch ol' Bandit run
By Jerry Reed

Birdie Daniels

On the night of the séance, Birdie Daniels was closing The Nest when the KISS pinball machine started. Bright red, gold, and white lights flashed, and the tune of *Shout It Out Loud*. Birdie was in the kitchen turning off lights when she heard the familiar sound of a pinball being released.

As it bounced off sensors and binged and dinged, racking up points, she grabbed her Colt 45 pistol and eased down the grocery aisle toward the video games. She noticed they were all dark. *Pac-Man* was dead to the world, along with *Mrs. and Baby Pac-Man* and *Burger Time*.

She would have to turn the corner to see who was playing pinball. Gripping the pistol tight, she pulled back the hammer, jumped around the corner, and said, "Freeze, asshole! I have a gun, and I sure ain't afraid to use it!"

A man stood with his back to her and continued to play, completely ignoring her threats. This pissed Birdie off something fierce. She called out again,

"I ain't kidding; get out now, or I'll shoot you full of lead!"

Without turning, the man confidently said, "No, you won't, momma; you know I'm your favorite."

Birdie's blood turned to ice, and she didn't think she'd ever be warm again. Because the man turned around and she was looking into her dead son's eyes. She thought maybe she must be dreaming or too drunk to see straight. Butchie, who had died in a car wreck five years earlier, cracked up at his mother's astonished face.

He said, "See what you did? I almost had a high score. Momma, you don't look so good. Maybe you should sit down."

Birdie's legs suddenly turned to jelly, and she crumpled to the tile floor. She put her head in her hands and wiped away tears she didn't know she'd shed. Butchie came toward her, shuffling a little bit at a steady pace.

When he was standing over her, she looked up at him, and all the grief of the last five years faded away like morning dew. Replacing it was a feeling of joy she didn't think she'd ever get to know again.

Butchie sat down Indian style and put his arms around his momma, and whispered, "I've missed you so much, momma. It's been so lonely without you, so cold and dark." Birdie's heart broke as the words he said sank in. She held him tight and breathed in the scent of her boy, but he didn't smell the same. She couldn't quite put her finger on that scent, but she knew she'd smelled it before. This was a fleeting thought. She didn't give a shit what he smelled like as long as he was back.

She had prayed so hard every night to have her child back. She guessed that maybe God really did answer prayers. However, a little voice in her head said, "Be careful what you wish for; you just might get it."

Birdie dismissed all these negative thoughts and basked in the glory of having Butchie back. Then her mothering instinct kicked in, and she asked him if he was hungry. He looked at her with glinting eyes and a sneer on his lips and nodded in agreement. Something about that look spooked Birdie, and she quickly got up and headed toward the kitchen.

Butchie followed her. She looked over her shoulder to ensure he was coming or still there, and he was, much to her relief.

Butchie Daniels was only nineteen years old when he wrecked his prized black 1979 Trans Am -just like the one The Bandit drove. It even had the Golden Eagle emblem and T-tops, which would be his undoing.

Butchie loved to drive fast, and his favorite route was around Dewey Lake at Jenny Wiley State Park. The hairpin curves and hidden entrances made this a perilous drive. Even Sunday drivers avoided it. Summertime made the road even more dangerous. Most folks spent their weekends packed on the shores. They parked their cars on the shoulder, narrowing the road. Arrowhead Point was a sharp, blind curve, a favorite of teenagers. Butchie loved to rev his engine before the curve so that all heads turned to see him flash by.

On the Fourth of July, the spot at Arrowhead Point was at capacity. Butchie had combed his long sandy blonde hair in a perfect feathered style. His sunglasses were shiny as the sun glinted off them. His bare, muscled chest was laden with a gold necklace with his initial dangling between his nipples.

With E.L.O. 's *Don't Bring Me Down* blasting out of his Pioneer stereo, Butchie lays on the gas as he shifts down, barking his tires. As usual, all heads turn his way, and more than one bikini-clad girl sighs as he goes by.

With his head turned to see who was admiring him, he took the curve too fast. Add the woman who darts before him; you've got the perfect recipe for disaster.

Butchie jerks the steering wheel hard left to miss the woman, but this move puts him in the path of another car. He slams his brakes as hard as possible, but it's too late. The impact is deafening. It catapulted him out of the T-tops and slammed into a tree, where he was left dead and dangling like the initial on his necklace. This all took place in front of loads of teenagers and kids. If there had been such a term as PTSD back then most kids there would have more than qualified. They had nightmares and were told to 'grow up!' or 'deal with it.' Being the children of parents who lived through WWII and took part in VietNam, there was little compassion for their emotions.

More than one parent preached, "I hope you learned a lesson by watching that fool drive like that. It was bound to happen, eventually. Butchie Daniels tried to cheat death whenever he was behind the wheel."

As Butchie entered the kitchen, Birdie asked if he wanted his favorite, and he replied, ", Yeah, Momma, just make it rare, bloody even." Birdie asked why he wanted it that way, and then she saw something that made her hold her tongue.

Butchie was wearing what he had on when he was buried; his favorite Kiss T-shirt and worn-out Levis'. This was emphasized when he turned his back to her, and she saw his shirt had a slit up the rear. Undertakers cut clothes that way so it's easier to dress a body, as she knew, seeing as how she helped dress him that awful day.

In her excitement to see her son, she hadn't considered how and why he was in what seemed to be the flesh. Then she noticed the sutures up his back where his skin had been put back together in a Frankenstein fashion.

All these thoughts went through her head as she stood, spatula in hand, frying up a rare burger for her dead son. Suddenly, she got chilled to the bone. What in God's name was she doing? Then he was by her side. The smell of him hit her like a freight train. She knew what it was now: dead flowers, moldy dirt, and decay. When she dared look at her son again, his eye had slid down his face and now rested on his cheek. There was a gaping hole in his chest with wood chips from where the tree branch had impaled him. He smiled at her, and there was blood in his teeth, the few he had left.

Birdie backed away, gagging at the sight of the shambling thing that was not her son anymore if it ever had been. When she was as far back as she could get, she stood with the spatula held out as if to parry with a sword.

Butchie grabbed the hamburger off the grill barehanded and crammed it into his maw. He chewed as it ran greasy and bloody down his chin. He threw back his head and cackled witch-like and said, "I got a message for you, momma: Baby Annie is coming for you and the whole fuckin' town. She says you gotta pay for the sins of your fathers."

Right up in her face now, Butchie leans in and kisses her on the cheek. At this, Birdie Daniels passes out on the floor. When she wakes up, the Mary Luck Volunteer Fire Dept is there, and Richard Collins is beside her. It's so smokey you can barely see as she searches for the Butchie thing with her eyes. Didn't look like he was there anymore, or did she imagine the whole thing?

Thankfully for Birdie, there was little to no damage to 'The Nest,' mostly only smoke. Due mainly to the frantic call made by Shiny (who told anyone who'd listen that they ought to be glad he was a loafer as he took another pull from the brown-bagged bottle of booze) to Richard Collins. Kate got the phone tree going, then called Beechie, who called everyone else. By the time Birdie walked outside, half the town was milling around. The haunted look in Birdie's eyes did not escape the notice of Claude Wells. He knew that look because he had the same one. He'd gotten a visit, too.

Claude Wells

When Claude got home from his evening stroll, he went inside to get the TV Guide and see what trash was on the idiot box that night. He never got to find out because he slipped in a puddle of water and nearly broke his hip. Claude uttered 'fuck' under his breath, a curse word he hadn't said in years. Tears came to his eyes as pain radiated up his left leg into his low back and fired up the sciatic nerve.

That's when his old Victrola began spinning and playing Benny Goodman's "*Goodnight, My Love*," Rebecca Jo's favorite song. Hell, it was her record. Claude sat in utter fright. He knew he was about to see a horror he'd never forget. He wanted to close his eyes but knew he deserved this: his long-awaited punishment for letting her die. And just like that, his leg and back pain went numb. A lamp in the parlor came on, and it illuminated the most beautiful sight he'd ever seen.

His little sister stood before him in all her glory. An enormous white bow in her hair pulled back on the side, wearing her Easter finery of pink and white lace. Legs clad in knee socks with Mary Janes on her feet. She danced to the music and beckoned him to join her.

Though he knew he was dreaming or dead, he felt like he could dance The Charleston if need be. He just wanted to be near her and bask in her loveliness. He righted himself from the floor and joined her in the parlor, where they danced with her standing on his shoes and him making all the moves. Rebecca said, "I've missed you, dear brother. Have you missed me?"

Claude responded with heartfelt sorrow, "I could never explain how much I missed you. Every day of my life, I have thought of you. I never forgot, I promise." Tears were coursing down the creases in his face, dripping off his chin. That's probably why he didn't notice the puddle of water at his feet until it was too late.

His shoe slipped, and he snapped his eyes open, and there was the honest Rebecca. Dripping wet with rancid pond water, muck all over the finery of her dress. Which was now a scummy green. The white bow was now deflated and sagged like a rotten tooth. Blue and gray splotches dotted her once pristine skin, turning her into a nightmare.

Her hand turned to ice as he held it. She tightened her grip, and he instinctively flung his arm to shake her off, but she held fast. Her strength had doubled as she pulled him to his knees. The pain was back and radiating through his body two-fold.

When they were eye to eye, he saw hers were like looking into a black coal mine. That's when the stench hit him, musty and sickeningly sweet mixed in with the moldy scent of a slurry pond.

He retched, making Rebecca giggle. That's when the natural person came through. "I warned you fools. You will pay for what yours did to me. There's hell to pay, and I will get mine."

Claude's left arm went numb, and he was hit with a punch to his heart that knocked him out.

He had a knot on his head when he came to but otherwise felt okay. That's when he saw the firetruck go screaming past his house. He walked onto his front porch and saw The Nest smoking up hell.

Claude left his house unlocked and walked down with the growing crowd. When he saw Birdie and the haunted look on her face, they locked eyes and nodded to each other. They'd get together soon: It was time to open the town records. As direct descendants of the men involved, it was their duty.

Ally-Fair Wells

After closing the store, Ally-Fair strolls down the sidewalk to her house at the end of the street. It's one of the few houses that had been enlarged. She has a long porch that lines the front of her house. She has added gingerbread trim that makes it look like a fairy tale house. As she approaches and dreams about what might have been, she loves to look at it.

She notices the porch light isn't on. The bulb must have burned out, she thinks. She opens the gate and walks up the steps, and that's when she sees someone on her swing. Since it's dark, she can't make out who it is.

Startled, she says, "Who's there?" When she gets no answer, she turns to go inside. That's when the person on the swing says, "Hello, my love. I'm finally home."

She knows that voice, and though she has dreamt many times and prayed every day to hear it, it chills her veins. She stops, reaches for the door, turns her head, and comes face to face with her long-lost love. He looks exactly the same as the day he left over forty years ago. How can this be, she wonders? She thinks she must be hallucinating.

Suddenly, his hand is on her arm. Her mind is whirring in a million different directions. Trying to swallow the fact that Jesse is here is overwhelming. But when she looks into his eyes, she sees he is real , and all doubt slips away.

She finishes opening the door, and they step inside. Jesse pulls her to him, and she hears his heartbeat. He whispers in her ear, "I knew you would wait for me, my beautiful darling."

"But Jesse, how can you look the same? I'm so old now; you couldn't possibly want me."

"Look in the mirror, my love. You are still the most beautiful woman I've ever known."

When Ally looks in the mirror, her gray hair is once again the dark brown it used to be. The crow's feet around her eyes are gone, and the wrinkles on her forehead and lips have disappeared. It's a miracle. She must have lost her mind or had a vivid dream.

Jesse spins her around to him, and she notices that his uniform has rips and tears. He nibbles at her ear, and she lets all those things slip away. Jesse was finally home. No matter how it happened, she didn't care. He has always been everything she ever wanted.

Suddenly, his hands grip her around the waist and squeeze. He waltzes with her. Music plays from the radio, Glenn Miller's *Moonlight Cocktail,* the last song they danced to before he shipped out. Hearing the strains of the orchestra and having his arms around her was ecstasy. He was awakening feelings in her she hadn't felt in decades.

As the song ended, she kept her eyes closed, wanting to hold on to this moment forever. Then his mouth was on hers, and she met his kiss with fervor. As his lips crushed hers, their tongues danced together. She melted like butter. He lifted her into his arms and carried her to the bedroom. All the while, her eyes are hooded and barely open.

Once on the bed, she flips on the bedside lamp to enjoy the sight of her love. What she sees almost rips her mind to shreds. Jesse seemed to decay right before her eyes. His jawbone is exposed, and his hair has fallen out in patches. His uniform is in tatters. But the worst part was his snake-like tongue. It is covered in mold and sores that ooze down his chin. He keeps flicking it in and out of his mouth like he's tasting her.

Ally is completely frozen. He zombie-walks over to her, and she is helpless to move. She thinks that if that thing touches her, she will become a raving lunatic. Instinct kicks in as he tries to lean in for a kiss. She kicks him in the stomach and runs for the door. Much to her surprise, he doesn't chase her. He simply laughs in a hellish manner. His voice is gravelly like he has rocks in his throat.

"Poor pitiful pearl Ally-Fair. Lost her lover. Boo-hoo! You're gonna lose more than that old woman. I have a surprise for all of you. You're all gonna pay for what was done to me. I'll have my vengeance. Just wait and see! You tell those other old fools that

Baby Annie is coming for them!" The gruesome thing that was once Jesse McCoy threw back what was left of his head and cackled a witch-like laugh.

Ally ran from her house as if it were on fire to the other end of town, where she met up with most of the neighborhood. Birdie's Nest was smoking something fierce.

Panting and breathless, she bent forward with her hands on her knees. Her legs seemed to melt as she collapsed. Edgar Wilcox caught her under the arm before she could fall entirely to the ground. She jerked her arm as if he had bitten her. Edgar let go and apologized.

"I'm sorry, Miss Ally. I was just afraid you'd hurt yourself. I didn't mean to scare ye." She smiled up at him and then burst into tears. Her whole body shook as she was wracked with tears.

This display of emotion from her shocked Edgar. She was always poised, almost to the point of being cold. Now, she looked like a wounded animal. He searched the crowd for Claude or Wilson, anyone who could help her. Because he didn't know what to do. Luckily, Birdie saw her and came over. They locked eyes, and that seemed to calm Ally.

"You saw Jesse, didn't you?" Ally nodded, "How did you know?"

"I got a visit from Butchie."

Ally digested that information and said, "Well, it was Jesse for a bit, then he changed. Oh my God, it was horrible."

She put her hands over her face and continued to weep. Birdie sat down beside her and rubbed her back. "I know, honey, I know."

Edgar was lost. What in God's name were they talking about? He didn't have to wonder too long because Claude came over and joined the women on the ground.

Wilson Mckenzie

Wilson McKenzie had just gotten out of the car he parked on the side of the road. Like everyone else in town, he came to see what all the commotion was about. That's when he saw her. She looked out of place with her ragged carpet bag and cloche hat. They made eye contact, and she turned to walk to the railroad tracks. A train coming, he had to save her this time. Without a glance back at his friends, he took off. The compulsion to follow her was overwhelming.

"Miss, Miss, wait! Don't go up there!" he shouted. People were turning to look at him and see who he was yelling at. They didn't see a woman, but Wilson sure did. He could hear the train coming, horn blaring at the Shotgun Holler crossing. It would be here in seconds. The woman kept up a steady stride. It was as if she wanted to be hit. Wilson almost caught up with her, but she stepped in front of the train anyway as he yelled with all his might, "STOP!"

However, the train didn't even slow down because the lady had vanished. Wilson waited while the coal cars sped past him. When the caboose was in sight, he glimpsed someone standing on the other side. He couldn't believe his eyes. There she stood, pregnant belly and all, in one piece. When the train passed, he stood gaping. There was no way to explain her being here. She simply stood there, staring back at him.

When he approached her to see if she was there, he noticed the gash on her neck. It was a clean cut but looked putrid. She bowed her head when he was within a few feet of her, and it fell off and rolled in front of him.

It landed face up, and the hideousness of it was the worst thing he had ever seen. The eyes were bulging and oozing yellow pus. But the mouth was the worst. It was trying to talk, but the lips were so swollen and purple that each word caused them to split. Her body remained standing, headless. Then suddenly, the pregnant belly squirmed. You could tell that whatever was inside was thrashing to get out.

The dress was slit down the middle as the baby used its claw-like little hands to shred his mother's stomach and fall out on the tracks. To say it was deformed would never compare to what that thing was. Its head was bulb-shaped, with the fat end pulsing with green veins. Its body was slimy with membranous fluid.

It dragged itself over to him, pulling the umbilical cord with it. It raised its bulbous head, and he saw its eyes were gone. There was nothing but black holes. When it was about a foot away, he bent over and lost his dinner. He backed away when he tripped over the lady's head. He fell hard on the steel rail but barely felt it. The head spoke, and a voice that wasn't its own said, "Baby Annie is coming. I'm gonna make you all pay. I'll take what is most precious to you. It's almost time, old boy. I'll see ye soon."

The next thing Wilson knew, he was alone on the tracks. No hellish baby or lady. Did he just imagine that? No way, he thinks. She was here, but she wasn't. That evil bitch just used her to get to me. He needed to talk to his friends, daughter, and granddaughter. Wilson didn't think he'd ever been so scared in his life.

Back at the 'Nest

When Wilson found his friends, Ally sat with Claude and Birdie on the ground. The crowd had dwindled down. Richard Collins was loading up the firetruck and glanced at the old people sitting on the road.

Wilson told them, "We need to get inside somewhere." Birdie ushered them inside the store and quickly locked the door behind them. She was the first to speak. "What in the name of God is going on here? I assume you all had a visit from someone who should've been long dead." Birdie fixed them all with her knowing eyes. They met her stare with nods.

"That's what I thought. I saw my boy, Butchie. At least, I thought it was him. Then he turned into something straight from hell!" Birdie's eyes teared up, and she finally just broke down completely.

Ally put her arm around her and patted her back while the men nervously looked at the floor and shuffled their feet. No one there had seen Birdie Daniels cry or show so much emotion other than anger. It did something to them all to see such a strong woman brought to her knees, though mostly, it broke their hearts.

Ally said. "Jesse looked the same as he did the day he left. And when I saw myself in the mirror, I was eighteen again. I should've known it was too good to be true. But I have yearned for him for so long that I wanted to believe it. No matter how impossible it was."

"When I realized it wasn't Jesse, he had turned into something so horrifying that I can't even describe it." Her voice hitched, and she sobbed with the memory of her beloved becoming a monster.

Claude hands her his hankie and says, "Well, my old friends, I saw my sister, and when she turned cold in my hands and spoke with that evil witch's voice, I nearly had a heart attack. I thought I was a goner for sure. I've had time to digest what it said, and I think we all know what to do."

Birdie and Ally shake their heads yes while Delano and Edgar look back and forth at each other, puzzled.

"What are you all talking about?" asks Delano and Edgar simultaneously.

Claude explained. "It's a sealed document passed down to us with instructions to not open until 1984. And then only if all three of us agreed. I got mine when my Momma passed away. It came down to her from her daddy."

Edgar becomes agitated by all the secretive talk and glances and finally loses his cool. "So, what in the hell has any document got to do with Baby Annie? I don't know what you's is a talkin' bout."

"Calm down, Edgar, Claude, and I will explain. First, though, I think we need to get the others. This pertains to the whole town. So, before we get ahead of ourselves, we need to get Matt and Mrs. Purdy." Claude raises a wrinkled and veined hand to shush Edgar, who is poised to ask another question at the mention of Purdy. Edgar grunts in frustration.

Wilson speaks up, "I have a document, too. My Pa gave it to me right before he passed. I haven't thought about that since I can't tell ya, but I think it's something extra. A what's it called, starts with a C.

Ally says, 'Do you mean a codicil?'

"Yes, yes, that's it. I was told to hide it and only open it after the other three had been read. I saw that poor wretch that got hit by the train just a few minutes ago. She looked like her, but then she turned monstrous. It was hands down the worst thing I have ever seen. I'll not sleep a wink tonight! When it spoke, it was the voice of that bitch Baby Annie." Wilson was still visibly shaking in his shoes.

"My Pap told me a story when I was a young feller. He was on his deathbed, dying of consumption. I put pillows behind him so he could sit up. He made everyone leave the room and made me promise to tell no one what he was about to say until the time was right… which I'm pretty sure is now."

"He knew that I'd heard the stories about Baby Annie since I was knee-high to a grasshopper, but he said there were things I needed to know. I thought maybe he wasn't in his right mind, and he must have read that in my face; cause then he grabbed my hand and pulled me to him. His strength surprised me and made me focus on his words."

He spoke steadily, "Mary Luck has its secrets, like most small towns. But this town has a curse. I never put much stock into that nonsense until I watched my daddy die an agonizing death. He died when Kate were just a babe, and I never talked much about him because of the way he died."

"My Daddy always had a haunted look about him. He wasn't very affectionate to his family. I always just thought he was a bitter man. Lived a hard life working in the mines and all. After my Ma passed, giving birth to Zelda, my Mammaw moved in and raised us. His eyes took on a far-away look, and his voice became almost a whisper."

He continued, "My daddy was hurt terribly in a mine accident; he lingered at home in and out of consciousness for three days. I was tending to him when he suddenly woke up, grabbed my hand, and pulled me to him. His breath had the smell of death on it, and I nearly gagged. He fixed me with a stare I didn't dare look away from. He said, 'Boy, go to the steamer trunk and bring me the Bible.' I did as he said, telling me to take out the folded document in the back. It was an old thing. Turned yellow from age and had a seal on it of a cross."

It said, "Only open when all three others are together." I was so scared; he was close to death, and I could see The Other Side in his eyes. But he told me it was to go to my eldest child, no matter if it was a boy or a girl. Only the eldest! I promised, and he closed his eyes, drew one last ragged breath, and died right before me.

Wilson wiped at his eyes. "When my daddy was on his deathbed, he gave me that document. He told me it was a sort of codicil to what I'm pretty sure you three have the other pieces. Our kin has done something unspeakable, and now I think we'll pay the price for it."

"But God has seen fit to give us a weapon in the form of my Ruby Lee. Kate told me a story today that you all have got to hear. It involves Willie Joe and Vera too. Also, someone else is involved that I don't think y'all are gonna be excited about, Mrs. Prudy."

"Hells Bells, why in God's name is she involved? She's directly descended from that Bitch Baby Annie. I don't think she can be trusted. If there is truly a curse on the town, she won't lift a finger to help us. Jesus, Wilson, why would you involve her?" Asks Birdie.

"Cam down, Birdie. I reckon I got enough sense to know that, but there's some stuff you don't know. Purdy delivered Ruby Lee if you'll recall. Saved her life when she was born. After what our young'uns got up to today, Kate is taking Ruby over to Purdy. There was something extraordinary about her birth. I won't get into all of it, but believe me, we will need Purdy."

Ruby Lee and Mrs. Purdy

Ruby is finishing the supper dishes when her momma tells her she wants her to walk with her over to the Bottom. Ruby had plans to meet with her friends, but her mom says she must wait. This is odd behavior for her, so Ruby drops the dish towel back in the sink and pulls her hair out of its ponytail.

Kate picks up her glass of Coke and grabs her cigarette case, and slides into her Aigner sandals. Ruby Lee puts on her flip-flops and joins her mother on the porch. She's scared that she's in trouble, so she shoots her mom sidelong glances every few moments but can read nothing on her face. Ruby thinks, dang! I must really be in deep crap over that stupid séance.

As they cross the tracks and start down the dusty lane, Ruby kicks loose rocks and slows down her walking. Her mother looks over her shoulder and throws her head in a "git moving" nod. Beechie is out on her porch, and they both wave and wish each other a good evening.

Ruby's heart leaps in her throat when her momma stops in front of Mrs. Purdy's house. To her disbelief, she opens the gate and motions for Ruby to join her on the porch. Ruby has always avoided Mrs. Purdy like the plague. Now, she is being forced to go to her house! What is going on with her mother?

Purdy eyes Ruby closely, then says, "Come here, child, and sit by me."

"Yes, Ma'am." With downcast eyes, Ruby does as she asks. Then, to her utter horror, her mother turns to leave. "Wait, Mommy, where are you going?"

"Ruby Lee, you'll be fine. I'll be back in a little while. You listen to Mrs. Purdy. She's gonna tell you some things that you need to hear. I love you, baby. I'll be back soon."

Kate Collins turns and leaves before the tears in her eyes betray her. She can't believe she just left her daughter alone with Mrs. Purdy. It's for the best, but she still regrets it. She turns the corner and starts walking down River Lane.

Thelma Blair is out on her porch swing, and she hollers to Kate to come sit for a spell. Relieved that she has somewhere to go that keeps Purdy's house in her eyesight, she climbs the steps and sits in a rocking chair by the door. She lights up a Salem, inhales the menthol smoke, and tries to relax even though she knows she won't until Ruby Lee returns.

Mrs. Purdy tells Ruby to follow her inside. She takes a bit to wallow out of the swing. She indeed weighs 400 pounds, Ruby thinks. The floorboards bend and creak as she approaches the screen door. It screeches on rusty hinges and adds to the creepiness of the house.

Ruby's hands are slick with sweat, so she wipes them on her cutoff jeans. She reluctantly follows Mrs. Purdy into the house. It smells like grease with an underlying scent of herbs and mold.

The house is shotgun-style. The living room is the first room, followed by a bedroom, then the kitchen. That's where Mrs. Purdy takes a seat in an oversized cane-backed chair. It creaks and sags when she sits down, and Ruby can't believe it can hold her, but

143

somehow it does.

Ruby takes the other chair without being asked, folds her hands in her lap, and keeps her eyes on the wooden table that's definitely seen better days.

After catching her breath from the short walk, Mrs. Purdy begins, "Look at me, child. I know you're probably scared of me, and if it was anybody except you, you'd have a reason. But you, my dear, are something special." Mrs. Purdy lets this sink in while she lights the pipe she's pulled out of the pocket of her blue gingham dress. She tamps it down so that it will smolder and release a scent that Ruby has never smelled before. It's fragrant with herbs.

"I don't know if you know this, but I was the one that brought you into this world." Ruby shakes her head no, while her eyes seem to get bigger. She definitely has Ruby's attention now.

"Yes, your mother was walking by my house when suddenly I was hit with an urgency to go to her. Her water broke right out there in the road. I got her inside, and you were already crowning. Your momma only pushed three times, and you slid into my arms. You were born with a caul. Do you know what that is?" Again, Ruby shakes her head no.

"I didn't figure you did, so let me explain. A caul is a layer of skin covering a baby's face when born. Your poor mother thought you didn't have a face when she first saw you." Mrs. Purdy slapped her knee and gave a cackle that startled Ruby Lee and made her jump in her seat. This made Purdy laugh louder, making Ruby even more on edge.

Sensing her discomfort, Purdy calmed herself and picked her story back up. "Well, anyway, I pulled the caul from your face easily enough, but you weren't breathing, so I blew breath in your mouth, and you took your first breath, opened your eyes, looked at me, and let out a fierce cry. It made me jump a little, and I almost dropped

144

ye. Damn, if you weren't a loud little thing."

Ruby finally speaks, "So what's so special about this caul thing?"

"I'm getting to it, so calm down. People born that way sometimes have the gift of second sight. So sometimes, they can see into the future through visions or dreams. Usually, they are omens of something bad that's gonna happen. Have you ever dreamed something that's come true?"

Ruby tries to process this information and slowly nods her head yes.

"Tell me."

"When my mamaw was sick, I dreamed that her cancer was all gone even though the doctors said she had eaten up with it and would die. I prayed hard that night, and then I dreamed that the cancer was all gone when she went for her tests. And it was. Mommy said it was a miracle from God."

"Child, I'm not gonna argue religion with you. But you had more to do with that than your prayers." Ruby shakes her head no but says nothing. This is a lot to take in. She's thinking back to other events in her life. And she tells Purdy.

"When I was about four, I used to tell my mommy that I lived in a house in Prestonsburg that I'd never been in before. I described the furniture and decorations. I can still see it in my mind. And I've always been good at finding things that go missing. Mammaw Lucy calls me her good luck charm. I can always find her watch that she loses all the time."

If I concentrate really hard, I can guess Christmas presents. I'm not sure how I can do it, but when I do, I can see Mommy at the store picking out toys and stuff in my mind. I just figured it was something everybody could do."

"Oh, no, child. That's something extraordinary. The caul is said to keep sailors safe from drowning, and they'd pay big money for one. Coal miners believe they can protect them from cave-ins."

"Do you still have mine?" asks Ruby

"I sure do. Someday, I thought you might need it. I wasn't born with a caul, but I have my ways of knowing things, too. It's a gift passed down through my family. But, I have more to tell you about your birth. Not only were you born with a caul, but you came on Beltane."

"Huh? What's Beltane?"

"It's the fire festival and the beginning of summer, but we can call it May Day- the day you were born. It's thought to be lucky to be born on this day. Also, there was a full moon which was also lucky. So, my dear, you have three things about your birth that make you very special. This is a lot for you to consider, so I'll get to the point. Tell me exactly what happened yesterday in the cemetery behind your house?"

"You mean the séance that me and Willie Joe and Vera had, don't ya?"

"Yes. Leave nothing out. The smallest detail could be significant."

"We didn't mean to do nothing wrong, honest. We just wanted to scare Willie Joe. He didn't believe we could work the Ouija board, which we can!" Purdy is nodding her head in agreement.

"That's when we dared Willie to have a séance in the graveyard. It was broad daylight, so I didn't think anything would happen, not for real, anyway. Boy, I was wrong!"

"Next thing I know, we've tried to contact somebody buried on the hill, and when nothing happened, I said, 'any spirit that wants to come back, come back?"

Mrs. Purdy draws in a deep rattling breath and rares back in her chair with her hand over her heart. For a minute there, Ruby thinks she's having a heart attack.

"What did I say?"

"Oh, child, you opened a door. Your mother said you saw three little boys. Tell me what they looked like."

"Uh, the first one had red hair, but not like mine. It was carrot red. The other two had brown hair, and the one in the back was pulling a little red wagon."

The look of horror on Purdy's face scared the shit out of Ruby. This was bad if it threatened the scariest person in town. Mrs. Purdy got up, and her chair fell to the side. She ran to the middle room of the house and returned with a jar of liquid with a filmy-looking piece of skin in it.

"What is it?"

"It's your caul!"

"EWWW! That's so gross."

"This is something that might help you against her."

"Who are you talking about?"

"Lordy mercy, you really don't know nothing at all, do you? You've opened a door by asking any spirit to come back, and since you didn't close out the séance, you've left that door open for twenty-four hours. I know she came back, too!"

Purdy visibly shudders and shakes her head back and forth. "I knew you should've come to me sooner, but your stubborn mother wouldn't have it. She said you were normal and that she had seen nothing weird."

"Mrs. Purdy, who are you talking about?"

"Why my Great-great-grandmother, of course. The notorious witch Baby Annie!"

Ruby recoils and staggers back a few steps, and her knees hit the chair seat. She sits down heavily and cries, her head in her hands, her shoulders racking with sobs.

"Mrs. Purdy, can't I just take it back? I really didn't mean for this to happen. I felt a jolt of energy in my hands as I said those words. I felt a sense of something, but I didn't think it was anything special. This is all my fault. That witch is gonna come and get us all."

"You can't take it back. Once opened, it can only be closed by another séance with the same people. Same place and time. But that doesn't put the ones back in that got out. And for that reason, you can't close that door until you can get them all back in. I don't think it will be hard to find them if you see those three little kids in broad daylight."

"So, they really were ghosts?"

"Yes, but I fear they aren't who they were. I'm fairly sure those are the kids that Baby Annie killed. Their spirits are being used by her. The voice they spoke to you with was hers. Baby Annie is loose, and we must capture her and force her back through that door, and then you three will have to close it."

The magnitude of what she's being told is something she can't even possibly process in her mind. This can't be real. Indeed, she's asleep. Right? How in the world did she open a door? She knew she felt something that day. It felt like static electricity flowed through their hands. It was like a jolt.

"We need to wait on the porch. Your momma will be here shortly. Then we need to have a meeting with a couple of other folks. No more questions, just sit tight."

Ruby does as she says and takes a seat on a wooden crate. Her heart still beats a mile a minute, but she tries to stay calm. She breathes deeply, exhales, and releases some of her fear. Ten minutes later, Kate pulls up in the family Jeep Wagoneer. Ruby jumps up and flies to the car. She climbs in the back seat and wraps her arms around her mother's neck.

"I know, baby, I know. I should've let you talk to her sooner.

Maybe this wouldn't have gotten so bad. It's my fault. I never should've let you play with that damn Ouija board!"

"It's ok; you couldn't have seen this coming. Nobody could've."

The Reading of the Documents

Later that evening, down at the 'Nest....

All five Yarn Spinners, Birdie, Ally-fair, Willie Joe, and Vera, gathered in the eating area when Ruby, Kate, and Mrs. Purdy pulled up front. Willie Joe jumped up and ran to open the locked door. He seemed relieved to see Ruby. She could see it in his face, as he could see it in hers. The last to enter the door was Ruby. Willie stood by, holding the door open for her.

"Come in, my fair lady," Willie said as he tried to do a fancy bow which he failed at miserably, but this brought a smile to her face and lightened the mood. That was to be the last smile Willie saw from her for the rest of the night.

Mrs. Purdy lumbered through the aisle, leaning heavily on her cane. It made a tapping sound that disturbed everyone there and sounded eerily like pebbles hitting a window. She sat on the wooden bench usually reserved for old men to sit on and whittle. That bench could hold four grown men, but Ruby would've had trouble fitting on it with Mrs. Purdy.

The kids were perched on the red stools at the soda counter. Everyone else sat at the oversized picnic table where they had had a thousand meals. But there wasn't any food today. This was big doin's. Edgar Allan Poe would have described the mood in that room as solemn and melancholy. And he would have been dead right!

With no prelude or display of formality, Claude pulls a folded piece of parchment paper with a red unbroken seal from the wooden box he held in his lap. Birdie and Ally produce the same wooden box and remove identical folded documents. Last, Wilson has his own wooden box that holds a similar parchment.

With grim faces, they all nod in agreement. Matthew, Del, and Edgar are empty-handed but slightly spooked. Matt had seen the face of Buddy Webb reaching out to him deep down in the old well where he still drew water. He almost pissed himself. He'd been thinking about that day in the mine since he told the fellers that story. Though he wasn't sure what he saw, it left him nervy and anxious.

Del also had a bad scare. Last night he heard scratching at his back door. So, thinking it was some hungry cat or dog, he opened the door. That's when he saw the shape of a man running into the woods through his yard. He shouted, "Who's there?" The response was that hellish screeching of the werecat, Sawblade. So, he is reasonably jumpy. He wrings his gnarled hands and seems ready to jump out of his skin at the slightest noise. The refrigerator kicks on, and he almost squeals out in fright.

Edgar had a scare as well. Being a widower, he usually ate his TV dinner in the living room watching Jeopardy. He suddenly caught the scent of a perfume he hadn't smelled in decades. Out of the corner of his eye, he saw a woman with raven black hair dart around the corner. After what the others told him, he didn't dare look to see who that was. He returned to his supper and listened to Alex Trebek ask questions he didn't know.

Wilson continues, "Let's try and get our ducks in a row. Does anyone know who goes first?"

Claude clears his throat and says, "Yes, that would be me. My Pa gave me this right before he died. Told me to never open what was inside unless the other two people agreed. He said I'd know when the time was right. After what some of us witnessed last night, I think we agree. Birdie, Ally, are you two agreed? They both nod yes.

For the first time in exactly one hundred years, what was written inside those documents will see the light of day. What they read will turn their world upside down and inside out.

Document One: Claude Wells

The seal on the document was brittle, crumbled to pieces when Claude broke it open. He unrolled the yellowed parchment using salt and pepper shakers to hold it open. Claude took a minute to clean his specs so he could see the handwriting in homemade pokeberry ink. With a steady voice, he began.

"To the descendant of Jackson Dean Wells, it is with a heavy heart that I must leave you with this terrible duty. The witch Baby Annie, owned land over by Jones Gap. Mine explorers found an enormous coal seam that ran directly under her house."

When she was approached to sell her land, she told them no. I never knew what the sum was that she eventually agreed to, but it was nowhere near what it was worth. She signed away her land and, because of her illiteracy, couldn't read the part about keeping her mineral rights.

It was shameful that they would take advantage of her ignorance, but they did. She hired a lawyer when she figured out she'd been swindled. I was the lawyer she hired, so I read the document to her, and she became irate. There was nothing I could do to help her. She declared she wouldn't move from her land. She held vigil on her porch with a shotgun.

Finally, Constable Grayson Wells went to her and ordered her to leave. She refused and threatened to shoot him. The Mine Foreman Sampson Goble tried to reason with her, but she still refused. She kicked me out of the house, saying I wasn't on her side. That's when she told us we'd be sorry! And God bless us all, we were sorry indeed.

Go to the next document for an account of the horrific deeds Baby Annie committed. Those words are not for the faint of heart. If ladies are present, I'd excuse them now.

Solemnly yours,
Jackson Dean Wells

"You can bet your sorry ass this here lady ain't going' nowhere!" stated Birdie. That drew a snort from Mrs. Purdy.

Ally-Fair asked, "Shall we finish this business? I want to be home before dark?"

"Sure thang, sugar britches. Let me break this seal and find out how deep the shit is we're in."

"Go ahead Birdie, we're all ears." Said Wilson

Document 2: Birdie Daniels

"Greetings, my descendant. If you've had to open these documents, then it means that she is back. Baby Annie, that is. As you've read in the first document, Baby Annie was swindled out of her land. The three men she blamed was me, Sampson Goble, mine foreman, Constable Grayson Wells and her lawyer, Jackson Wells.

When we left her shack, we met up in town and tried to come up with a way to make amends. I'd already offered to let her live in one of the company houses so she could be in town, but she turned me down flat. The next day was when they were going to blast, so she had to leave. Constable Wells had an eviction notice, so me and Jack Wells went with him the next morning, bright and early.

We could only drive the wagon to the bottom of the hill because of the steepness of the mountain. She lived almost at the top. When we got to her dooryard, we were met with a sight that no man should ever have to see. I find it hard to put into words the horror that was before us.

Hanging disemboweled from a red maple that was bursting with red leaves were the bodies of three children. They were the sons of us men. Baby Annie had gotten her revenge. She made our children pay for our sins. This simple fact compounded the grief and sorrow I was already drowning in and still am to this day.

All three of us fell to our knees and threw up our breakfast. The howl of pain that came from us echoed through the mountains. It was the most gruesome thing I had ever seen, and I'm a war veteran. We each cut down our son and tried to place his innards back in as best we could. She had stitched their eyes and mouths closed and filled their ears with sand. See no evil, speak no evil, hear no evil was carved into the ground beneath their bodies.

I was so grief stricken that I'd forgotten about the witch. I wanted to torture her like she had my son. She was sitting on the porch with her shotgun. The sneer on her face was purely demonic. Jack and Gray finally joined me, and we approached her with guns of our own.

She shot at us but missed by a mile, so we three rushed her and God help me, I punched her right in the face, breaking her jaw. Gray put the shotgun to her head and was about to blow her head off when Jack stopped him. "Let's take her to town and let everyone get a whack at her. She's been nothing but a filthy witch, so she can die like one."

"The whole time she never said a word to us, she just kept muttering to herself. This made Gray scared, so he used the butt of his gun to smash her face in and knock out the two teeth she had left. We bound her wrists with rope and tied her to the wagon."

This concludes document number two. The third document will finish our tale. GodSpeed.

Throughout the reading of this document, Birdie was stoic. When it was over, she joined everyone in the room as they cried tears of sorrow for those poor, innocent children. Mrs. Purdy, however, was crying tears over her ancestor, Baby Annie.

"I don't know about you'uns, but I need a stiff drink after that." as she reaches under the counter and pulls out a bottle of Jim Beam and a jar of 'shine. "Pick your poison folks. As for me, I'm having whiskey and lots of it." she said as she poured two fingers in a glass.

All the adults raised their hand for a shot, even Ms. Allie. Mrs. Purdy pulled out a flask that she had hidden in her mammoth bosom. Not sure what was in it, but I bet it was better than what Birdie was offering.

"Alrighty folks, let's have that third document read so's we can figure out what to do to put these spooks back to where they belong!" declares Birdie.

Everyone takes their seat and Allie puts her specs on and clears her throat. Her hands are visibly shaking. She's not used to reading in front of a crowd; especially not one listening so intently.

Document 3: Ally-fair

Descendants, blood of my blood, my name is Grayson Wells. It is with the utmost regret that you've had to open this document. If there is help that I can give from heaven, I certainly will do all that I can. The end of this saga starts with us men dragging that filthy witch to town. As soon as we started down the mountain, the heavens opened up and it rained harder than I had ever seen. The creek was rising quick and if we hadn't hurried, the bridge would've washed out. We made it just in time. I knew she was muttering some kind of spell. But we foiled her plan, and we got to town anyway.

I lay the pitiful bodies of our children out in the back of the wagon, covered with a canvas tarp. I was thankful for the rain; it hid my tears. I suspect Jack and Sam were grateful for the rain, too. The worst part was having to tell our families. I figured the wives missed the children as soon as dawn broke and were frantic to find them.

The howls of agony and screams of pain that filled the town were something I'll never forget. But when the townspeople got wind of what had happened, a mob formed. A gang of men grabbed some old cross ties which were soaked with creosote and built a pyre.

The rain still hadn't quit, so it was gonna be hard to get the wood to burn. The witch was tied to a wooden post, and the townspeople gathered around her and threw rocks at her, spit on her and called her vicious names. I was the Constable of the town, but I was a father first, so I allowed this vigilante justice to take place. As the witch wavered and lost consciousness, the rain slacked off and she was doused with lamp oil, so she'd burn even though she was wet. Dry kindling was laid at her feet, doused in oil as well.

Everyone in town was present, even the children. I, along with Jack and Sam, lit torches and approached her. She raised her head and locked eyes with me and said,

"You will all pay for what you do to me. I'll have my revenge, not today, but in a hundred years, one of your own will raise me from the pits of hell and I'll torture your kin."

I told her to get ready to burn in Hell for eternity. When she tried to talk again, I threw the lamp oil in her face and she was quiet. Gray stepped forward and said, "Thou shalt not suffer a witch to live." The crowd ramped up and chanted, burn, burn, burn! Everyone was in a fever.

We lit the kindling and miraculously, the fire spread as if the wood were dry. The witch went up in flames quickly, but not before we all got to hear her scream in agony. That seemed to quell the anger in my soul. But then I had to face my grief.

It is my greatest wish that you never read this, but if you do, please heed this warning. Do not let anyone try to conjure up a witch! But if you're reading this, it's too late. I wish I had some wise words for you, but I don't. I turned the words the witch said to me over and over in my mind and the best I can figure is that someone will be born with the power to call her up. Beware of any person who is descended from the witch, she had children. But amongst our ancestors is where you'll find either your destroyer or savior. Best of luck to you and all the residents of Mary Luck.

Best Regards,
Grayson Wells

"Well, shit a brick. Ain't this a fine mess!" exclaimed Birdie.

"I have something to add if ya care to hear it?" said Wilson.

All heads turned to look at him as he stepped forward and presented his own rolled parchment.

"My daddy gave this to me when he got sick with the black lung. He said he didn't know how much longer he had so he thought it best to give it to me while he could still talk and be at hisself. I've had this hid away in the steamer trunk out in the smokehouse. He told me to only open it if the other three were opened and it had to come last. So here goes."

Codicil to the Documents

Wilson McKenzie

"*I suppose if you're reading this, it's the dreaded day of the return of the witch known as Baby Annie. Sadly, it will be one of our descendants that will have the power to resurrect her. It will be a girl and she will either do it on purpose or hopefully by accident. This child will come into her powers at the crux of her becoming a woman. Her menarche will give her the ability to summon the dead. She will communicate with spirits, good and bad. She can see into the future and predict things. If she tells you something is going to happen, heed her warning, for she will seldom ever be wrong.*"

"*How do I know these things? I am like her and she will have these powers through my blood and the blood of her ancestors from the highlands of Scotland. It is a gift passed down for centuries. I see this child being special. She will be your savior, but she will have a choice to choose either white or black magic. She will be powerful at either.*"

"*This time in her life will be when she is at her full power. As she ages, it will slowly fade, but she will always have her gifts. I pray you heed my warning when I tell you that a battle is coming. This town has seen a heinous crime committed on innocents. The echo of that pain will forever tarnish the town of Mary Luck. Do not let the witch win. She must be sent to Hell. Her soul is trapped here in the in-between, so she has never left. She's been able to influence certain events. I am certain that any ill luck that has struck can be traced back to her.*"

"*Breaking the curse will be difficult, but not impossible. I was present at her burning and heard her muttering. She was cursing the whole town. Every man, woman and child at her execution was party to her demise and was set with the evil eye. Before she was burned, the men of those poor children gave her a chance to ask God for forgiveness, but she just spit at them and said that she would have her revenge in one hundred years so that their kin would pay for their sins. She started muttering until her voice became shrieks of agony once the fire reached her."*

And if you're wondering how in the world a document passed down through the generations could last without someone peeking inside, that would be because of me. I placed a warding off spell on each of them. They could only be opened after one hundred years. Anyone who attempted to open them would be struck sick with a headache and dizziness and temporarily the memory of the document would vanish, only to return when the time was right, or if they were on their deathbed. When the time to open it drew nigh, nightmares and hauntings would make you remember.

Good Luck and God Bless you all.
Elspeth McKenzie Collins
31 Oct. 1884

Conflicts and Confusion

After Wilson finished his document, all eyes turned to Ruby Lee. She seemed to shrink before their very eyes. Birdie spoke up and said, "Well, child, mayhap you tell us what happened at your séance?"

Ruby hung her head and cried. No one spoke so that she could gather her wits about her. Finally, after one last sniffle, she straightened on her stool and told them all what had happened. Willie and Vera sat silent, only nodding when appropriate. All around, people were stunned in silence. It appeared everyone was lost in their thoughts, imagining what it was like for these kids to have seen the impossible in broad daylight, no less.

Mrs. Purdy said, "Now, don't you all blame little Ruby. She knew not what she did. Her momma should have brought her to me years ago, and we could've avoided all of this. So, any blame should be on her." She said this last with a hmph and fixed Kate with an 'I told you so' glare.

Now it was Kate's turn to hang her head in shame. She took it well and admitted that it was her fault. "If I hadn't been a fool and let my prejudice against Mrs. Purdy cloud my judgment, I'd have done what they asked me to, but I didn't have any idea something like this could happen.

When you told me she was special, I didn't realize what that meant. My ignorance caused this."

Wilson said, "Purdy, don't be pointing the finger of blame just on Kate. If you knew the dangers, you should have warned her when Ruby was of age. We ain't all practiced in the ways of witchery like you. How could she have known unless you told her?"

Claude jumped in before things could heat up, and somebody broke red.

"Let's all calm down. It doesn't matter who's to blame; it was probably a little of all of us, truth be known. The problem is, how do we fix it?"

All eyes turned to Purdy on this question, and she wasn't saying anything. After a pregnant pause, she finally spoke. "That's something I will have to ponder on for a while. Keep your heads on, and don't do anything stupid like trying to have another séance." She looks at the trio one at a time.

"Ruby, I'm going to need you to come to my house tomorrow so I can work with you and see how we can reverse this. I admit this is way past my learning, but I may have something from the old country that could help. You be at my house in the morning, and we'll get to work. If you see more spooks, turn your back on them and don't let them smell your fear. They feed on that. And they are hungry!"

"Make no mistake, Baby Annie is a powerful spirit, but she is still a spirit. She has no earthly body unless you invite her in. So, whatever you do, don't entertain her demons by falling for their tricks." With this last, she wallows out of her chair and tells Kate to fetch her back to the house. Chastened, Kate does as they tell her.

The trio leave together and head to the park to find their friends. Ruby stops before they get to the entrance, saying, "I really don't think we should tell anyone about this." "Why not?" asks Vera. "I know Josie would want to know. And Whitney."

"But they ain't from here, Vera. They wouldn't understand, and I don't want anyone but you all to know about how I was born."

Vera says, dripping with sarcasm, "Oh, I thought you'd love to tell everyone how SPECIAL you are." Vera's tone appalls Ruby.

"Vera, how can you say that? I'd give anything not to have this curse on me."

"Yeah, right; I know you're loving every minute of the attention you're getting. You can bring back ghosts!" Vera says as she skips off, declaring, "I'm meeting Tammy, and we're going to have a sleepover at her house. I'll catch you all on the flip side." She heads to the park, where Tammy waits for her by the swings. Ruby and Willie stand with their mouths hanging agape.

"What the hell just happened?" asked Ruby.

"Beats me," says Willie.

"Vera has never talked to me like that. She seems like a different person."

"Oh God," says Willie, "you don't think she's possessed, do you?"

"I don't know. But I bet it's possible. With all the weird shit going on around here, it wouldn't surprise me a bit. I will try to talk to

Vera again and see if I can make her see sense. All we need is for her to tell Tammy about this 'cause she will spread it all over town."

They head to the park, and when they get there, Tammy and Vera sit at the picnic table with the Catlettsburg brothers. Tammy has her boom box on full blast playing Footloose. She and Vera sing their hearts out, and Ruby's spirit breaks a bit. That's her and Vera's favorite song. How can she sing it without her? Ruby walks over and tries to talk to her, but the music is too loud, and Vera ignores her.

Finally, when the song is over, Vera looks her way. "What?" she says hatefully.

Ruby flinches from the hateful tone and says, "Vera, can we talk for a minute?"

"I go by V now, so never call me Vera again." She says snarkily, and Tammy and the boys giggle. Ruby is in shock and hurt.

Willie sees her pain and says, "What is up with you, Vera? Oh, excuse me, V? You're not acting like yourself?"

"Well, that's a good thing. I'm new and improved." She says proudly.

"Vera, I'm worried about you. You're not acting right," states Ruby.

"Well, this is the new V. She's tired of walking in your shadow, Ruby." Tammy spits out. She and Vera slap high fives and giggle together.

Then Vera pierces Ruby's heart and says, "Run along, Ruby and go be special somewhere else."

Tears well up in Ruby's eyes, and this pisses Willie Joe off.

"That was harsh, Vera; you're acting like a pure bitch!" Willie declares.

Vera fakes a hurt heart by clutching her hands to her chest, which suddenly looks fuller as Ruby observes. Typically, this kind of insult from Willie would have broken her spirit, but today she takes it in stride and seems to care less.

She says, "Surprise, surprise. Willie Joe is taking up for poor little Ruby. Boo Hoo." She mimics, rubbing her eyes, and the table erupts into laughter. Willie Joe flips her off, and she gives it right back. Ruby has never seen Vera do that. What the hell is wrong with her?

Willie and Ruby leave, and as they get to the gate, Josie, Josh, and Whitney catch up to them and say they heard what Vera said. They were as perplexed as Willie and Ruby. "Dang! Vera has flipped her wig! She barely spoke to us, just gave us a little wave and went back to talking to Tammy!" said Whitney.

"I can't believe it. I went one day without seeing her, and now she's V. It's like *Invasion of the Body Snatchers*," states Ruby while wiping away tears.

"It's almost dark, so we better head home. We'll see you guys tomorrow." Willie gives Ruby a ride back to the mouth of Shot Gun Holler on the back of his bike. allowing her to have a seat and him to stand up to pedal.

When Ruby hops off, she asks Willie if he wants to come to sit with her for a bit on her Papaw's swing. He jumps at the chance, and they sit down and enjoy the evening sound of crickets and jar flies. As dusk falls, the lightning bugs show up, leaving tiny glints of light that look like fairy dust.

Ruby asks Willie if everything is alright with him at home. He shrugs and hangs his head. "It's gotten pretty bad these last few months. Since the bank took his truck, he's been drinking more than ever. We all try to avoid him if we can. I hate it so bad. I want my dad back. He never asks me about school or what I've been up to. He doesn't care if I live or die!" Tears pour down his face, and

Ruby hugs him tight and tells him it'll be okay. But will it?

"Why don't you go stay with your Pappaw Claude? He would love the company. I bet he's afraid to be alone after everything."

"I've thought about that, but I'm afraid to leave my sisters and my Mom with him alone. He's gotten violent, Ruby. Sometimes I'm the only protection they have."

Ruby inhales sharply and says, "Oh, Will, I'm so sorry. That has to be awful. I wish you'd tell someone, like your Pappaw. That's your Dad's Dad. Surely he will listen to him."

"I suppose he might, but if I tell, they'll put him in jail, and I couldn't ever do that. I'm just hoping the mines open up again soon, and he can return to work. We've had to resort to food stamps. And when school starts, I'll be on the free lunch program. That embarrasses me to death."

Ruby turns red, knowing that this is a humiliating thing to admit. So she tries her best to console him. "Willie, everybody loves you. Nobody is going to care if you get free lunch. You'll still be the crush of every girl at school."

"Every girl, huh? Does that include you?" Ruby flushes again and starts to say something snippy, but the look on his face stops her. He looks so tender and sincere that she can only think to say, "Yeah, that includes me, too."

He takes a chance and leans over, and gives her a quick peck on the lips. It happened so fast and unexpectedly that Ruby didn't have time to dodge him. But why would she want to, she muses? That kiss, her first kiss, felt like magic. She suddenly wants another, so she leans in this time, which lasts a little longer. Willie reaches up and grabs a piece of her hair and lets it slide through his fingers like silk.

There was an uneasy silence that fell between them. Then they returned to swinging on the back porch sipping on their Faygo Pop.

Next thing she knew, Willie was holding her hand. They didn't need to say anything out loud. Things had changed between them. They were no longer just best friends. They were more and always had been. The bond between them could take them through anything. And they were going to need that kind of love. They were getting ready to face a witch and try to bring her down. Being tied to the land in Mary Luck through the blood of their kin made them culpable to Baby Annie.

Ruby heard her Pappaw coming through the house, so she quickly let go of Willie's hand, much to his regret and hers. Pappaw stuck his head out the door and told Willie Joe it was time to go home. He told him to throw his bike in the back of his truck, and he would drive him home. He didn't want him out alone after dark. With all that had happened, it wasn't safe.

Willie did as he was told and climbed into the front seat. Ruby waved goodbye from the porch. Her stomach was full of butterflies, and she suddenly felt half empty once he was gone. There were significant changes in her life in the last 48 hours. She discovered she had a specialness that could bring back witches; her best friend had dumped her, and now Willie Joe might be her boyfriend.

Vera's Transformation

When Vera woke up the morning of the reading, she looked different and felt different. Visibly, her body had changed. Her boobs were fuller, her acne was gone, and her teeth were straight. She bet the orthodontist would take them off at her next appointment. But the most significant difference was her newfound confidence and hatred of Ruby.

Her dreams the night before hadn't been about Willie Joe but about a woman who lived in a cottage in the hills. She had cookies and milk and a beautiful table set for a tea party. Vera joined her, and the woman told her she could make her attractive and have any boy she wanted. All she had to do was tell her what Ruby was doing and what powers she had.

In return, she would be the prettiest girl in town. The more information she gave her, the better she would look. So Vera offered that Mrs. Purdy would help Ruby defeat her. The ordeal made the woman mad; the angrier she got, the uglier. When Vera looked around, she wasn't in a cottage but a filthy, stinking shack. The woman, who now looked like a witch, said, "So my kin has turned on me. I'll fix her. Wait and see."

"Run on now, child, you keep me in the know, and I'll make you pretty."

Vera shook her head yes and didn't have any qualms at all about trading secrets for beauty. Ruby had been at the top too long. It was her turn now. The dream ended, and upon waking, she felt exuberant.

Ruby Has A Vision

That night, as she lies in bed trying to get that kiss out of her mind, she hears a knock on her window. Her bedroom was on the second story, so she knew that if she looked out, she would see something unnatural. That scene from 'Salem's Lot goes through her mind, and she's suddenly so scared she can hardly breathe. Another knock sounds followed by giggles that are high-pitched and eerily loud. Scared out of her mind, she can only think to banish them with her thoughts. She envisions those three little kids, and then she says to herself, "Get thee behind me, ye devils, and be gone!" she screams this last in her mind. The giggles outside stop, and there aren't more knocks at the window. Feeling as though she got rid of them, she can drift off to sleep, where she will encounter another obstacle. This time, she will face the witch.

As she falls into REM sleep, Ruby begins to dream. The only thing is, it doesn't feel like a dream. It seems real. The first thing she notices is that she's cold. Then the smells of wood fire and body odor assaulted her senses. She's in a crowd, and everyone seems much taller than her. She looks down at her hands, and they aren't hers. They're childlike. She realizes she is no longer thirteen; she's maybe four. Rough, calloused hands grab her shoulders, shove her to the front of the crowd, and tell her to watch.

That's when she sees her, a woman, or what's left of her, seeing as how she has been shaved bald, with burn marks all over her body. She is barely dressed in what was once white but now is a dingy gray gown. Barefoot, she can tell that her feet are crushed, and her fingers all lay in different directions. They are dragging this poor wretch to the pyre. They will burn her for being a witch. Ruby hears all this from a man in a plaid skirt. . He's standing in front of the pole they will tie her to. He tells them there will be no mercy for this witch. She will be burnt alive without first being strangled since she didn't confess to being a witch. .

This last declaration tears Ruby up. She will have to watch this woman die through her daughter's eyes. As the men reach the pyre with the pitiful woman, the crowd gathers around, throws stones, and spits on her. She makes no move to dodge any of the rocks and doesn't even wipe the spittle off her face. She has a stoic look. Ruby can't help but think she is brave and wonders what courage you need to have to face being burned alive.

Once fastened to the pole, the men light torches and start the fire. Ruby shuts her eyes, but a hand roughly grabs her chin. She locks eyes with the woman she finds out is named Agnes McKenzie. It seems the woman looks straight into her soul, and she smirks as if she knows her daughter has a passenger inside watching the show. Then the smirk is gone, and the shrieks and howls of agony replace it. Thankfully, they don't last long, and her misery ends quickly. During this last, Ruby is pushed to the back of the crowd as they chant with fervor. "Burn Witch Burn!" Then another pair of hands hefts her off her feet, and she is thrown inside a wooden carriage piled with quilts and woolen blankets that stink like a wet dog. A soft pair of hands covers her eyes and tells her, "Look no more upon thy mother's face."

Suddenly, it finally made sense. She was in the daughter's body of the witch. But who was she? It didn't take long before the horses pulled them as the carriage creaked on crudely made wooden wheels. It was warm inside, and the woman holding her seemed kind. Her hands were old but soft, and she began stroking her hair and said her name. "Now, now, sweet Baby Annie. Dry your tears, we'll be in America soon, and you won't ever have to worry about being burnt at the stake."

Ruby sat straight up in bed. Her heart was hammering, and she was gasping for air. As she became fully awake, she could still smell the wood smoke and the wet dog wool blankets. It was daylight, but just barely. She glanced at her hands to make sure they were hers. She pulled back her covers and saw a dark stain on her nightgown. Thinking it was soot or ash, she ran to the bathroom to look. That's when she saw the blood. During the night, Ruby Lee had become a woman.

The much-expected and dreaded day t had finally arrived. Suddenly, overcome with fear and embarrassment, she removed her clothes and washed them in cold water. She suddenly felt a cramp that almost doubled her over. Though it was painful, she couldn't help but smile just a little. She thought, Wow! My first cramp the day after my first kiss. Then another pain hit her, but this one was in her heart. Her first thought was to call and tell Vera. They had prepared for their period since the fifth grade when the health department nurses came to school and gave all the girls a booklet called "Personally Yours" that explained menstruation. If they went anywhere, movies, football games, etc., they made sure that they had a Kotex pad in their monogrammed wooden handle reversible cover purse. Your first period could happen anyplace, anytime. But now, would Vera even care? Also, Ruby and Willie were different now. Would Vera hate her forever?

Ruby couldn't imagine her life without Vera. They'd been best friends since first grade. Vera was painfully shy and odd with her thick-lensed glasses. She was an easy target to be picked on by Tammy Turner. On the first day of school, Tammy had seen Vera pick her nose, and she and her cronies circled her, singing,

"Everybody's doin' it, doin' it, doin' it. Pickin' their nose and chewin' it, chewin' it, thinking it's candy, but it's not. It's a hot snot sundae with a booger on top!"

Vera was mortified and crying, so Ruby went over to help her, along with big sister Rosie. Rosie took care of the teasing by threatening to beat the shit out of them and sent them packing. From that day on, they'd been best friends. Vera had many beautiful qualities, but her shyness kept them secret from most of the world. Ruby had wished that everyone else could see the honest Vera.

After what happened yesterday, it seemed Vera had finally come out of her shell. It was just so uncharacteristically not like her. The person Ruby knew was no longer present with this new girl known as V. She would have to tell Mrs. Purdy about Vera's odd behavior. Maybe there was something she could do to help her. After her last night's dream, it didn't seem so impossible for Baby Annie to possess Vera. The thoughts of that scared Ruby something fierce.

After her daddy went to work, Ruby crept into bed with her Mom. Kate gathered her to her without opening her eyes and just hugged her. Ruby cried, and so did her Mom. "Baby, I'm so sorry that this has happened to you. I was a fool, and that has put you in this mess. I hope you've learned from my mistakes. Never judge a book by its cover; don't worry so much about what people think or say. Pride is not only one of the seven deadly sins; it's an ugly word. Just always remember, 'pride comes before the fall.'"

"I will, Mommy. I'll never worry about what people think again. I feel sorry for Mrs. Purdy. I feel stupid for always being so scared of her. I mean, she is weird. But so are a lot of people."

"That's right. Don't judge people. That's for God to do, not us."

"My period started this morning."

"Oh wow. Do you know what to do?"

"Yes, ma'am. Rosie told me all about it. We probably need more pads, though, and my stomach is cramping."

"Okay, well, I can help with that. Let me get you some Tylenol, and you go back to bed and rest before you go to Mrs. Purdy's. Rosie's been asking questions about what's going on. I told her it was nothing to worry about, so don't tell her too much. She can't keep a secret to save her life." Kate says this last while shaking her head and shrugging her shoulders as she walks out of the room.

Ruby giggles to herself because it's true. Rosie loves to gossip! She goes back to bed but doesn't fall asleep. The remnants of her dream were still very vivid in her mind. Instead, she replays the kiss she shared with Willie Joe. Her cramps were gone, but the butterflies were back, and those left her feeling giddy and nervous. But in a good way.

Later at the Park

When Ruby got to the park, it was hoppin'. A late July afternoon was the prime time for fun. Kids packed the courts, and the baseball field had loaded bases. It looked like every piece of athletic equipment in the town was in use. Ruby spied Willie Joe as he was sinking a three-pointer. He high-fived and was cheered for, but his biggest reward was the smile he got from Ruby Lee. Seeing Vera sitting on a picnic table snuggled up to George almost made Ruby lose her courage to speak to her. But Ruby wanted to save Vera. Undoubtedly, their friendship was strong enough to overcome Baby Annie's influence.

Coming up behind her, Ruby asks. "Hey, Vera, can I talk to you for a sec ?"

"I told you yesterday, the name's V!" she says snottily, then turns back and ignores Ruby.

Ruby is in shock. Vera didn't even look the same. She was chewing gum with her freshly permed hair. Vera hadn't chewed gum since before her braces, which could only mean the braces were off. A year early? Ruby reached for Vera's shoulder but paused before she got her when she saw what she had on. She cropped a shirt she'd had since third grade to make a belly shirt. It was super tight, which drew Ruby's eye to her chest. Vera had boobs now, too? What was going on?

Ruby walks around before Vera and asks, "V. Can I talk to you for a minute."

"Since you used my name right, I can spare a few minutes."

They walk to the side, and Vee says, "So what's so important you had to drag me over here?"

"Uh, well, I just wanted to tell you I started my period today," Ruby whispers.

"Hey everybody, Ruby Lee's on the rag!" Vera shouts to the entire park.

To Ruby, every head turned to look at her mortified face. Then came the laughter and teasing. George started a chant saying bloody Ruby. She turned and ran as fast as her legs would carry her. Willie yelled at her to stop, but she got on her bike and took off. The pain in her heart was almost too much to bear. It was matched only by the embarrassment she was feeling. Vera must genuinely hate her.

Willie Joe slammed down the basketball he was holding, went over to Vera, and got right up in her face. Holding clenched fists by his side, he said, "What the fuck is wrong with you, Vera? How could you say something like that about your best friend? That was about the meanest thing I've ever heard."

"Well, in case you haven't noticed, I have a new best friend," Vera says while pointing at Tammy.

"Yeah, V doesn't need bloody Ruby hanging around," Tammy snickers.

"You bitches deserve each other."

"Hey man, that's my girl you're talking about," George says while standing up slowly.

Willie gives him a look that changes his mind. He lowers himself back down as Willie says, "That's right, Georgie, don't even think about it." George is taller than Willie, but he is all skin and bones. Willie was a country boy, muscled and strong from outside work. It would have been a bloodbath.

Jerry Crider hollers over from the basketball court, "Kick that city boy's ass, Willie."

Willie eyes Vera and Tammy, and then his eye falls on George. "If I hear you repeat bloody Ruby, I'll beat the shit out of you!" Nothing more needed to be said. Willie's face said it all.

"Ooh, yeah. Tell 'em, Willie." Sammy Price yells as he attempts a three-pointer, which strikes the rim with a resounding 'thunk.' The kids all laughed at this pitiful display of suckiness.

"Give it up, Sammy: you'll never be as good as Willie Joe." Says Jerry. And just like that, the action was over, and he was on to tease someone else. Kids at that age have the attention span of a gnat. They had most likely already forgotten Ruby's humiliation, but for Ruby, her embarrassment almost felt tangible, like a cloak surrounding her.

Ruby Lee went straight upstairs and flopped down on her bed. She put her face in her pillow and screamed.

Rosie walks out of the bathroom, slumps in the door frame, and says, "What's wrong with you?"

Ruby knew better than not to answer. Rosie would get it out of her anyway, so she'd might as well get it over with. So, Ruby told her. When she finished, Rosie was in shock!

"You mean to tell me that mousey Vera said that to you?" Ruby nods.

"I'll kick her ass. After all the times I took up for that little twerp. I should've let Tammy tease her."

"Rosie, please don't say anything to her," Ruby begs.

"Why not? She deserves it."

"If I let my big sister fight my battles, I will never live it down. I can take up for myself." Ruby calls off her sister because even though Vera has broken her heart, she knows something is wrong with her. Something supernatural.

Ruby goes down and sits on her front porch swing and tries to calm her nerves. She lets the wind caress her face, and the scents of the mountains flood her senses. Nature had always been her refuge. Even as a small child, she was content to play outside regardless of the weather. The rustle of leaves on the trees were whispers from imaginary friends. The birds were her choir mates, the insects, rhythm, and thunder percussion. Ruby Lee had always been in perfect harmony with nature. It's where she drew her strength. She'd never thought about it before, but now it was as though everything felt more intense. The sun is brighter, sounds louder, and scents stronger. Ruby had found her calm.

She heard Whitney and Josie before she could see them. Their laughter is riding the wind. When they came into view, Ruby said, "Y'all come on up."

"Hey, Ruby." They said in unison.

"Are you okay?" asks Josie.

"Not really, but I guess I'm gonna have to be."

Whitney scowls, "I can't believe Vera is acting so awful. What the hell is wrong with her?"

Josie chuckles, "I think I know what's wrong with her. She's just turned into a snotty little bitch."

"You got that right."

"Y'all, I have to tell you something. But you have to promise, cross your heart and hope to die, stick a needle in your eye, that you won't tell another soul. Josie, you can tell Josh if Willie Joe hasn't already, but nobody else. This is serious-like. Someone could get hurt or even die." Ruby fixes her eyes on her friends with a look so stone-cold that all smiles and giggles are immediately gone.

"Okay, okay, I promise."

"Me too." Says Whitney.

Ruby then gives her friends the abridged version of the last few days' events. She can tell they are in shock by the slack-jawed expressions on their faces. When she's finished, she turns her head, closes her eyes, and waits to hear if they think she's crazy.

Josie speaks first. "Ruby, that is the wildest story I've ever heard, but I believe every word. I've always thought there was more to this town than what meets the eye. I always catch glimpses of things out of the corner of my eye. But when I turn to see them, they're gone."

"Well, I haven't seen any ghosts, but I believe you too, Ruby. That story is too crazy to make up," Whitney states.

"It almost makes me feel sorry for Vera." She adds with a snicker, "Almost."

"Yeah, I know. It's the only reason I didn't punch her in the face earlier." says Ruby Lee.

"Speaking of punching faces, you missed it, Ruby; Willie Joe cussed Vera out and threatened to beat up George after you left. Talk about a knight in shining armor. He was furious," Whitney says as she wiggles her eyebrows.

Ruby turns red, hides her face then peeks out from under her bangs. "Willie Joe kissed me yesterday." She quickly covers her face again, and the other girls squeal and start oohing and awing.

"I think you guys are perfect for each other. I never said anything before since it was painfully obvious that Vera was in love with him."

"Yeah, Ruby, I've always thought he liked you. Josh says he talks about you all the time."

"Really?" asks Ruby.

Whitney teases, "Well, Duh. He's always looking at you with this dreamy look."

"I never really paid any attention to him in that way because of Vera. I just thought we were best friends."

Josie was curious, "Are you going to ask him to the Sadie Hawkins dance?"

"I guess I will. I hadn't even considered it, but it's this weekend."

"Why don't you see if you can spend the night with me tonight, and we can catch Willie on his way home since you don't want to go to the park this evening?"

At that time, Kate opens the door, tells Ruby supper is almost ready, and asks the girls to join them. "Thanks, Mrs. Collins, but my Gran is cooking."

"My Paps and I are going to Jerry's tonight. It's the all-you-can-eat catfish special, and he never misses that. But, thanks anyway. Can Ruby spend the night with me tonight?" She smiles her sweetest suck-up-to-the-parents smile.

"Sure, as long as she does the dishes and cleans up her room."

"I will," she says and gives the girls a high-five.

"Alright, get in here and set the table. Bye, girls."

Staying the night at Whitney's

Ruby pulls her bike up in front of Whitney's house. She's never been here before. The Burkett house had always been her favorite. It was once the home of the coal company's doctor. It had two front doors - one for patients and the family, a wrap-around porch with a swing and wicker rocking chairs. It had gingerbread trim and wooden shutters with hearts carved on the corners. It was a fairy-tale house that had always captured Ruby's eye.

That evening, as the sun set behind the mountains, the white house had a red glow, and the fiery sun was reflected in the top windows, giving them a hellish glare—a jolt of fear shot through Ruby. The feeling was so intense she couldn't move. So, when Willie Joe shook her shoulder, she yelped and jumped. She hadn't even heard him.

"Sorry! I didn't mean to scare you." Says Willie Joe with earnestness.

"It's okay. This house scares me to death."

"I thought this was your favorite house."

"It is or was. It just looks like it wants to eat me up. And those top windows look like eyes."

"You're right; it looks like a face."

"Yeah, and I'm spending the night here too."

"Better you than me." Willie teases.

"Gee, thanks."

Ruby looks down at the ground and gathers her courage, and before she can change her mind, she blurts out, "Do you want to go to the Sadie Hawkins Dance with me?"

The abruptness of her question takes Willie aback. He stammers for a second and then says. "Yes. I was getting nervous. Thought maybe you wanted to go with someone else." He looks relieved.

"Okay. And who else would I ask, anyway?"

Willie shrugs his shoulders and says, "I don't know. Anybody would go with you."

Ruby blushes and says, "Yeah, I know. I can't help that I'm special."

They both break up in laughter, and all's right with the world again.

When Willie Joe gets out of sight, Whitney and Josie run out on the porch, squeal as only teenage girls can, and ask, "Did you ask him? What did he say?"

"Yes, and yes." She confirms with a squeal.

Upstairs in Whitney's room, she has Prince singing "Let's Go Crazy" on her stereo. She dances around, singing along with her hairbrush as a microphone. Soon, all three of them are dancing and singing. Their pure joy at just being young was infectious.

Brother Burkett was tapping his foot with the beat before he knew what he was doing. When the guitar solo came on, all three girls fell to their knees, playing to beat the devil on their air guitars. Little did they know that this would be the last day they would feel this happy and carefree.

Later that night, the girls are all sacked out in sleeping bags on the bedroom floor. The windows are open to let in the cool night air. The moon is out full and bright. It's the perfect night to take your Yankee cousin Snipe hunting, and that's what Keith and Joey Frasure did. Their cousin, Bryan from Michigan, had bragged about how great he was at hunting for a week. The Frasure boys decided they'd test his skills by taking him up in the hills and getting him lost.

When Ruby reaches REM sleep, she opens her eyes but is not herself anymore. She thinks she's up on the mountain behind her house. When Ruby sees the tombstone obelisk in the moonlight, she's sure. Whoever she's with is running and sweating, and they seem to be in a panic. That's when she hears a roar that sounds like an enormous cat. The person runs faster. In his haste, he trips over a root and goes sprawling.

He loses his breath, and it takes a minute to right himself. He hears the roar again and tries to stand. Kudzo held his foot captive. When he reaches to get free, the Kudzo ensnares his arm. He is pulled off his feet and hangs with all four appendages, pulling him in four directions. Ruby uses his eyes, looks around, and then sees that the Kudzu monsters have come alive. Kudzu shapes around power lines and telephone poles look like gelatinous blobs of green vines. Their vast size and random shape give them a loathsome aura that had always scared Ruby. All of her fears came true when she saw that not only were the shapes alive, but they were also mobile.

It was more than Ruby could fathom seeing these horrors move from their stationary positions. But top that with a roar that sounded way too close. When Ruby saw what was making the roar, she couldn't believe it. She didn't need an explanation of what or who it was. She knew by all the descriptions she'd heard her whole life. It was Sawblade. The white fur and claws for hands were second only to the fangs gleaming in the moonlight when he threw his head back and screeched loudly. His eyes shine, but not like an animal's will do at night if hit by headlights. His eyes were pure silver. They glistened and seemed to swirl hypnotically.

But the animal smell was the worst. It was musky and sweaty, worse than any wet dog Ruby'd ever smelled. But the underlying smell, which was way more pungent, was the stench of death, like the putrid flyblown corpse of a groundhog that had been hit on the road and left to swell up and rot. When Sawblade spied his prize caught in the Kudzu like a fly in a spider's web, he drooled. As he crouched down on all fours, Ruby knew whoever she saw this through was a goner.

Sawblade leaped into the air with superhuman agility. As his fangs punctured the skin of his neck, Ruby Lee was thrust back into reality and gave out an ear-splitting scream that mirrored the one happening on the mountain. The combined scream woke the Burkett household, Widow Stephens next door, and Birdie Daniels as she nursed her Makers and Coke.

The scream on the mountain made the Frasure boys giggle at first, and then their blood turned cold when they heard the cat's roar longer and louder.

Ruby clutched her heart, which seemed about to leap from her chest. Her breathing was labored but quick. Like she was almost panting, Whitney and Josie were trying to console her when the bedroom light came on, and Whitney's Pappaw came in brandishing a shotgun and wearing an ancient nightshirt that Ebenezer Scrooge could've owned.

"Paps, we're okay! No need for a shotgun!" Whitney says with a huff.

"Are you sure there weren't any boys trying to peek at you girls?" asks Pappaw.

"No!" Whitney says with an exaggerated eye roll.

"Ruby had a nightmare, is all. Go back to bed! You need your rest, Pap." Whitney's tone was kinder, and her true feelings were shining through. She may often fuss about her Pappaw, but she loved him fiercely. He was the father figure she needed since her dad was too busy to be bothered. Whitney led him back to his room, promising to shut and lock the windows. When she returned, Ruby was in tears.

"What happened, Ruby? Did you have another vision?"

"Oh my God, you all. I think somebody is dead. If my vision is right, it happened as I was dreaming." Ruby hugs herself as tears run down her face.

"Who was it?"

"I don't know. I was seeing it through their eyes. I'm pretty sure it was a boy, a teenager. Sawblade ripped him apart."

"Who is Sawblade?" asked Whitney and Josie simultaneously.

Ruby filled them in on who and what he was, and the look of horror on their faces told her they believed.

"What should we do?" asked Whitney.

"There's nothing to do now. He's dead. I'm sure of it. I felt the fangs go in his neck right before I woke up. All we can do is wait till morning and see if it happened."

The girls were huddled on the floor together. As an ambulance siren wailed through the nearby window, they all turned their heads. Cold chills broke out on their skin. It must be true. Someone had heard the screams of agony from the boy, but it was too late to save him. Ruby knew she had to see Mrs. Purdy first thing in the morning. Baby Annie was getting stronger. No one would be safe if her spooks could now harm the living.

Mrs. Purdy's House

The news was all over town when the girls woke up from a restless sleep. The police were saying it was an animal attack, probably a bobcat. If they only knew what happened, they'd be more afraid. A group of men were out scouring the mountain, looking for the animal so they could kill it and put the town at ease. However, they'd never find Sawblade. He'd been hiding in those hills for decades, and if Baby Annie was animating him, he had probably already vanished.

At breakfast, Mr. Burkett told the girls that Brian Frasure, a cousin visiting from Michigan, had died. His cousins had taken him snipe hunting and lost him in the woods. By the time they got to him, he was already dead. The boys and their families were devastated. The whole town was in a panic to find the animal responsible. Ruby Lee knew it was a waste of time because it would take more than a gun to bring down Sawblade. How could you kill something already dead?

With promises to meet up later, the girls parted ways, and Ruby Lee went straight to the 'Bottom to see Mrs. Purdy. She was on the porch swing when Ruby arrived.

"I was wondering when you were going to get here. Come on up here and tell me what you saw."

Mrs. Purdy never failed to amaze Ruby with her intuition. She always knew when something wasn't right.

Ruby plopped down in the rickety rocker and told her about her vision and the real culprit.

"Good Lord!" Mrs. Purdy exclaimed. This moment was only the second time Ruby had ever seen her flustered or even look worried, which turned her blood cold.

"You were right to come here. If Baby Annie is strong enough to use her spooks to take the life of the living, then she is almost ready to walk the earth in her true form. We have to figure out how she is harnessing this power. I know that fear is an energy Annie can pull from, but this stunt took more than fear. She is using other people besides Vera to do her bidding. Can you think of anybody else who is acting odd?"

Ruby ponders this for a minute, "Willie Joe said his dad has been mean and drinking a lot. He has beat on the whole family."

"Yep, that fits the bill. Maybe someone who's been missing for a while?"

"Miss Ally hasn't been at her store in a few days since reading the documents. Maybe she's possessed now too?"

"She's probably too scared to leave. She's such a sad little mouse." Mrs. Purdy says with a sneer.

"Somebody should probably go check on the old biddy, though."

"I'll tell Pappaw to do it. I need to fill him in on Saw Blade, anyway."

"Run along then, but let me know if you have more visions. Things have gotten bad, and they'll get worse before they get better."

Ruby got to her Papaw's and went in the back door. She let the screen door slam and got a dark look from her Mammaw, sitting at the table breaking up beans. Before she could get scolded, Ruby ran to the living room where Pappaw was leaning back in his recliner, smoking his pipe, watching *Gunsmoke*. He sat up, startled when Ruby bounded into the room with a crash as she sat on the floor at his feet.

"What's going on? You scared me half to death!" Pappaw said as he righted himself in his chair. He buttoned his pants and refastened his belt since he liked to let his belly out after breakfast.

"Did you hear about that boy getting killed last night?" she asks.

"Yeah, they said it was likely a bobcat or a panther," Pap stated.

"Well, they're wrong. I saw it all through his eyes in one of my dream visions. It was awful, Pappaw." Ruby broke down in tears, wrapping her whole body with sobs.

"Tell me what you saw, honey."

"It was Sawblade Pap. Except it was Baby Annie acting through him. Mrs. Purdy said that if she could take a life using her spooks, she was almost strong enough to be in the flesh again. Then she will be able to hurt people herself soon. I'm so scared, Pappaw. How am I supposed to beat her? I'm just a kid!" Ruby is getting hysterical after realizing what she's up against, and only her Papaw's embrace keeps her from a total meltdown.

"Now, now, don't get so worked up. You aren't the only one that's gotta beat her. You've got all kinds of folks that are going to help. You're the bright star that's going to put an end to that old hag. Elsbeth said you'd know what to do when the time was right. Just believe that. Good always defeats evil, always!"

Pappaw pets Ruby's head like you'd pet a loyal dog, which calms her like nothing else. She dries her eyes and blows her nose on his hanky. "I hope you're right. I don't know what I'm doing, and I'm scared that someone else will die because I'm too stupid to stop her."

"If that happens, it ain't your fault, honey. We can only do what we can. No more, no less."

Ruby tells him how Mrs. Purdy used people for their energy and had them do her bidding. They decided they should check on Miss Ally. "I'll go see her. You go home and get some sleep. Leave the checking to me and the 'Spinners. That's the least we can do."

"Okay, thanks, Pap. I love you."

"I love you too, honey."

When Ruby gets home, she tells her mom what's happening and then goes to her room to nap. As sleep descends upon her, she is whisked away to another vision. This time, she's in the body of a woman. She can tell by her hands and the fact that she is wearing a long dress. Then a voice inside her head says, 'Walk over to the mirror so I can get a look at myself.' Ruby obeys, and when she looks through the eyes of the person, she sees a beautiful redheaded woman with long hair, just like hers. The eyes are the same, but she knows this isn't her.

The voice then says, 'Wasn't I a beauty?' Ruby thinks, yes, you sure are. "Thank you, dear. In case you haven't figured it out, I'm Elspeth McKenzie. I need to show you where something is hidden

The Mary Luck Tales

for your eyes only. Do not share this with anyone. No one can know that you have this." Elspeth walks over to a steamer trunk and lifts the lid. At the top, there is a panel that, when pressed down, slides over and reveals a hidden compartment. Inside is an ancient-looking parchment with words on it she can not read. "What is it?" Ruby asks.

"It's a spell written in Elven. It is meant only for the chosen one, which is you."

"What does it do?"

"It will give you the power to read Baby Annie's grimoire. A spell inside will cast her out of the world should she gain the power to become flesh again. It will take your energy, love, and strength to perform the spell, and you can only perform it once. It's a dangerous spell and one you should only do as a last resort because there will be a price for using it. All gods require sacrifices, and this is no different. For it to work, you must lose something you love. You don't get to choose what it is either."

"Why all the secrecy? Can't I tell Pappaw or Purdy?"

"Not! Having the ability to read the grimoire is very enticing. The spells in the book are powerful and ancient. These are things coveted by weaker people. Purdy would double-cross you in a second to perform the spells in the grimoire. Even someone as pure of heart as your Pap would be tempted by the fountain of youth spell. Baby Annie knows what spells are in the book but cannot cast them because she can't read them. Do you understand?"

"Yes. But how can I read this spell? I don't even know what language this is." Ruby says while looking at the faded parchment.

"When the time is right, it will reveal itself to you. When you need it, if you are pure of heart and want to use it for good, it will be readable, but only to you. But, once you speak the spell, it will become blank and can never be used again. You can read the

187

grimoire and perform the spell to banish the hag to hell. But only if she is made flesh. And don't forget; there will be a sacrifice."

"Thank you, Elspeth. I hope I won't disappoint you."

"I have faith in you. Just believe in yourself and what you are."

"Oh, one more thing, let your Pap know that mother nature was the Green Lady, and she was not happy that the hag used her embodiment to deliver her message. That was the test she gave the town, and their kindness to a desperate stranger earned them the weapon to save themselves, you."

Then, Ruby relaxed into a dreamless sleep that left her rested and restored. When she awoke, she wrote everything she could remember from Elspeth in her diary. Leaving out any clues as to the spell's purpose just in case her diary should fall into the wrong hands. Papaw was going to flip out over the G reen L ady's true identity.

After supper, Ruby went to the park to meet up with her friends. Vera, thankfully, was not around. There were a few snickers when she walked in, but a side look from Willie Joe stopped any teasing that could've happened. She couldn't believe that after yesterday's humiliation, she could go to the park and face her shame. But, after the murder by Sawblade, her embarrassment paled in comparison.

Ruby filled Willie Joe in on her vision and the truth about what killed Brian Frasure. When she finished speaking, Willie looked visibly shaken. He looked pale under his tanned skin as he reached over and took Ruby's hand to comfort her as much as himself. He couldn't help but feel stronger when he was with her. She radiated strength and didn't even know it.

"What are we gonna do, Ruby?"

"I don't know. We have to be very careful and keep an eye out for anyone acting strange. Like Vera."

"She's a whacko!" Willie says.

"I know she was awful to me yesterday, but a part of me can't be mad at her because I know it isn't her fault. Baby Annie is using her, and I don't know how to stop her."

"You're too nice, Ruby. I don't think I could be after what she did."

"Yes, you would. You've got a big heart, Willie Joe. Under your tough guy act, you're an old softy!" Ruby teased while punching him in the arm.

"Willie, promise me you won't be out after dark. It isn't safe." Ruby begs.

"Oh, don't worry. I'm scared to death. I'll be home before the streetlights are on." He assures her.

Ruby is satisfied that he will be careful, but so many others won't be. She looks around at the twenty-five-odd kids at the park and wonders who will be next.

Sadie Hawkins Dance 1984

Two days after the attack by Sawblade, Ruby is in her room getting ready for the dance. It was a tradition in Mary Luck to dress up as the fictional 'Hillbilly' ugly duckling Sadie Hawkins. After all, Dogpatch was supposed to be in Kentucky, so the girls would braid their hair in pigtails, black out one of their front teeth with eyeliner, and paint red dots that were supposed to be acne or freckles on their cheeks. Attire ran anything from cut-off jeans to flour sack dresses leftover from the thirties. People in these parts didn't throw away anything. The boys usually wore overalls or short britches with holes and patches, plaid shirts, and straw hats.

When Ruby's mom finishes braiding her red hair, blacking out her tooth, and applying her freckles, she looks in the mirror and almost doesn't recognize herself. It seems like weeks since she looked at herself. She looks older, and it startles her. She flashes back to the dream about Elspeth. Suddenly she knows why she looks different. She seems like Elspeth, which is scary and exciting all at the same time.

Her mom allowed her to wear mascara to accent her green eyes and light pink lip gloss. Her worn-out cut-off Levis' cinched around the waist with a piece of straw rope from Pap. Next is her faded pink and purple plaid button-down shirt with a patch on the left elbow. She leaves the last three buttons undone to tie up her shirt in the front. On her feet were her pink flip-flops, which she planned to remove the minute she walked into the gym. Another tradition in Mary Luck, at a hillbilly dance, you couldn't wear shoes.

Ruby's mom takes her to Whitney's house, where the girls meet to walk to the dance together. Kate has made Ruby promise not to go anywhere alone. They were staying at Whitney's again, and the boys would walk them home. Whitney and Josie were on the porch waiting for her. They looked great! Neither had ever been to a Sadie Hawkins dance. Whitney had asked Josh so that he wouldn't have to go stag, and Josie asked Kevin Goble, Willie's cousin, come to stay the week at Claude's. Willie frequently visited with his Pap to avoid his father's wrath.

Whitney had to opt for pigtails since her hair was only shoulder length, but Josie had her dark crown in two braids like Ruby. She looked like Pocahontas with her dark eyes and hair and golden tan. They both had cut-offs with plaid shirts rolled up sleeves tied up in front. Ruby gave them each a piece of rope to tie around their waist to complete their outfits.

Whitney came outside with a straw cowboy hat identical to the oneAerial in *Footloose wore*. They all squealed and were instantly envious. Whitney looked great, and she knew it. When the boys arrived, she strolled down the sidewalk like a runway model.

As the girls exited the gate and joined the boys, they had an indescribable air of innocence. A feeling of living in the moment that would never come again.

Life is like that sometimes, a moment arrives, and things seem to lock into place like the last piece of a jigsaw puzzle. Try to savor it and hold on to it. Save it for another day. It could be the one thing that gets you through a cold night.

The boys park their bikes in front of the house, each with a surprise for the girls. Josh brought Whitney a yellow rose freshly picked from his yard, which she deftly placed in her hat band. She gives him a peck on the cheek, making him blush fire engine red. Kevin brought Josie a necklace made from clover flowers, which she slipped around her neck. Willie got Ruby two perfect daisies, her favorite, which he placed behind each ear. Admiring his handiwork, he pronounces her beautiful. With all eyes upon her, it was her turn to blush. "Thanks, Willie, you're not so bad yourself."

Willie wore overalls rolled up above the ankle. They are worn out, with holes in the knees and patches on the seat. He is shirtless underneath, and his muscles are displayed, which he arrogantly refers to as his guns. The sight drew a much-needed gagging noise from the girls and a sneer from the boys. Try as she might not to ogle him, Ruby has to tear her eyes away. He truly is a beautiful boy.

Josh didn't own a pair of overalls, so he had on cut-off shorts that were new and barely had any threads dangling. He made up for it with his straw hat and a hawk feather in the band. He and Whitney looked great together with their matching hats. Kevin had on overalls and a sleeveless Def-Leppard t-shirt underneath.

The community development club sponsors the dance. They focus on doing activities to give the folks something to do now that the park is complete. The club decorated the gym with hay bales and streamers. Edith had the popcorn machine fired up. It smells like popcorn, hot dogs, and chili. Admission was $2 for kids and $5 for adults, all proceeds going to the club. Kate Collins was one of the volunteers that night. She'd be in the lunchroom tending to the soup bean supper for the old-timers. Something for the whole town, you could say.

Ruby reaches into her pocket for money at the door, but Willie Joe jumps ahead of her, hands them a five-dollar bill, and says, "Two, please." Ruby starts to give him money, but he stops her by saying, "My treat. I mowed two lawns today so we can eat whatever we want, and it's all on me." He's so proud. Ruby doesn't argue. She feels so different with him now. He brought her flowers and was going to buy her treats. His gesture made it feel like it was an actual date! She's sure when he grabs her hand, and their fingers clap together. His palms are sweaty, but so are hers. The butterflies in her stomach felt like hummingbirds now.

When they got inside and their eyes adjusted to the gym's dimness, the sight they saw took Ruby's breath. Vera was in high heels, and her hair was teased and laden with hairspray. Her make-up looked like she'd applied it with the lights off. Ruby halted and squeezed Willie's hand. When he saw Vera, he covered his mouth to hold the laugh he wanted to let loose. Vera looked clownish. Everyone was staring at her and whispering. Ruby was embarrassed for her. Undoubtedly somewhere inside, the honest Vera still existed.

Sensing her pity, Willie pulled her to him, and they started slow dancing to "*Crazy For You*" by Madonna. Ruby looked around and realized how crowded the gym was. There was barely room to get on the floor.

They had lost the rest of their group, and it seemed to Ruby that the crowd had swallowed them up. It was hard to see in the dimness, but for a moment, she thought she saw the redheaded kid back from the dead. But when she looked closer, he was gone.

While looking at Willie Joe, he melted into the mass of dancers. She squeezed between two people she'd never seen in her life. She grabbed Willie's hand and pulled him to her. The DJ was laying out the hits. He seemed to have his finger on the pulse of what the kids wanted to hear. Then he would switch it up and play some oldies. Some of them old folks could still do *The Charleston*.

"Willie, come outside with me. I'm scared. Something just isn't right here," Ruby begs.

"Okay, yeah, let's go."

As they made their way out, they looked for the rest of their group but couldn't see them. Ruby's mind was whirling, trying to process what she'd just witnessed. She had to get her friends out. Still holding hands and drawing stares and whispers, Ruby pulled Willie over to the back stoop of the lunchroom. When she sat down, she was trembling. Willie squatted in front of her, holding both her hands, and said, "Just breathe, Ruby. Calm down and tell me what's wrong."

"Oh God, Willie, I think that entire gym of people has been spelled or cursed. I thought I saw the redheaded kid in the crowd. Then he disappeared. And there were people I'd never seen before not dressed in the Sadie Hawkins theme. The men were wearing suits! But the main thing was the feeling of being swallowed up in the crowd. I haven't seen our friends since we got here."

"I know what you mean. It was so crowded, and I thought people were pushing and pulling me. What do you think is going on?"

"I think Baby Annie has put a spell on the gym, and those people we don't know are some of her spooks. From what Pap says, the spooks can look normal, too. They look out of place, and they are the ones doing the pushing and shoving."

Willie was adamant. "We have to go back and get our friends, Ruby!"

Still kneeling in front of her, he tries to assure her they will be okay, Willie puffs out his chest. "Just hold on to my hand and don't let go. We can beat those spooks. We're both tougher than they are."

Despite the situation, she gives him a small smile. He grabs her hand and pulls her to her feet, and they land chest to chest, and both instantly pull apart. Then, Willie pulls her close to him and gives her a kiss that lasts only seconds but sets his body on fire. Caught up in the moment, he whispers, "I love you." She knows that in her heart, she has always loved Willie Joe, so she isn't afraid to tell him because it's the truth, "I love you too, Willie Joe Wells. Now let's go get our friends!"

With hands clasped, they marched up to the gym door, and once again, Ruby felt the magic in the air and knew it was black magic, intended only for evil. She tightened her grip on Willie's hand and pushed inside. The men in suits were everywhere, dancing with the living. Ruby saw Cheryl Stone and Marjorie Burke swept up in the arms of the men in suits, who immediately turned to Ruby and sneered. After a quick crowd scan, Willie Joe calls out, "I see Josh, and I think Whit, let's go!"

Willie leads, parting the crowd like the Red Sea. When he stops, Ruby sees Josh's head. Willie shoves past two spooks, trying to squish him like a bug, but he gets through and pulls Ruby to him. Josh reaches out his hand and grabs onto Willie's. Josh was in a panic. His eyes were darting around like he was watching a ping-pong match. He asks, "What the hell is going on? I've been looking for you since we got here. I lost Whitney as soon as we went out to dance. And what's up with Vera? She looks like Tammy Faye Baker!"

"Josh, listen to me!" Ruby shouts. She fixed him with her eyes when he looks at her and pleads, "Josh, don't let go of our hands. It's the only way we can stay together. The gym has a spell."

"What? A spell?"

"Just hold on to my hand. We have to find everybody. And DO NOT LET GO!"

He grabs her hand and squeezes it almost too hard. At his touch, Ruby could feel how panicked he was. Then Josh spotted his twin and let go of her hand as he dove through the crowd of spooks. Ruby couldn't see where he went, but Willie Joe found a clear path, but she's afraid of what will be at the end. The crowd shoves them, and they are propelled to the edge of the dance floor in front of the door to the dressing rooms.

Ruby and Willie were terrified. There was no way she was going through that door. Nope! No way! Suddenly, the door opened, and a small, stooped older woman stood. Her hair was long, gray, and stringy. Her face wrinkled, her hands gnarled, and she could barely grasp her cane. Even though she was stooped, she held her head up and cackled her now infamous laugh. Ruby knew immediately that this was her nemesis, Baby Annie. She was finally going to see what she was up against.

At first glance, she looked like a feather would knock her over, but when she spoke, it wasn't what you'd think. She said with a strong, clear voice that radiated authority.

"Well, look who we have. The chosen one, the one the people say can put an end to me." She cackled again and then spat on the floor at Ruby's feet. She got up in her face, and the stench of death was so pungent that she gagged and turned her head, but suddenly her face jerked back around, and she was face to face with the legendary Baby Annie. Her claw-like fingers dug into her skin, and she winced. That tickled the witch, and she laughed some more, then said, "Can't take any bit of pain. You wait. I have some plans for you, sis."

Stung by Baby Annie's insult, Ruby pulls up her chin and says, "Bring it on, you old hag!" She is squeezing Willie's hand so hard it'll be bruised. As her courage shrinks, the witch turns her back and hobbles away.

Before she is out of sight, she yells back in a booming voice. "It's almost time. Just wait." The gap closed, and all the surrounding people were men in suits.

The men in suits stared at them, then bent down to be eye-level with them. The false face they had worn all night slipped away, leaving nothing but rot. Teeth that had raw meat stuck between them. It dangled there like a curtain. None of them had eyeballs, just a dried-out socket. They stayed that way for seconds, but Ruby took it all in, burning the moment into her brain forever. Just before she was ready to scream bloody murder, they returned to normal and faded into the crowd.

With jaws hanging agape, Ruby and Willie, wide-eyed, faced each other and let out a breath they didn't know they were holding.

They embraced and clung to each other with racing hearts. "Total Eclipse of the Heart," by Bonnie Tyler, began to play, which was one of Ruby's favorite songs. She put her arms around Willie's neck, and he automatically cinched her waist. Though they are at a tender age, they can still fall in love, and this is not your average crush. Their love is a love that will last through anything. As they sway to the music, they look into each other's eyes. Ruby sings along to the part, "Turn around bright eyes." Willie looks at her with dazzling blue eyes that bore into her soul. She now sees what all the other girls have seen. He was beautiful. And his heart was as pure as the driven snow.

She hugs him, puts her head on his shoulder, and closes her eyes. She is determined to enjoy herself, even if just for a few minutes. She sensed him near, and her eyes flew open, and there he was, again, the redheaded boy from the séance. Ruby can only see him from behind, but when he turns, he has on his regular face.

He has tears on his cheeks and looks frightened; then the sneer returns while his eyeballs slide down his face like a pair of sunny-side eggs. His skin looked like *Silly Puddy*, that's been stretched and distorted. Then he was gone. It happened so fast that she wondered if it had happened at all. Then she spotted her friends, all four of them. "Willie, there they are!" They both waved and yelled for them. This time, they got through the crowd much more effortlessly. Before they answered any of their questions, Ruby and Willie grabbed onto them and pulled them out of the gym.

Once outside and out of earshot, Ruby caught her breath and then held up her hand for silence, which she got, albeit with wide eyes and the look of fright on all their faces.

"The gym had a spell. To make this a long story short, Baby Annie sent her spooks to make the gym like a spider web. Once you were in, getting out was almost impossible because her spooks constantly pushed and shoved you back in. She did this to lure me back inside once I got out. She knew I'd come back in for you all. I had a sort of face-to-face with her. She wanted to size me up, I guess. She's not at full power, or she would've killed me right there." Ruby says with a look of puzzlement on her face.

Josh was the first to speak. "I was having a hard time believing all this spooky shit, but I'm a believer now. Those spooks were so creepy. You saw their eyes dead once you looked at them long enough." Josh shivers and puts his arm around his sister.

Willie's cousin Kevin says, "I've always sensed this town is haunted. Since I've been at Papaw's, I've heard a little kid laughing late at night, and then I saw a little girl on the swing when I was coming in from the park. I saw her as plain as day, but she was gone when I got to the gate. I had thought she was just a neighbor kid, but now I don't know."

"That was Rebecca Jo, our aunt that died when she was ten," Willie says solemnly. Kevin looks at him like he's speaking Chinese. "Who is that?"

Willie ignores Kevin's attempts to ask more questions. "Never mind, it's too much to tell right now."

"What we need to do now is get home behind locked doors. We can walk home most of the way together. I have to tell my mom bye." Ruby runs to the lunchroom and finds her mom.

"Mommy!" she yells. When she sees her pale face, she drops the spoon back in the vat of soup beans and heads to her daughter, wiping her hands on the blue and white flowered apron she's wearing.

Kate hugs her daughter, knowing that's what she needs. Ruby is so relieved to be in the arms of her mother. She doesn't go into too much detail; she tells her that Baby Annie is stronger and sending out her spooks. After more hugs and kisses and a promise to go straight to Whitney's house, Ruby rejoins her friends, feeling revived.

Ruby and Willie clasp hands again and don't even care that

everyone can see. That is until Vera makes herself known. "Well, isn't this just precious? Look at these two lovebirds." Her voice is shrill, and her tone is grating. Ruby tries her best to let it go, but after everything that has happened, she just can't.

"Well, look who showed up, guys; it's Bozo the Clown." Everyone within earshot breaks into laughter.

"I'm glad somebody finally called out the elephant in the room!" said Minerva Daniels as she shuffled down the sidewalk in her orthopedic shoes.

Then Vera took it too far and yelled at her back, "At least I ain't as big as an elephant, you old bag!" Vera was wobbly in her too-high heels and almost tumbled over when she whipped back around to continue her fight with Ruby.

Josh pitches in and says, "Watch it there, Ronald McDonald,"

Whitney high-fives his sarcasm, and Vera glares at him.

"Y'all just keep it up. Your time is coming. She told me so tonight."

"Who told you, Vera?" demands Ruby.

"Oh, just a little birdy, that's all."

Ruby wanted to ask her more, but they were all washed in high-beam headlights from a car hitting a mean lick. The engine revved, and Vera turned on her heels and said as she left, "There's my ride. See you losers never, I hope!" She was gone in a flash. She hopped into the car with what looked like a grown man driving a black Trans-Am.

As Ruby looked, she thought she saw it change from pristine to a total wreck, then back again. She walked closer and saw who was driving. It was Butchie Daniels. His face morphed from ordinary to grotesque. Vera didn't seem to care. The Butchie thing revved the engine and blasted "Highway to Hell" as he laid rubber and threw gravel all over the crowd standing outside. No one else noticed who was driving because it was dark, and they were distracted by the mess and noise.

By the time Willie Joe reached her, she was trembling again. She didn't think she could take much more excitement tonight. Willie grabbed her hand, and they started walking. The touch of his hand calmed her, and she realized she felt safer with him, with all of them. There was safety in numbers, she'd heard.

They were a little behind the others, and Ruby said to Willie, "I feel bad about what I said to Vera. But I don't think it's her I'm talking to. It's that old hag. Vera would never say or do the things she did tonight. Willie, do you know who was driving that car she got into?"

"No. Looked like a man, though, not a kid."

"It wasn't a kid; it wasn't even human, at least not anymore. It was Butchie Daniels. Birdie's son that died years ago."

"Oh, God! Why would she go anywhere with him? Did he look dead?"

"Not at first, but he did like those spooks in the gym, changed his face. It was awful." Ruby says as she covers her eyes, trying to rid her mind of the mental image. "We have to save her, Willie. Vera is still in there somewhere. We have to figure out how to get her back in control. Baby Annie has possessed her, and her sweet soul cannot compete with that power."

They reached the gate to Whitney's house, and the nerves from earlier returned. She was on her first date, and what a disaster it was. But there was an upside; Willie Joe said he loved her, and she was sure now that she loved him too. So, when he leaned over, brushed her lips with his, and whispered 'I Love You' again, her heart swelled as she returned the sentiment.

The Next Day at Mrs. Purdy's House

As Ruby steps up to the porch, Mrs. Purdy speaks to her from the shadowed swing and startles her. How in the world did she not see her sitting there? "I see that you're different today, Miss Ruby. I believe you've become a woman." Mrs. Purdy says this last with a smug look on her face.

"How do you know that? Did my mom call and tell you?"

"No, child, I could just tell. You look different to me. You are a little pale around the eyes, probably because of the blood loss, but you carry yourself differently. It's hard to explain. It's just something I can do. I can tell when somebody's lying, too. It's just one of my many gifts."

"What else can you do?" asked Ruby.

"What've you heard I can do?"

"Uh…"

"Don't lie. I'll know."

"Okay, I heard you can make tables walk at seances."

"And…."

"put spells on people and make their peckers fall off," Ruby says this last with a red face, and she won't make eye contact. Mrs. Purdy threw back her head and cackled, which led to a coughing fit that made Ruby w ince it was so bad.

"You've been talking to Delano Goble, ain'tcha?"

"No, Ma'am, just heard him telling a story to his buddies." Ruby knew better than to lie. It seemed like Mrs. Purdy really could tell when someone wasn't truthful.

"You weren't eavesdropping, were ye?"

"Oh yes. I know it ain't right to listen in, but sometimes that's the only way to hear the truth." Ruby explained.

"Well, you're right about that. Folks think young'uns can't handle hearing certain things, but I think sometimes that's what they need. You may be young, but you aren't going to break. But that's enough about me. I want to hear more about you. Since the last time we talked, there's been a lot happened. Have ye had any visions, child?"

"Visions? You mean like a dream?"

"Well, it could be considered a dream, but sometimes a vision can come when you're wide awake." Said Purdy.

"Last night, I dreamed I was in somebody else's body."

"Do you know who it was?"

"It was Baby Annie…but she was a little kid in the dream. Through her eyes, I watched a woman burn at the stake. I think it was in Scotland cause all the men had on skirts or kilts, or whatever people call them. It was terrible."

Ruby wrinkled her nose. "I could smell the smoke from the fire, and the people all smelled like wet dogs."

"Was there anyone else there that you knew?" asked Purdy, suddenly interested.

"Not that I knew their names, but I think they were gypsies. They looked like the ones I'd seen on TV, anyway. They saved me/her by hiding in their wagon. I remember there was a book in my hands that I gave to the older woman who held me in her lap. It was brown leather and looked ancient."

"That book was Baby Annie's ticket to America. Her mother, the woman burnt at the stake, bribed the gypsies with her grimoire so they'd take her daughter to the new world. She figured it wouldn't be long before the villagers would accuse her of witchcraft, and she would suffer the same fate." Mrs. Purdy said this while wiping a tear from her cheek.

"Ya see, Ruby, people will always treat our kind like dogs. Even today, the least bit different from the crowd will be shunned. Your mother had to learn that the hard way. If she'd treated me respectfully instead of judging me, we might not be in this mess."

Ruby's cheeks burned with embarrassment, but her spirit fired up, and she was on the defensive. "My mommy knows she did wrong. No need to beat a dead horse."

"Hmph! If you say so."

"I do!"

"Well, now, is there anything else I need to hear about?" asked Purdy.

"I'm worried about Vera. She's not acting like herself. She's been my best friend forever, and since the séance, she's been different."

"Different, how?"

"She was mean to me at the park the other night and made fun of me for being special."

"Ah, that sounds like pure old jealousy to me." Mrs. Purdy said and waved her hand in a shooing manner as if it were of little importance.

"No, that's not it. Vera has never acted like this. She's even become friends with her mortal enemy, Tammy Turner."

"Well, now, that is strange. That little girl is one child I never could abide. Anyone who'd pal around with her must have something wrong with them. I don't think even a good whoopin' would fix her."

"See, that should be enough right there. But it's more than that. Vera's entire personality has changed. She walks differently and uses cuss words, and gives people the finger. I have never seen Vera do that. She couldn't have changed that much in a few days. Do you think she might be possessed?" asked Ruby while pacing the floor.

"Possessed? I hate to admit it, but you're probably right. If I were a vengeful spirit, I'd want to get to the person closest to my enemy. And you say Vera's the closest person to you?"

"For sure! She's always been my best friend."

"Anybody else?"

"Willie Joe and my Pappaw."

Mrs. Purdy studied Ruby's face, "Wilson, I'm not worried about it, but Willie Joe might be a problem." Ponders Mrs. Purdy.

"Why? We've been friends for a long time, even though he's a boy."

"That's why I say it. I saw the way he was lookin' at you yesterday. He likes you for more'n a friend, doesn't he?"

"Yeah, I think he does and has for a while now. I just kept ignoring it. Until the other night."

"What changed?"

Ruby avoided her eyes and said almost under her breath, "Willie kissed me, and then I kissed him back. But please don't tell mommy. I'm sure it won't happen again."

Mrs. Purdy chuckled and said, "Oh, I doubt that. Don't fret; I won't tell ye, Mommy. But you make sure kissin' is all that boy does. I was already a momma at your age."

"Gross! That ain't happening!" Ruby says while looking appalled.

"All in due time. All in due time." Says Purdy.

"Mrs. Purdy, are you a witch?"

Purdy takes it in stride and sits back to mull over the question. Finally, she answers, "I guess I am a witch. My bloodline returns to Scotland, and the woman you saw burnt at the stake. I won't get on a broom and ride across the sky but I believe in magic and spells. I've seen too much in my life not to believe. Witches aren't all bad or all good. Even Baby Annie had a good side once upon a time."

"She made her living by healing the sick and delivering babies. That's what our line was known for. That book you saw in your vision was our family grimoire. And before you ask, I'll tell ye. It's a witch's spell book of sorts. There are recipes for healin' and hurtin'. For some of these spells to work, you must have witch blood. A family line begins when a member gets in league with the devil and signs their name in his book. At least, that's what I've heard. The family is then forever linked to the dark lord.

"You, though, are a natural witch because of how you were born—the significance of the day, Beltane, the full moon, and the caul. Greatness is your destiny. Most witches are born with one special gift. But you, my dear, have many gifts: you can call up spirits, have visions, thwart the weather, and any spell you wish to cast will be like eating pie. It's just that simple."

Ruby lets all this information sink in before she speaks again. "So how am I supposed to use this against Baby Annie?"

"I ain't figured that out yet. I was aiming to see if we could reach Baby Annie's spirit together and try to reason with her. The only thing is, she's my blood. She could take me over and use me against you. My kin, I'm not particularly eager to go against, but I don't hold with hurting young'uns. The little boys were just babies. And now she's using them again to hurt the town. I only hope their spirits are in a good place, and it's just their bodies she's using." Mrs. Purdy shakes her head in disgust.

"I don't think it's a good idea to reach her. At least not today. Maybe she just wanted to scare everybody with the spooks she sent back. It might be all she can do. And that was enough. Miss Ally, Birdie, and Claude were sad and scared to see their kin like that. I'm surprised one of them didn't die of fright." Ruby spoke with an air of maturity that was well beyond her years. Mrs. Purdy took note of that.

"You're right. I keep waiting for someone to appear to me. I figure it will be Baby Annie herself, seeing how she's blood, especially if she finds out I'm helping you."

"Does that book say anything that can help us?" asks Ruby.

"It might, but it's written in another tongue. Some spells translate into English, but it's mainly in Gaelic, the old language of Scotland. My mother could read some of it, but I can't, so I can't tell you what most of it means."

"Maybe we can find someone who can read it. Like a teacher at the college." Ruby suggests.

"I don't think that's how it works. The book has a spell on it. Only direct descendants of the one who wrote it can see the words. If you were to look at it, the pages would be blank. It was a warding spell. That's why the gypsies let Baby Annie keep it. When they opened it, it was blank. There was nothing in it but a family tree, or so they thought."

"What made her so mean? I know people shunned her because she was strange. But, to murder those kids like that, she had to have a mean streak a mile long."

"You don't know the half of it. To hear my Ma talk about her, why she was forever cursing people and their animals just for looking at her crosswise. When someone called upon her to deliver a baby , if anyone in the family had ever slighted her, she would ensure the woman suffered. She was known to let more than one woman bleed to death in the child bed if she thought they weren't treating her right. That's one reason people stopped using her as a midwife, but if you were looking to hex somebody, she was more than happy to oblige. If your enemy went to see her, expect your days to be on the chopping block."

Ruby gulped air and stared big-eyed at Mrs. Purdy. "Was there no one that could undo her spells? Like maybe that woman in

Papaw's document, Elspeth?"

"Maybe she did what she could, but she was only used to doing good with her magic. She was a true healer. She took most of Baby Annie's patients after she became so vengeful. I believe that she delivered my grandmother."

August:
The Taking of Jarvis Spears

Three weeks after the dance, the town had quietened down. Ruby and Mrs. Purdy reckoned Baby Annie had used most of her power with the cat attack, the spooks at the gym, and her making an appearance, which had zapped her energy. Mrs. Purdy also believed that the culmination would come on Samhain, or Halloween, as we call it. She said it was a sacred and powerful day in the pagan belief. It was when the veil between the living and the dead was the thinnest. Ruby had always loved Halloween. It was fitting that Baby Annie would try to ruin her favorite holiday.

The school would start the next day, August 20th. Mary Luck Grade School was getting two new students, Josh and Josie Baldridge. Their parents were staying in Guam on their missionary trip. People desperately needed them because of the malaria outbreak. The twins were thrilled. They loved Mary Luck and didn't miss the mall at all. Ruby couldn't believe little Mary Luck could be more fun than Lexington. But she was happy she wouldn't have to go to school alone with Vera.

Then another surprise left Whitney with a decision. Should she stay, or should she go? Her dad, an attorney, was working on a case in Washington, DC, and would be gone for several months. Her mother was on her third honeymoon in the Bahamas, and the thought of meeting daddy number three was about as appealing as sticking a needle in her eye. She talked it over with her Pappaw, and he was happy to have her. He said she brought life back to the house. He'd been depressed for years, ever since he lost his wife to cancer. So, Whitney would go to Prestonsburg High School with the horrible Tammy Turner.

The weekend before school started, Kate surprised Ruby with the news that they would go to the Huntington Mall to go school shopping. Rosie didn't want to take anyone with her, so that she could invite Josie and Whitney. The Sunday before school started, Kate picked the girls up and headed down Route 23. An hour and a half later, they pulled into the crowded parking lot, and the girls bounded out in a flash of big hair and enough pink to make Pepto Bismol jealous. Kate, with Ruthie, brought up the rear. They were both giggling, too.

It was a rare occurrence to go to the mall. It was big doings to leave their n est. Richard had given enough warnings about safety to scare Kate to death. She homed in on her girls inside the mall and made them promise to meet her at three at the entrance to Lazarus. Whitney assured her that her Swatch Watch was running great and that they wouldn't be late. Then they were gone, mixed in with all the other teenagers bustling through the corridors.

Ruby and Rosie were wide-eyed; this was their first time at the Huntington Mall. It seemed so huge. The only other mall they had been to was The Turfland Mall in Lexington. This one was newer and had all the stores they'd seen in magazines and movies. It wasn't as fancy as the one in *Fast Times At Ridgemont High*, but it was good enough for them.

Whitney seemed unfazed by the mall. She was disappointed that The Limited didn't have her size in a pair of acid-washed jeans, but it didn't stop her from practically buying out the store.

She put the hurt on her daddy's credit card and even threw in matching earrings for all three of them.

Ruby had never seen anyone shop like that; her budget was one-hundred dollars. Whitney spent close to a thousand, and that was just in one store. She hit up Foot Locker and bought Reeboks and Tretorns, then went to The Limited Express and spent almost as much. This was her getting even with her dad for never being around. She bought a new Swatch Watch that was white and pink with a wide band, two Liz Claiborne purses, and a bottle of Gucci perfume. This display of wealth floored Ruby. She'd only seen these things in Vogue and Cosmopolitan magazines.

Next, the girls ate at Chick-fil-A and got a chicken sandwich, like tasting heaven to Ruby and Rosie. They then bought cream-filled chocolate chip cookies from The Cookie Factory. This was the most fun the girls had had all summer and the last enjoyable day any of them would have for some time.

Ruby bought her first pair of Guess jeans which ate up most of her spending money, so she had to shop on the clearance rack at Lazarus for a few shirts. Her Nike's from last year still fit, so her mom would work her magic and make them look almost new. Rosie bought two Esprit outfits on sale and a pair of espadrilles. Josie got a twist-a-bead necklace and a pink Izod dress. She purchased a Guess T-shirt and Chic jeans. With bags and bags of clothes, the girls had to help Whitney with all of her purchases. The best thing she bought all day was the Purple Rain soundtrack on cassette and a Walkman. It was so much fun seeing someone go on a shopping spree. Even though they weren't getting all the goods, the other girls felt rich that day too.

When they had all returned to the Jeep, their chatter sounded like a hive of bees. Kate graciously let them play their music on the way home. When they got to Mary Luck, they knew all the words to "Let's Go Crazy," including Kate and Ruthie. Crossing the bridge, they met a crowd gathered around the turnoff to Shotgun Hollow. Fear ripped through Kate at the thought of something happening to her family. She pulled alongside the group, rolled down her window, and asked Beechie what was happening.

"Lord honey, I hate to tell you this, but they've found your cousin Jarvis dead by the tracks."

With a shaky voice, Kate asked, "What happened to him?"

"I'm not sure, but they say it was a snake bite. It got him in the neck, and when he pulled it loose, he laid his jugular vein wide open and bled to death."

Kate drew a breath and held it while her hand covered her mouth. The girls all sat there, stunned. Ruby had a jolt of fear run through her body that paralyzed her. She cast her eyes to the side and met the stoic face of Mrs. Purdy. Her barely perceptible nod told Ruby that her fears were correct. This wasn't random. Baby Annie was behind it.

Beechie continued her commentary. "Now Kate, you know I ain't one to spread tales, but we all know that Jarvis Spears was an accident waiting to happen. I'm just surprised the poor loony made it this long. No offense. I know he's your kin, but I don't think his poor mother will be too surprised."

"Has anyone told her yet?" asked Kate.

"Yeah, your daddy went as soon as he found out. Him and Minerva being first cousins and her being a widow, he broke the news to her. I haven't heard how she took it, but like I said, she had to expect something like this."

"Thanks, Beechie. I have to take the kids home, and then I'll go over and be with her. I'll let you know when the wake will be."

"Yeah, let me know so I can get the neighbors organized. They'll all want to get the food going soon."

Kate rolled up the window and started driving. The car was silent till Ruthie spoke up and asked her mother what a loony was. "Honey, that just means that he had a mental problem. Like he was a grown man, but his thoughts were like someone in kindergarten."

Ruthie mulled this over in her young mind. "So, someone touched him on the head?" Kate was astounded that her seven-year-old knew that term. "Where did you hear that?" "Mammaw saw him walking on the tracks, and she said someone touched him in the head. I didn't know that he was crazy. I thought that meant that he got touched by somebody."

The girls all giggled, and Kate struggled to keep a straight face. "It's okay, Ruthie. Those are things you don't have to worry about." She patted her knee and drove on, dropping off Whitney and her payload of packages and Josie with her two bags. When they returned to their turnoff, the coroner from Prestonsburg was there, along with an ambulance and Constable Flannery. The crowd moved so that she could pass, and they saw poor old Jarvis covered with a sheet with bloody patches on it.

Jarvis Spears was the only son of Minerva and Percy Spears. Percy was killed in a mine blast when Jarvis was a baby, and his mother never got over it. She never remarried and was forced to live on what little severance the mine paid for the accident. Their once pleasant house in the 'Bottom is now shabby.

Jarvis started showing signs of ignorance as a toddler and only got worse. When he started school, he was so disruptive they expelled him, and he never returned. He could do simple jobs like digging ditches and hauling things. His size was an issue, too. He stood about six feet five and weighed about two- seventy-five, like a giant with the mental capacity of a five-year-old. He wasn't ever violent unless he got into some alcohol.

When he was twelve, he found his dad's moonshine out in the smokehouse and nearly tore the door off of the house. Some neighbor men tackled him before he could get at his mother. He could scream and holler with the best of them. His distinguishing trait was his laugh. A cross between a squeal and a howl would echo all over the 'Bottom and up to the head of the holler . Ruby had heard him laugh like that more than once, and each time, she'd cover her ears and cringe. He scared her to death when she was little and still did.

That evening, when they pulled up in front of her house, it was packed with people. Most of them just wanted some gory details. Kate got out and went up on the porch, and shouldered her way inside. There was Nervie in her threadbare house dress sitting in her rocking chair. Her eyes were red and swollen from crying. Her gnarled fingers worried a handkerchief with lace trim. Kate knelt before her, took her hands, and whispered words of sympathy.

Nervie repeated repeatedly, "I never should've let that woman in here."

"What woman?" asked Kate

"That little skinny woman. She brought me a few jars of canned apples. She said she was a new neighbor and heard I liked apples. You know I love some fried apples on my biscuits, and it's been a long time since I had any, so I let her in. As soon as she stepped in, Jarvis perked up and approached her. He got excited and started squealing, but she silenced him with a touch on the cheek with her tiny hand. She told him to bend to her, whispering something in his ear. He turned and walked out like he was in a trance. That was the last time I saw him, yesterday just before dark."

Kate turned to the neighbors in the room and asked, "Do any of you know who she's talking about?" Jordy Powers said, "They ain't been nobody moved here in twenty years. I ain't seen no little woman, neither." Nods of agreement went around the room, and then Kate made eye contact with her father, who then turned his eyes to Ruby. When Kate saw her ashen face, she knew who had been there. But why?

"Nervie, where are those apples?" Kate asked.

"In the cupboard above the sink."

"Daddy, come with me. Ruby, you sit with Nervie."

Kate found the jelly jars filled with apples in the primarily barren cabinet. She took one down and pried off the sealed lid. The smell that escaped was putrid. The apples turned black with green mold spots when they spilled out. It was as if the air itself was like acid. Kate and Wilson covered their noses and gagged at the stench and sight of the apples. Their eyes watered, and their noses ran. Wilson grabbed the jars and bowl with the poured-out apples and flung them off the back porch. When he came back, Kate had recovered but still shook.

"It was Baby Annie, wasn't it?" she asked her father.

Ruby spoke from the door. "It was her. I can feel her in the room still."

She was very matter-of-fact in her mannerism. There wasn't a question in her statement. She looked different, Kate thought. She seemed resigned to the queerness of her gift. Wilson stared at her with a look of pride and dread. "Yes, it was her. I can't figure out why she'd want to hurt poor, feeble-minded Jarvis?"

"She's building an army. Jarvis would be easy to control, and his size could benefit her in a fight."

"And out of the mouths of babes, the truth shall be spoken. I'll be damned if you didn't hit the nail on the head, Ruby Lee." Wilson states.

"What do you mean by an army?" asked Kate.

"Mommy, she wants to hurt as many people in this town as she can. Her revenge makes her so evil, and that gives her power. She only knows darkness and is consumed by hate. She's getting stronger every day. She is almost ready to walk among us if she can show herself to someone. Right now, though, she can't stay real for long because it drains her power. She won't do anything else for a little while."

"Ruby, how do you know all of this?" asks Kate

"I don't know. I do. Mrs. Purdy has taught me a lot, but it's mainly things I know in my heart. I can't explain it." Ruby sinks into a nearby chair and shrugs her shoulders.

Kate tries to console her. "That's okay, baby. You don't have to explain anything. I know you're doing the best you can. I wish I could take this burden from you."

They all head back to the sitting room and check on Nervie. The crowd has thinned out, and they make plans for the wake. The family belief did not hold with embalming, so Jarvis would have to be laid to rest l the next day. He got torn up pretty badly, and he'd already been dead for twelve-plus hours when they found him. It would take a lot of flowers to mask the stench of death to hold a wake.

Food had already arrived. There were cakes, cobblers, and pies of every variety. Someone will deliver the food tomorrow. Edith would bring her chicken and dumplings, and the church ladies would fill in the rest with green beans, corn, mashed potatoes, and yams. A turkey and a chicken would be killed and roasted with cornbread dressing. Yeast rolls would rise in the morning, and collard, mustard, poke, and rape would be picked and cooked down and kilt with bacon grease.

It's a tradition in the mountains to feed grief. The wake would be short, but the funeral could go on for hours if Brother Burkett felt up to it. When one of their own died, whether he was a community pillar or a simpleton, the pomp and circumstance were the same. Junior and Clint Wells would already be sanding down a coffin. They would make it unique to accommodate Jarvis. Beechie would coordinate the making of the batting and netting for the inside of the coffin and flower arrangements, which would need to be considerable.

At the end of August, most flowers were on their last legs. Wildflowers like goldenrod, daisies, Rose of Sharon, and tea roses are plentiful. Someone would bunch herbs like rosemary, thyme, basil, and lavender clustered into a bouquet and place inside the coffin. By the time they delivered the corpse home the next day, they had everything in place.

They postponed the start of school until the next day, so most everyone in Mary Luck attended the day-long funeral and wake. Nervie wore her finest which may have been in style about 1932. She had on her cloche hat and a white rose pinned to her breast. Wilson and Kate walked her into the church, and she looked almost regal as she stoically went down the aisle to the front pew to bury her only child. They always say no parent should ever have to bury their child. It was unnatural and not in the way of things. There was an upset in the balance of nature when something like that happened. There would be a reckoning, and it would be soon.

That night, Ruby Lee sat on the back porch swing curled up like a cat by her daddy's side. She had been reading Anne of Green Gables for the third time and had almost drifted off to sleep, feeling the contentment of love and safety as lunatic laughter broke the quiet as it echoed through the mountains, her comfort shattered. The full moon shone brightly and made shadows out of the darkness. The unique laughter was none other than the recently departed and buried Jarvis Spears. Ruby sat up and turned to her father, who was rigid beside her. His face showed an emotion she'd never seen before, fear.

Knowing that his daughter saw him falter, he quickly gathered her in his arms and hurriedly entered the back door. He closed and locked the door, deadbolt and all, something he rarely did. He shook, so Ruby took his hand and, without a word, assured him they were safe. He hugged her, kissed her curly head, and said, "Night, Night. Daddy loves you."

Ruby turned and headed to her room, still hearing the lunatic laughter in her mind. She climbed into bed and pulled the covers up tight under her chin, though it was muggy outside. Jarvis' laughter scared her when he was alive, and now that he was dead, it terrified her. She closed her eyes and hoped she could dream about John Taylor from Duran Duran with all her heart, but that wasn't in the cards for her.

As REM sleep took her over, she tumbled back to the night of Jarvis' death. Being in his mind would be disturbing but informative. Baby Annie didn't know Ruby could hit the rewind button and watch everything she did. She'd hold That trump card near and dear to her heart.

Ninety-nine bottles of beer on the wall
Ninety-nine bottles of beer
Take one down and pass it around
Ninety-eight bottles of beer on the wall

September:
Ball Games, Bus Rides, and Boogeymen

The first day of the last year at Mary Luck Grade School for Ruby and her friends began with little fanfare. The death of Jarvis and then the subsequent resurrection of his spirit left Ruby shaken and weary. Josh and Josie fit right in, even though they weren't used to having only one teacher all day instead of getting to change classes and have a locker. The cloakroom was the best they had to offer. Mr. Music led the class with familiar anecdotes and the wisdom of his fifty-plus years in Mary Luck.

The morning started with the bell ringing, and then all would rise, face the flag, and recite the pledge of allegiance. They spent an hour on English and reading, then a half hour of PE, then lunch. Recess after lunch for fifteen minutes, then classes resumed. They had math for an hour, then either history or science. Then it was time for a pop break. Edith would pop up some corn, and you could buy a Coke for thirty-five cents. Then go out to the park and play some more. Afterward, Mr. Music would tell them some current events for the day or maybe a story about growing up in Mary Luck.

After school was basketball practice and cheerleading practice. Since Josh and Josie enrolled, we had another player on the basketball team and a new cheerleader. Josh was nearly six feet tall, and Josie could do back handsprings up and down the court. Vera tried out this year. She was always an excellent dancer and skater, but she struggled with learning cheers, and her gymnastics consisted of splits and a cartwheel.

At the tryouts, Vera performed flawlessly, much to Ruby's

dismay. This overnight difference proved more and more to her that Vera was possessed. It took real magic to transform a shy, quiet, introverted person into this loud, brash, nimble-bodied woman-child. But it made for a much better cheer team this year. Ruby was captain, which rubbed Vera the wrong way, but Mrs. Webb wasn't having any of her nonsense and threatened to kick her off the team if she gave her any more lip. Vera wisely let it go.

The first game was at home against Clark Elementary. The atmosphere at these games was a testament to how important basketball is to the mountain people of Eastern Kentucky. It wasn't just a school function; it was a community event. The gymnasium stays packed, with most of the town in attendance. A haze of smoke at the ceiling mingled with the aroma of popcorn and chili dog sauce. The squeak of Converse on the newly oiled wooden floor is the background noise of hollerin' and cussin' from the fans. The cheerleaders on both sides are chanting as loud as they can to the beat of the dribbled basketball. The humid air inside causes the stench of sweat to sting the air. An industrial fan on the wall carries the scent to the back of the gym. Chicken wire encases the concession stand to keep stray balls from hitting Edith and the new prized popcorn machine. The game's second half would open the gym's back door to create a draft. The scents and sounds that emanate from the little gym make a lasting impression on your senses. You will forever relate any of those triggers to this place and time.

Most of the time, seeing as there are only a handful of students to play, the Mary Luck Miners are an easy win for visiting teams. This year, however, with the addition of Josh, Willie Joe can take over as point guard, and together they are the dynamic duo. They beat the Clark Indians 38-22. The gym was rocking! Mary Luck hadn't had a winning team in years, and it seemed this would be the year.

After the game, Ruby ran up to Willie, hugged him, and told him how proud she was of him. He was radiant as he basked in

Ruby's praise until he saw his father staggering over to him. His face was ruddy and sweaty from the alcohol he had drank and was still sipping on from a brown paper bag. He tried little to conceal his drunk behavior, which mortified Willie Joe. His dad bear-hugged and lifted him off his feet as he swung him around and nearly dropped him.

Willie tried to shrug him off, and that lit a fire. "Don't you turn away from me? I'm talking to you, boy!"

His dad growled this last part, and fear took over Willie Joe. Ruby stepped in and said, "Hey there, Mr. Wells. Did you see our last cheer? I thought it was one of the best we've ever done."

Steven Wells looked perplexed by Ruby's words. He was confused and visibly baffled. "What did you say, Red?"

Ruby took him by his arm and walked him to the concession stand where her mom and Edith were cleaning up. "Mommy, are there any hot dogs left? Cause Mr. Wells didn't get one, and he's starving."

A light seemed to dawn on him as realization hit him. "Geez, I am hungry. Kat, give me two dogs if you got them."

Suspecting something was happening, Kate hurriedly fixed up two dogs with a chili mound. Ruby had her hand on his arm guiding him; she felt a wave of power when she touched him, and she was sure Baby Annie was forcing him to mistreat his family.

Without knowing what she was doing, she closed her eyes and mumbled some words she didn't know she knew, and suddenly, Steven was back to his old self. He shoveled in the food like he hadn't eaten in years. He turned to her and said, "I don't think I've ever eaten anything so delicious."

"I'm glad. You look like you feel better already."

"I do. It's the strangest thing. I feel like I've been asleep for months and am just now awake. How can that be?"

"I ain't sure, but you know this town is weird, and we have things that happen here that don't happen anywhere else. It's a bad time here right now. Be careful and don't let anyone in your house if you don't know them. Better yet, don't let anyone in." Without a question, Steven assured her he would do as she said. He then went back to eating his hot dogs.

Ruby spies Willie Joe and goes to him. She tells him, "Your Daddy is going to be alright now. I don't know how I did it, but I think I broke Baby Annie's hold on him. He seemed like his old self." Willie has a look of pure relief, and finally, a smile that reaches his eyes spreads across his face.

He hugs Ruby tight and whispers, "I love you. I hope you're right, Ruby. Guess I'll find out when I get home. My mom should be home from work now, so at least I'll have someone in my corner. "I truly think everything is going to be okay. It's so hard to describe what it felt like. I know in my heart that he's okay." Willie gives her a peck on the cheek and goes to his dad, who greets him with a hug.

With a victory, the Mary Luck Miners head out for their first away game of the season. It's late September, and the leaves are just starting to change as the bus winds through the mountains to Garrett Elementary, home of the Black Devils. On the bus, Willie and Ruby sit together while Josie and Whitney are across the aisle. Josh is stretched out in a seat by himself while over his shoulder, Vera tries to flirt with him, but he ignores her and keeps reading *Catcher in the Rye*.

Vera is leaning over the seat, smacking obnoxiously on her Bubblicious wild strawberry gum.

The scent of her gum mixed with the gallon of Love's Baby Soft perfume is nauseating. Josh tells her to be like Michael Jackson and "Beat It." She takes the jab and laughs it off. Her ego is so inflated that nothing bothers her. Ruby is amazed at how much more she has changed. She hopes to fix Vera the way she did Willie's dad. Mr. Wells has wholly turned himself around. He has a job and has quit drinking cold turkey. Willie Joe is so much happier now. His intense, worried look was gone and replaced with the visage of calm.

When they arrive, the sun is already setting behind the mountains. The crimson glow sets the leaves ablaze, making it look like the hills are on fire. The Autumn breeze carries the familiar scents of popcorn and chili and the sounds of twangy chatter.

It's a packed house tonight, and the whole town showed up. This year, Garret has a good team, so it should be a real barn burner. As the Miners head out to center court, there are some low cheers but booming boos while the Devils come out to a roaring crowd. The atmosphere was intense from the second that Josh won the Jump ball and tipped the ball to Willie Joe, and he scored a 3-pointer in the first seconds of the game. Suddenly, the mood changed to full-on anger. Ruby observed the shift and saw the faces change to hatefulness. As the game went on, nothing could slow down the momentum, and the Miners kept on scoring while the Devils barely hit any shots. At half-time, the Miners were up 33-15.

The bus to the games usually served as a team bus and a pep bus. Therefore, about twenty fans from Mary Luck were at the game. They screamed, hoot'n, and holler'n to beat the band. When one of the devils air-balled a foul shot, Shiny yelled, "You couldn't hit the broad side of a barn." As the crowd laughed, someone lit a fire under the Garrett side of the gym.

Ruby could sense the anger turning to rage on the faces in the crowd. Even the old folks looked furious. She thought the crowd was pressing in and getting closer to the court. As she cheered on the team, she kept a wary eye on the coach of the devils. He was kicking chairs and cussin' worse than Bobby Knight. He grabbed one of their players by his jersey, lifting him off his feet.

Fortunately, time ran out before the anger could boil over and cause a full-on brawl. Ruby gathered pom poms, and Willie Joe went to the dressing room. She looked around for her mom and couldn't see her. Then she heard raised voices and saw a crowd at the gym door. 'Shiny was in the middle of several men yelling and screaming at him. It was odd for 'Shiny to turn on like that, so Ruby immediately attributed his behavior to Baby Annie. She seemed like she could control people outside of Mary Luck as well.

Mr. Goble, the basketball coach, broke it up and dragged 'Shiny to the bus. He was still ranting as he made his way to a seat. Ruby saw her mom, took her the cheerleading gear, and whispered, "Mommy, I think that 'Shiny' might be acting up because of Baby Annie. The crowd was so angry tonight. It seemed like they were itching for a fight. Almost like it had nothing to do with the game."

"I noticed that too. It just doesn't feel right," said Kate.

"I think we better round up Polecat and get us home. I'm getting scared."

"Okay, baby. I'll get him."

Willie Joe came up about that time and was white in the face. "What's wrong?" asked Ruby.

"I just saw one of those little kids. While we were changing, he looked out from behind a bathroom stall. He looked all cut up and gross. He pointed at me and started laughing. Josh was close by, but he didn't seem to notice him. I just threw on my clothes and ran out as fast as possible. He was so scary. I swear I don't think I'll sleep for a week."

Ruby consoled him by patting his back, and her touch alone calmed him. He looked at her, smiled, and said, "Some big tough guy I turned out to be, huh?" He shrugged his shoulders and looked defeated.

"Yes, you are. You're facing things that would make grown men pee their pants. We need to get out of here. There is something bad in the air here, and Baby Annie feeds on it, making her stronger."

They were almost the last ones on the bus, so they went to nearly the back seat. Ruby saw Vera, and she wanted so badly to help her. She was so strange now. She was in the back, sitting alone, staring out the window blankly, almost like she was in a trance.

Ruby and Willie sat together, holding hands, trying to be calm and not scared to death. Josh had brought his boom box and played his Bryan Adams cassette. As the sound of "Run to You" permeates the air, Ruby is lulled by the sway of the bus as it twists and turns its way through the dark mountain road. With her head on Willie's shoulder, she drifts into a restless sleep.

The dream begins, and she is on the railroad tracks, walking by herself. She is near the coal mines, and she can hear the chink and ting of the pick ax striking the wall. Then the earth trembles as the roof of the mine collapses. The collective cries and screams of the miners shake her to her core. The desperation of the ones trapped alive spur her to run toward the mine opening to help as if she could. She sees a familiar shape when she looks inside the dark gaping maw of the mine. It's small and bent and hobbling with a cane. She knows her at once. Baby Annie, in all her wickedness, is standing at the scene with a look of triumph on her face.

At once, Ruby knows who caused the collapse. She is in such a panic that she wakes herself up. She comes to with a jolt and scares Willie to death. She looks around and takes a minute to realize where she is. Then she sees Vera in the seat two rows back. She isn't alone anymore.

Butchie has her around the throat, whispering in her ear. He looks at Ruby and runs his putrid green pus-riddled tongue down Vera's neck. And all the while, Vera is oblivious to what is happening. Butchie silently mouths, "Mine." Ruby sharply inhales and looks away. She can't stand to see that abomination violate Vera. Vera is alone when Willie turns to see what she's looking at.

Ruby is in tears as she relates her dream to Willie. Josie and Whitney are in the seat in front of them, and they, along with Josh, try to console her.

"I think Baby Annie is going to cause a mine collapse. I saw it in my dream. But it was at the old Mary Luck mine. It's been closed for fifty years."

Then Willie says, "Remember the story that Mr. Honeycutt told? Where he swore Baby Annie caused the cave-in?"

"Yeah, maybe that was what I saw. She just looked so proud of herself. Laughing as those men cried for help." Ruby shook her head and looked out the window.

Then the bus jolted to a stop with a squeal of brakes. Everyone shot forward into the seat in front of them. Polecat held tight to the steering wheel, fighting the curve the bus was trying to navigate. When they finally stopped, everyone was on their feet, trying to see what was happening. There was a roadblock as railroad cross-ties set ablaze.

In the Fall of the year, this was a common prank played by teenagers in the mountains. While you try to move them out of the way, you may be pelted with hardened corn kernels or get the windows on your car soaped. It was a dangerous thing to do, seeing as how the road was narrow and dark with no guardrail in sight. The men on the bus got off and used the fire extinguisher to put out the blaze. 'Shiny staggered over to the edge of the road and yelled, "Come out of there and help us, you wretched heathens." Willie Joe snickered, "Yeah, like 'Shiny is helping so much." Another few cars pulled up, and they had the road cleared pretty quickly. Back in motion, Ruby settled back and hoped with all her heart that nothing else would happen that night. She would get her wish, but her journey was beginning. When October dawned, the end would be near.

The Yarn Spinners Get Spooked

Sitting on his front porch, Edgar Wilcox rocked back and forth in his rocking chair made by his father almost seventy-five years ago. It creaked and cracked as he adjusted his sizable rump in the seat. Once comfortable, he lit his pipe and settled back to enjoy his smoke while watching the sunset. His mind wandered back to his first love, Mrs. Phillips.

Unlike the other Yarn Spinners, Edgar had had no visits from the dead. The fine memories of his love were pure. He believed every word his friends had told him, but it was one thing to hear about something and quite another to experience it. He knew he saw the hag Baby Annie the day Mrs. Phillips fell off the ladder.

And something was going on with his niece, Vera. He saw her just yesterday and thought she looked like a clown with all the make-up she had on. He had a mind to call his nephew and say something, but that was for his wife to handle: women's worries. But if Ruby was right, Baby Annie had a hold on her, and that was something that he could not abide by.

Edgar's wife Patsy was gone to a Tupperware party in Prestonsburg and would be out until at least nine. Leaving him a casserole in the oven and a peck on the cheek, she left out at five. He was content to sit and enjoy his little piece of the world. The breeze turned chilly as shadows fell, and Edgar felt it in his bones. Old folks can feel the weather change coming by the aching in their bones. He didn't need Superstitious Sally to tell him when the rain was coming.

As the last of the kids from the park rode past on bicycles, he got up with a groan. His knees popped, and his back cracked; getting old bit the big one. If only he could feel young again. He envied the kids on the bikes with their young, muscular bodies. They'd never understand how precious that time in their life is. He'd give almost anything to have that time back. Sixty-six wasn't ancient, but he felt every bit of those years when he moved.

It was time to eat supper, so he shuffled in the door, letting it slam on its frame. Patsy wasn't there to fuss at him for it, so he paid it no mind. The casserole was chicken and broccoli. In *Woman's Day* magazine, Patsy read that broccoli is the healthiest vegetable and that red meat causes heart attacks. So now, she refuses to fix hamburgers, pot roasts, or steak. It was always chicken, fish, or pork loin these days. He had half a mind to go up the road to the 'Nest and have a double cheeseburger, maybe even two. He laughs and thinks. I wouldn't return to the house before everybody in town knew I was cheating on my diet. As the PostMistress, Patsy talked to all who entered the Post Office. Everyone in the town knew about her new way of cooking and that she had put me on a diet. His eating a hamburger at the 'Nest would be popular gossip.

Regrettably, he dug into the chicken casserole. It was tasty, but he had it at least once a week, sometimes twice. He took his plate into the living room, another No-No in Patsy's book, sat in his *LazyBoy* recliner, switched on the TV, and tuned into *Wheel of Fortune*.

Taking his fourth bite, that's when he heard it. Someone was calling his name. EEEDDDIIIEEE. It was very faint, but he knew he heard it. He turned the TV off and sat up in his chair. There it was again, but this time it was louder and closer. It sounded like a woman. He sat his plate on the kitchen table and climbed the stairs. That's where it was coming from. Again and again, the voice called his name, so he rose faster.

Thinking someone had broken in, he grabbed the baseball bat from the upstairs closet. He walked into his bedroom, which was so dark he couldn't see. Suddenly, the door shut behind him, and he broke out coldly. His knees were on the verge of buckling, and his heart was pounding too fast. He reached behind him, flipped on the light, and saw her. She sat up in the bed like she did in her coffin. She turned her head, looked him in the eye, and said, "Eddie, finally, we can be together. Now that you're a big boy come over here and give me a big wet sloppy kiss.

She made lip-puckered kissing sounds and laughed a laugh that was more of a cackle.

Edgar was in awe of seeing Mrs. Phillips again. She was just as beautiful as she was back then. He knew it wasn't her, but it was tricky to refuse her beckoning arms and pursed lips to call his name. Suddenly, the scenery changed, and they were back in the church, and she was in her coffin, sitting up, reaching out to not her husband but him. He was no longer an older man, nor was he a child. He was a strapping young man of twenty-three. He looked at himself, and his senses came to him, and he rushed to her, lifting her out of that hideous box that almost killed her.

She lovingly gazed into his eyes and said, "You were always the one I wanted. Kiss me, darling, so I can feel how much you love me." He leaned down, pressed his lips against hers, and their tongues danced The Samba. The kiss seemed to last forever, and as he pulled back from her, he got weak. His knees gave out, and he almost dropped her, but he lay her down gently. The arthritis in his hands burned like fire from holding her in his arms for so long. His back was a battleground of pain. He had a herniated disc that loved to pinch his sciatic nerve, degenerative disc disease, and good old arthritis. Let's not forget old Arthur.

Riddled with pain, he still tried to smile at her. She lay there looking like Liz Taylor from *Cat on a Hot Tin Roof.* Then she changed. The facade of Mrs. Phillips melted, and what was left was the hag, Baby Annie. She reached out to him in all her wicked glory and said, "Give me some sugar, Loverboy!" The look of horror and disgust on Edgar's face made her cackle. It was earsplitting, like a rooster with a sore throat.

Baby Annie stood up and, with Edgar on his knees, they were eye-to-eye. "I'm warning you, Loverboy, stay out of my way. You old fools can't stop me. I'll have my revenge; I've already got little Vera." Edgar's heart gave a spasm mid-pump, and he clutched his heart, and then his left arm as pain coursed through his veins. Baby Annie reached out with a gnarled finger and touched his chest. "I guess I'll start with you, Old Eddie. Let this be a warning to all of you." She faded away in a swirl of orbs of energy. Eddie, wracked with pain, couldn't process the show of magic he just witnessed.

He got to the phone by the bed and called for an ambulance. He slid onto the floor next to his bed and lay there wondering if he died, would he go to heaven? He couldn't think of any sin he'd committed to send him to hell. Just in case, he prayed for forgiveness. As he ended The Lord's Prayer, he heard the ambulance's siren. As the sound grew louder, he got sleepier and sleepier until he was entirely unconscious.

When he woke up, wires surrounded him. Machines were beeping, and people were standing all around him. Doctors and nurses with worried looks poked and prodded him. He felt like he was watching this on TV like a bystander. A jolt went through his entire body. He thought it so intensely he felt it in his soul. Then there was a pain in his chest, and he heard the Doctor say, "He's back; we have a regular heartbeat. That was a close one."

Realization hit Edgar like a sledgehammer. "I almost died. I think I died for a minute." He said aloud to no one. They were tears of pain, joy, fear, and anger. He resolved to take a shot at that old hag if he could. Ruby Lee would have her hands full, so he hoped he'd be able to help. That witch belonged in hell!

October 1, 1984

On October 1, it dawned crisp and cool. September had felt like summer to the Autumnal Solstice. Suddenly, the humid air turned to cool breezes, and the early mornings were on the cusp of bearing frost. It wouldn't be long before the grass would be crunchy and dry, and the mums would turn brown. Kentucky is known for its quick temperature change. It is a common occurrence to use both the heat and air conditioning on the same day. Allergy season was on the way out, and flu and cold season ushered in with the cold snap that had begun.

When Ruby awoke that morning, she shivered and burrowed back underneath her favorite quilt. It was thick, warm, and, best of all, worn. It had been in her family for generations, made by her great-great-grandmother's loving hands. Though Ruby had never met her, she felt close to her when she used her quilt. Holding it up to her face, she could almost imagine the scene of her grand-mother rocking in her rocker, pulled up close to the wood-burning fireplace. It was as if she could smell the smoke from the fire and the cornbread in the oven. How could that be, thought Ruby. Is this another vision while I'm awake?

Ruby opened her eyes in a flash, and suddenly, the feeling was gone. What was that? It wasn't a scary vision; it was a good feeling; it made her feel loved. "It's about time I had a good vision." she thought out loud. Suddenly, she felt alive more so than ever before. She ran to her window and raised it to watch the sunrise and feel the cool breeze. Rosie rolled over, put her pillow over her head, and said, "Go back to bed. We don't have school today!" It was a teacher in-service day, so Ruby ignored her and returned to her window.

She felt invigorated by her hollow's sights, sounds, and scents.

In all its glory, the rising sun illuminated the changing color of the leaves on the swaying trees. Sounds of the whippoorwill, loon, and bluebirds gave a cadence to the wind, and they seemed in tune with each other.

The wind caressed her face and hair and brought familiar scents of wood smoke, bacon frying, and the earthiness of the woods outside her window. It was almost more than she could stand, and she wondered why she had never noticed all of this before. Maybe this was the change Mrs. Purdy had discussed or what Elsbeth meant when she said, 'When the time is near, you will feel it in your soul.'

When she dressed and went to the kitchen, her senses went into overdrive from the feast before her. Mounds of bacon and a plate full of hot biscuits, a bowl of gravy, and scrambled eggs in a skillet just being put out on plates. Ruby kissed her mommy, plopped in her chair, and filled her container.

Her daddy smiled. "Whoa, their wild cat, plenty to eat, no need in gobbling like a hog."

"I know, it just all looks so good. I could eat it all!"

"Didn't you eat a big supper last night and have popcorn?"

"Yes, but I must've had a dream where I was hungry 'cause I'm starving!"

Her dad laughed at her while he slathered his biscuit with butter and then dunked it in gravy.

"Well, we are lucky to have what we have, so just remember that. I'll never let my girls be hungry. You can bet your bottom dollar on it!"

After breakfast, Ruby told her mom she was going for a walk and be home later. Kate paused before she spoke, a worried look on her face…"Be careful. You know better than us what could be out there in the hills. Take Major with you, and don't go too far."

"Yes, Ma'am." Bounding out the door with a full belly and nothing but high hopes for the day ahead, Ruby called to her German Shepard Major, and they disappeared into the trees.

Once on the trail that served as a shortcut to the cemetery road, Ruby breathed deep, and her senses seemed to awaken. It was a powerful feeling hard to explain to someone who wasn't receiving it. She beheld a spectacular view when she reached the top of the mountain.

Mary Luck lay before her; from this vantage point, it looked peaceful and picturesque. Hidden from view were the shabbiness and squalor of the 'Bottom and the back row of shotgun houses with their muddy yards and homes with peeling paint. The two church steeples had a backdrop of thousands of trees with leaves ready to burst with autumn color. It was gorgeous, and it was home.

Ruby sat down and leaned her back against an ancient oak tree that had probably been there since Jenny Wiley walked by on her trail of tears, massive with a great big hollowed-out trunk that fit her perfectly. This far up the mountain, the sounds were entirely natural. Even the train going by blowing its horn barely reached her ears. Major snuggled up on her feet and laid his nose on her knees. Ruby ran her hand through his thick black and gray fur coat and, as she did so, got a sense of freedom. It was as if she could feel what it would be like to run fast and chase butterflies and rabbits- freedom to be in a natural state and not have any human worries. It was a fleeting moment, but it happened. What was going on?

She didn't have long to wonder because, just then, the tree behind her slowly melded to her body, holding her in an all-consuming embrace. Her senses again opened up, and she could feel what it was like only to move when the wind blew but simultaneously be so alive all the time.

No sleep, just awake constantly. Memories stored inside the

trees were ancient, passed down through the seeds from which they came. Trees were all-knowing but always a silent witness to the actions of the world. They couldn't speak to warn them, offer advice, or pass the time. They had all the world's secrets but no way to share them. Ruby sensed all this and was sad for the tree until it spoke to her.

"I am the keeper. My kind always has been. There is no other path for us: we do what nature intended. We keep on living. On and on we go, the knowledge passed to our saplings. But we can be called upon when she allows it."

"When who allows it?"

"Why, Gaia, of course. She is the keeper of balance in the world."

"Like on its axis?"

"No, let me explain. You might know her as Mother Nature. It is she who keeps a balance between good and evil. She has to intervene whenever there is too much of one. We are called upon to help her at certain times, like now."

"Beggin' your pardon, but how can you help?"

"We, along with the wind and the water, can create terrible storms. They call it a freak of nature, I believe, in your tongue."

"You've been given several gifts. To use them, you must convene and converse with them. I represent the earth. You will talk to the other three momentarily. This conversation will be the easiest for you to understand since I speak every language. The other three will not be so easy. You must open yourself up to them."

"Who are the other three?" For a second, Ruby was afraid the tree was talking about the three little kids from the seance. His reply was, "Wind, water, and fire. Run along now, little Ruby Red. I'll be here standing guard."

"Do you have a name?" "I am the oldest tree on this mountain,

Caucus."

"Wow! I wish I could talk to you all day. I bet you've got some killer stories to tell."

"I do indeed. Maybe I will share them with you someday, but time is of the essence for now, and you have the other elements to speak with."

"Okay, but how do I do that?" she asks.

"Just stand up, Ruby Lee. Close your eyes and open your mind- and your soul."

"Okay, thank you, Caucus. . It was sure good talking to you." The tree did not respond, so Ruby assumed it was time to move on.

Even though talking to a tree in her mind was not what she expected to happen that morning, she wasn't freaked out by it. With her new mindset, she took it in stride. Standing up, she dusted off her Levis' and walked along the ridge, taking in the surrounding beauty. When she came to a clearing, she turned her face to the sun, closed her eyes, and opened her mind.

A gale of wind whooshed over her, and whispers consumed her. She tried to listen, but the words were so faint she couldn't understand what was said. Concentrating with all her heart, she tried to open her soul. Suddenly the words were more transparent.

"I am the air that causes the wind. I am the bringer of storms that drive the rain, the snow, the sleet, and hail. My task is to move things on the earth. When the need arises, I am yours to command. But use me wisely because once I'm in motion, it is hard to stop. Before you harness my power, know I can bring harm and aid.

The quick release of the wind staggered Ruby and left her breathless. She bent over, put her hands on her knees, and deeply breathed. Once her heart slowed, she stood up and felt a little dizzy. What the air told her sank in. She would have to be careful before she called on the wind to help her. Major came over and nuzzled her hand, trotting ahead and looking back at her as if to say, 'Come on.'

Ruby followed, and soon they were at the creek, where Major helped himself to a refreshing gulp of water. Ruby lay down on her back and looked at the sky. A few clouds were out, floating by lazily. Then the babbling of the water as it flowed down the mountain formed words. They were quick, cluttered, and hard to understand, but the harder she listened, the clearer they became.

"Water is my name. I am the biggest part of you. I feed the world. Nothing would live without me. But I have the power to destroy as well. I lend you the use of my power. Use it only if you mean to destroy something to restore balance- not for your amusement or gain." Then it was gone, and once again, you could hear just a water flow tumbling over rocks and soil.

Ruby sat up and looked around. She had the sense that someone or something was watching her. Peering through a thick grove of trees was a figure composed of wood that looked like someone had bent branches to create a shape that shifted to hide among the trees. You had to be still and watch without blinking to see it move. Ruby didn't feel afraid of it, just highly curious. It was fleeting and left her to wonder if it was ever there.

Ruby walked on toward the old Mary Luck Mine, reached by going down through a valley that barely had a path big enough for two people to walk abreast. Her Pappaw always told her to be careful of snakes, the authentic kind and the other, which are low-class people out to harm you. Homeless people built old rusted cars and huts. Transients hopped in boxcars and had to get off when the train stopped. They'd be there a while, then hop on another. That's why Pap thought they were dangerous. "Hobos are no account trash. Always with their hand out. Get a job, you lazy bum!" he'd chant.

At the entrance to the mine, there was a smoldering campfire. Ruby knelt and warmed her hands. Suddenly, roaring flames leaped from the ashes. Ruby jumped back but wasn't afraid. The roar of the fire was hard to hear, but it was talking to her, that was for sure. The glow from the flames illuminated her hair, and her eyes danced as she watched the fire burn. A voice became clear, but it was so loud she had to concentrate.

It roared at her and said, "I am your twin. I can be yours to command as you wish. You were born on my festival day when I am revered: I am a destroyer and a necessity. Without me, there would be darkness and cold when night falls. I am a consumer of all that is in my path. Air and earth feed my strength: Only water can stop me. You are a child of Beltane and therefore have my mark upon you. Beware my use unless you are certain something should be destroyed. Once it is gone, there is no going back. Harness my power and use it to restore the balance."

The words came in a sizzle and then returned to just a smoldering pit from the previous night. Ruby sat hard by the pond where Claude's sister Rebecca Jo drowned. There were cattails by the bank taller than her. The frogs and dragonflies were amongst the weeds, hopping and flying. Her head felt cluttered with all of this new information. She thought she should see Mrs. Purdy, but a figure arose from the pond just then.

Ruby sat in shock as the figure emerged from the murky water. It had a human shape that included everything around it- sticks, plants, and leaves. There were swirling sections of water and places held open by air that whooshed, but its eyes were fiery pits. Flames jumped in them and danced. Its mouth opened, and a voice spoke.

At once, she understood that this was Mother Nature. She said, "I am the keeper of balance in the world. I am a judge and jury for good and evil. Neither one can win all the time. Too much of either, and I must intervene. I do not make it a habit of showing myself to humans, but I couldn't resist in your case. I've watched you your entire life. When you came on, Beltane, I knew you were the one. I and your kin, Elsbeth, created the magic that put you on your path even before your conception."

"You are the restorer of balance in human form. Therefore, I have given you the power of all four elements. I am confident you will use them well. Remember, there can be no balance if one is bigger. I cannot intervene anymore after this. You must use what has been given to you by blood. Make your magic."

"One last thing, the old woman Purdy is not all she seems. She is struggling between what is right and wrong. She is tempted by the evil one. Do not reveal to her you have these powers over the elements. She could betray you and join forces with her kin. The grimoire is all that she can be helpful with. Fare thee well, Ruby Red." And just like that, the shape collapsed into the water and floated away. Ruby thinks, "What a way to start the first day of October."

She left the pond and walked down the railroad tracks to Shotgun Hollow with Major close on her heels. One foot in front of the other, she balanced on a rail and could walk home without falling off. Thoughts raced through her mind, trying to recall everything she had learned. She felt invigorated with life and wanted to soak it all like a dry sponge. She had a renewed sense of confidence and, for the first time, felt like she could win the battle she was born to fight.

Mrs. Purdy and Baby Annie

While Edgar Wilcox was convalescing in his home and being catered to by his loving wife Patsy, Mrs. Purdy tried to commune with her wicked great-great-grandmother, Baby Annie. The other four Spinners were on edge after what happened to Edgar. They'd all been allowed to visit him when he got home, but Patsy hovered nearby, so he had to relay his ordeal in an abridged version. It was night on October 17, two weeks until Halloween, and they still didn't have a plan of action.

Over at the 'Bottom, there was a feeling of magic in the air. Ordinary people may have a niggling of something off-kilter, but nothing that would make them sit up and take notice.

As dusk fell, Purdy lit three black candles. She was boiling some herbs in a kettle hung over her fireplace, making the air smell like cinnamon, sage, and clove. Purdy perched on the edge of her chair. With closed eyes and head tilted back, she began mumbling words that sounded like nonsense. She brought them to a staccato rhythm that grew louder and louder.

Suddenly the candle flames shot up almost to the ceiling, and Baby Annie sat across the table in shadow form. "Who calls for me with the blood chant?"

"It is your great-great-granddaughter, Petunia. I have called you to warn you about the girl. I know what she can do, and if you want to make sure you can defeat her and have your revenge, you'll need to know what I know."

"Well, don't keep me waiting. Spit it out."

"I require something in return."

"Ain't you the cunning fruit of my loins? What can I give you?"

"More power, of course. I want to read the grimoire and cast the spells. These townspeople have always snubbed me. They've only come to me now so that I can betray my blood to help them!"

"I know you have the gift of sight and can commune with the dead. It is spell casting you want. I can pass on some power to you, but use it only if you must."

A shock moves through her body. When she inhaled and breathed air, she was nose to nose with her ancestor.

"Now, what have you got for me?"

Purdy is shaken, being this close to her, and can barely speak. "I was the one who delivered her. She was born with a caul. I saved it in a jar. Her momma didn't know what it was and what it could do. I knew it would come in handy someday, and so it has."

Baby Annie chuckles, "Looks like you ain't worthless after all. That will stop her in her tracks. Bring it to the town carnival on Halloween, and I'll put her back where she belongs. Bring my grimoire, for I may make it work too." with a swirl of air, she disappeared. Mrs. Purdy felt a tug on her heart because she liked Ruby Lee. And even though she felt used, she still enjoyed being part of the town and being revered for her talents in the occult.

Still, her need for power and revenge was more potent than any soft feelings she may have for a child with powers she'd never understand how to use. Serves this town right for all the sneers, pranks, and snubbing they'd given her for almost sixty-five years. She came here as a bride of fourteen, and now, at seventy-nine, it was still the same: once they got what they needed from her, they'd all go back to snubbing her.

With her mind hell-bent on betrayal, she tried her new powers by casting a spell on herself. It worked exactly the way it was supposed to. Finally, she had what she wanted, and it felt beautiful. She muses that this town won't know what hit them.

Ruby and Willie Joe: Laying the Plans 10/18/84

Ruby told Willie a watered-down version of what happened while communing with The Elements. Willie seemed surprised but took it in stride, just like her. Ruby's ability to see visions by touching someone or something helped her realize what was at stake. Everyone she touched was depending on her to defeat Baby Annie. When she touched Willie Joe, she felt loved and cherished and, most of all, safe. He was her touchstone to reality. She knew she needed him by her side to win. Just his presence strengthened her.

"Willie, I want to help Vera. Maybe I can break Baby Annie's hold on her if I can talk to and touch her. The only thing is, she won't come around me. It's as if she knows I can release her from the spell, and Baby Annie won't let her come around me. Even at cheerleading practice, she says mean things to me and hangs around the younger girls, who follow her like puppies. Who knows, maybe they're spelled too."

"I don't think I'd mess with Vera right now. Once you banish that old hag back to hell, the curse will be over, and Vera will return to being our friend."

"So you think I can beat her?" Ruby asks doubtfully.

"Of course, you can. Baby Annie might be evil, but you have so much goodness in you, Ruby. There's no way she can win against you. And you have a secret weapon."

"What's that?"

"Me!"

They both giggle and join hands as they walk through the park to meet up with their friends. The love they share is so pure. Not just with each other but with their friends, family, and town. Ruby has filled the twins and Whitney in on what's been happening lately and asks for their help.

"Hey, you two lovebirds," Whitney says while raising her eyebrows up and down and lowering her *Wayfarers*.

They both blush and release their hands. Willie jumps up on the picnic table bench they are all lounging around and says, "Wherefore art thou, Juliet?"

"I think that's her line there, Romeo." Josh points out while punching him on the arm. Josie rolls her eyes and says,

"Dorks!" The girls all giggle and start talking about the Halloween Carnival. Whitney asks, "So, what's the deal with this carnival stuff, anyway? I've never heard of such a thing."

"Me either," says Josie.

"What do you mean? asks Ruby. "Don't y'all celebrate Halloween in Lexington?"

"Well, sure, but it's just costume parties, trick or treat , and usually just for kids. There isn't a carnival. Where will they set up all the rides and stuff?"

Ruby laughs, slaps her knee, and says, "Oh no, you got it all wrong. The carnival is at the gym. They set up booths with games like dart throw, fish pond, knocking over bowling pins, the basketball toss, the spook house, and the best cakewalk." Ruby says all of this with such enthusiasm that they stare at her in wonderment.

"Wow! That sounds great! But what the heck is a cakewalk?" asked Josie.

"In the center of the gym, they outline the circle with the mascot in the middle with masking tape and then block it off in spaces with a number on each one. Everyone chooses a number to start on, or you take whichever one is open and walk around the circle while music plays. When it stops, you stop, and they draw out a number, and if you're on the number called, you win a cake. Almost everyone in town makes a cake to donate, and if you win, you get to choose the one you want."

"That sounds awesome!" Says Whitney.

"A lot of people dress up. Not just the kids, but the grown-ups, too. They have the best costume contest, and the winner gets a free chili or soup bean dinner."

The adults play bingo in the lunchroom, and the little kids bob for apples. Mrs. Purdy is the fortune teller, big surprise, and her booth usually brings in the most money." Ruby says all of this with pride. This is typically the highlight of her year, but this time, she's more scared than she ever has been in her life.

The costumes this year will be more elaborate than ever before.

As their ancestors did, the residents have a reason to disguise themselves: To hide their identity from evil spirits that may seek revenge or cause mischief. You could avoid their malice if they didn't know who you were. Samhain, the pagan name for Halloween, was when the veil between the living and the dead was said to be at its thinnest. This allowed spirits to cross into our world and do as they pleased.

Before Christianity had reached the highlands of Scotland, the pagans believed that fire cleansed the land, and they worshiped gods of the elements; earth, air, water, and fire. They observed four crucial dates: the Vernal (spring) equinox, summer solstice, autumnal equinox, and winter solstice. The festivals they celebrated and offered sacrifices to were mostly Beltane, the fire festival, and Samhain, the most powerful day to use magic.

"Ruby has got a plan, so you'll come closer and let her tell you," said Willie as he sat beside her. The twins and Whitney sit down too. When they settle, Ruby starts to lay out her plan.

"I'm going to need your help if I pull this off. I'm going to Mrs. Purdy's later to get a look at the grimoire if she will let me. I have to have it at the carnival to cast the spell. That's where you guys come in. I have a feeling Mrs. Purdy is going to switch sides. Baby Annie is her kin after all, and who knows if maybe she's been promised something in return."

"Geez, Louise Ruby, you think she'd do that? After everything that's happened?" asks Josie.

Josie guessed, "I hate to think about it, but something tells me she has a grudge against the town for always shunning her, just like Baby Annie."

Ruby sighed, "And now we are asking her to help banish a member of her family back to hell. I don't trust her as I did."

"In the mountains, blood is thicker than water, and you always care for your own. Most of the town is of Scottish descent, so they have always been clannish. It will be hard for her not to side with her blood."

Josh seems doubtful, "So what can we do to help?"

"Okay, so when Baby Annie shows up, I'll need the grimoire. That's the key. I have to have it to open the portal. So, when Purdy has the book in her hand, if she tries to give it to Baby Annie, one of you has to take it from her. I'll only need a minute with it to say the spell."

Willie Joe puffed out his chest, "I'm your man, Ruby. I'll wrestle that old woman to the ground before I let Baby Annie have it."

Josh snickers beside him and says, "And when she gets the best of you, I'll be there to take it from her and save the day."

Josie chuckles, "Oh my Lord! I'm the smallest and the fastest, so I can sneak up and grab it before she knows what hit her."

Whitney flips her hair over her shoulder and offers, "I guess I'll be a distraction. If nothing else, I can talk her to death. Like totally!"

They all burst out laughing, and this moment is a priceless thing that has the power to take down ten witches. Their pure love and camaraderie give off an indestructible aura of power.

The Grimoire

Reluctantly, Ruby left the safety and warmth of her friends and rode her bike to Mrs. Purdy's. She didn't tell the others that she saw Baby Annie with her. She couldn't hear what they were saying but knew it wasn't anything good. A thing as rotten as Baby Annie could never be associated with anything good. She was evil through and through, so Ruby had to go to her house. If Baby Annie had been there, she would feel her presence, almost like a sour, moldy essence. She was permeating the furniture, curtains, and walls.

She could sense the magic in the air as she pulled up on her bike. It nibbled on her skin like the goldfish at Superstitious Sally's house. Light touches that gave off energy and heightened her senses. She stepped to the door and was poised to knock when a familiar voice called, "No need to knock, Ruby Lee. You're always welcome at my house." This threw Ruby off. Mrs. Purdy was never this nice: evil is afoot.

"What brings you to my door today?"

"I have some questions about using spells."

"Well, now, I'm not much of a spell-caster; My gifts lie elsewhere.. but my ma could cook up potions. That cauldron hanging in the fireplace was hers, but I only use it for soup these days. Mayhap when I die, I'll leave it to you." Mrs. Purdy laughed and then broke into a coughing fit.

Ruby cringed away from her. The phlegmy sound of her lungs made her want to puke.

Ruby needed to get her hands on the grimoire. Now that her sense of touch could give her visions, it could show her something that would help her defeat Baby Annie. Mrs. Purdy left the room, and when she returned, she had the worn dark brown leather book in her hands. Its pages were parchment filled with spells in an unknown language.

Outside, a fight broke out between two men. One had a brick trying to destroy the other over the head. They staggered to the backyard and started trampling Purdy's herb garden, and out she went, but not before she handed the book to Ruby. Once in her hands, she closed her eyes, and another world appeared in her mind.

The Taking of the Three

Ruby's mind opened like a flower: She saw a scene that appeared to be on a mountainside. There was a shack with a porch and a rocker. A well and a hitching post was in the yard with no horse. Close to the porch stood an iron tripod. Hanging from it was a cauldron like the one she had just seen at Mrs. Purdy's house. The fire underneath it was roaring, a bubbling brew.

She was free to move about in this vision and moved closer to the shack. Who lived there was unknown, but she didn't have to wait long. The door creaked open, and out hobbled Baby Annie in a homemade house dress and a bright red shawl mixed with a green and black pattern. The stark contrast between the shabby to the brightly colored shawl was jarring; there was a reason, and it wasn't anything good.

Baby Annie moved to the cauldron, and Ruby followed. She drew the shawl from her head and exposed her thin, balding scalp. Peering inside the pot, she saw murky water that bubbled and hissed, sloshing and sizzling when it hit the burning wood below. Baby Annie threw back her head and raised her hands skyward.

Come to me, come to me, on dark wings you fly
cometh to me and do my bidding
I've been wronged, and I need my
vengeance.
I call on thee, oh mighty dark one
the demon of Hamelin of old
I summon thee to help me
and give you your three
you were wronged, and so was I
lend me your tune
and it's an eye for an eye.

She repeated this mantra three times, each more demanding. Then a solid black shape appeared that looked like a shadow but had a full-bodied mass. From the cauldron, it stepped out and faced her. Shimmering and changing shape as if it couldn't stay the same. It finally spoke, "Who has called upon me, and what do you ask?"

Baby Annie humbly knelt, "I am but a low thing that comes before thee. I ask that you lend me your tune so I can complete what Hamelin did not. You got all the children except for three. They wronged you when they did not honor the deal ye struck. I, too, have been wronged by the town below. They tricked me and took my land. Three men who were the worst to me each have a son that hasn't yet turned ten. I wish to honor you with them. If only you would lend me the use of your tune, I would do what Hamelin did not."

The figure seemed to ponder the request and then said, "I will lend you my tune, but you must first give me a sacrifice. You will cut off a finger and throw it in the cauldron and out will come my flute. You need only to blow into it, and it will produce the tune to lure the children away and to their doom."

Baby Annie fell to her knees, thanking him as he looked down upon her and demanded. "Give me the finger." And then stepped back into the boiling pot melting away until only the head was visible.

Baby Annie shuffled over to the chopping block and, with no hesitation, grabbed the hatchet. She laid down her left hand and hacked off her pinky finger as blood trickled from her hand. She ran back to the pot, tossed it in. The black shape gobbling it up before sinking inside. The pot boiled so hard and fast it swung back and forth on its tripod. Baby Annie backed away from it. For the first time, even she looked afraid.

Just as suddenly, it just stopped. The fire died down, and floating on top of the brew was a flute made of bone. Long and thin, with four holes for playing. She picked it out of the water and turned it this way and that as Ruby studied it. Putting it up to her lips, she blew. The sound that came out was the sweetest melody she'd ever heard. Ruby couldn't believe it: She was listening to the tune of The Pied Piper. That story had haunted her as a child, and now seeing and knowing how she lured those three little boys sent chills up her spine.

In 1284 a German town called Hamelin had a rat infestation. A man in a multi-colored suit came to town, offering to take care of the rats for a large amount of money. The mayor agreed, and the Piper went through the city playing his tune on a wooden flute. Soon all the rats were following him, and he led them to a river, where they all jumped in and drowned. When he returned to collect his money, the mayor refused to pay him the sum they agreed on, only giving him a small portion of what they owed.

The Piper walked outside in the street and played another tune. This time, instead of rats, children were his followers. They followed him up the hill outside town, where a portal had appeared. One by one, all the children of the village went inside the mountain and were gone forever- All except for three:

1. Deaf and couldn't hear the tune.
2. Blind and could not see where to go.
3. Disabled and couldn't keep up.

Ruby now understood: The children were sacrifices. She was offering them up to the Piper, who she now believed to be a demon that only took the shape of the Piper. What had always scared her about that story was that it was supposed to be true.

Ruby felt sick. She was about to witness the murder of three innocent children and the heinous crime that cursed her town and people. There was a flash, and suddenly it was dawn; just a sliver of sun peeped over the mountain, enough so that Ruby could see the hag getting ready for her murder spree. She put the flute in her dress pocket, drew the shawl around her body, and covered her head: She looked like a gypsy. Surefooted from living her whole life on a mountainside, she slunk down the hill.

The first house she visited was that of her lawyer, J.D. Wells. His son Morgan had just turned seven. His carrot-red hair was passed to him by his mother, Mercy. Tall for his age and reed-thin, he was always ready for a game of war or marbles. That morning as he lay sleeping, unbeknownst to him, he was being stalked by a witch with a deep hatred that turned her heart black without sympathy for anyone. It didn't bother her at all that this child was innocent. She figured he'd grow up just like his father, and the world didn't need another like him.

She drew out her flute, and the musical sound passed through the window and into the ears of the sleeping child. From that moment on, he felt doomed. He arose from his bed and shuffled to his window, and when he looked out, he did not see a witch. The man with the colorful coat played the flute and danced to the music. Without hesitation, Morgan raised his window and slipped out, wearing nothing but his nightshirt. His bare feet walked across the frost-hardened grass without feeling a thing. He took the proffered hand and, with a smile, skipped along to the tune.

The next house she and Morgan visited was that of Davy Goble. His father, Sampson, was the mine foreman and the company's right-hand man. He knowingly took advantage of her ignorance and did not inform her she was selling the mineral rights along with her land for a small sum. This angered her more than all the rest: Not only was it dirty and underhanded, he was stealing from one of his own. That unspoken bond between mountaineers was to "take care of their own." She guessed he got a hefty bonus for his bargain deal. She might not read but she could count and knew when someone wronged her.

Therefore, his son would suffer the most: she'd spend time with him. Little Davy was six years old. He still liked to sit in his momma's lap when she read him stories at night. Right now, he lay in his child's bed with brown wavy curls that his momma couldn't bear to cut. He had a cupid's bow for a mouth, and his chubby cheeks were rosy and plump. Baby Annie played the flute, and when the tune hit his ears, his eyes flashed open to reveal brilliant green eyes. He sat up, ran to the window, and saw a man dressed in bright colors playing a tune he couldn't resist. Also, his pal Morgan was outside, beckoning him to come out and play. "Come on, Davy, hurry. You'll love this game called "Follow the Leader." Morgan's eyes were open but opaque, and his face was gleeful.

Davy didn't hesitate. He couldn't wait to join his friend and follow that fantastic tune. He was dressed the same as Morgan in his nightshirt, without shoes, and still, the cold didn't bother him. As soon as he stepped on the ground, his eyes rolled back and turned fish-belly white. He'd run away as fast as the gingerbread man if he'd only known what was in store for him. But the tune mesmerized him, and he was helpless against its magical pull.

The last house they visited was that of Grayson Wells, the town constable and the lawman that would force Baby Annie off her land. Taking his son would crush him, and she couldn't wait to see him crumble. Zeke was only five years old with Blond hair and dark brown eyes that were in stark contrast to his pale skin, making him look sickly. His bedroom was on the second story of his house, so the witch had to get the other two boys to toss up some pebbles to awaken him. The flute began its tune, and a moment later, Zeke appeared at his window. Little Zeke was thrilled by the colorful Piper and his two pals outside. He threw open the sash and leaned out to hear better. The boys called to him, "Come on, Zeke, it's wonderful. We're playing a new game, 'follow the leader.' Hurry so that you won't miss out."

Zeke clapped his hands and threw his leg over the window. He placed his foot on the trellis, and halfway down, he fell and snapped his ankle. His eyes had already turned white, so he felt no pain but couldn't walk right. Spying his little red wagon, the Piper had him climb in, and the other two pulled him along. And off they went to Rattlesnake Hollow, never to be seen alive again.

The melodious tune filled their heads with happiness and images of sweets and treats they had never dreamed of. Every day was a holiday, and all they had to do was play. At the bottom of the hill that led up to the witch's shack, Zeke was lifted out by the other two boys since there was no way they could pull the wagon up the steep incline.

When they got to her yard, they didn't see the shack but a field of flowers and a bright, sunny day. There were tables heaped with their favorite foods and toys to play with. Ruby was the silent witness to this and, for a moment, saw it as they did, a child's paradise.

The witch brought a stool and a black leather bag with torture tools. Ruby wanted to stop her, grab those boys, and run off the mountain. This was the worst vision yet. She could still see it in her head even if she closed her eyes. She tried to brace herself for what she knew was coming, but nothing could prepare her. It was beyond evil.

The boys were still frolicking in the yard when suddenly the witch stopped playing the flute. They stopped playing and looked around and recognized nothing. While in their dream state, the witch tied them to a tree. Morgan was the first to speak. "Where are we? Why are we tied to a tree?"

"I don't know," said Davy. Zeke looked around as his legs trembled, "I want to go home." He said this with a lip that was quivering.

"Me too. My ankle hurts bad," whined Davy.

They didn't have to wait long to learn their fate: The witch appeared. "Now, who wants to go first?"

Morgan yanked at the rope around his waist, binding him to the tree, "First for what? Who are you, and why are we tied to a tree?"

"Oh, I think I have a volunteer." the witch said with a sneer. "You've got too many questions. But I'll answer you one: I am Baby Annie, the witch of Rattlesnake Hollow. Mayhap you've heard of me?" The fear on their faces made her cackle. Ruby cringed right along with the boys. Tears flowed down her face as they cried.

When Little Zeke hollered for his mommy, the witch responded by slashing his throat, and his cries turned to gurgles as his life's blood coursed down his white nightshirt. Morgan thrashed against his ropes and screamed for help when the witch turned her eyes upon him.

"Be still, and I'll be quick, or suffer like this one's gonna." She took her rusty blade and sawed into Davy's angelic face. His mouth was open, so she cut the corners to keep him from opening wide to yell. No one lived close enough to hear them anyway.

"Now, do you want to know why you're here?" They didn't answer.

"It's because of your fathers and what they did to me, stealing my land, and nobody tried to help me. They tricked me; they did. I'll show them, though. They'll see what they paid for when they come to boot me off my land. You three will be hanging from my tree." She threw her head back and laughed.

Davy passed out from the pain and fright, but the witch wanted him awake, so she slapped his face until he came around. She grabbed his chin and jerked it up to face her. "You open those eyes, or I'll cut the lids off." He kept on whining, and she gave up. Morgan was different, though. He was the oldest and had been the leader of their gang of friends. He wasn't going to let this hag see him cry.

When she approached him, he looked her in the eye and didn't back down. "You're a contentious one. I can tell you'd have grown up just like your daddy. Good thing I'm putting a stop to you."

Morgan spits in her face- his only way of retaliating . Infuriated, she wiped the drool off with her hand and smeared it all over Davy's face. Morgan winced.

"Okay, you little bastard, you're next." She turned to Davy and said, "I want you to watch what's coming for you. But I'm going to have some fun with this one now."

She took her blade and split Morgan's nightshirt down the middle. She eyed him and said, "I want to see what your insides look like." Before realization hit him, baby Annie plunged in her blade and sliced him open from the groin to the sternum. His innards spilled out while he was still aware. He saw his intestines hit the ground, and then, mercifully, his eyes closed forever.

Wiping her blade on her dress, she turned her gaze to Davy, who was in complete shock. She untied him and led him by his hand to the stump beside the boiling cauldron.

He sat there, numb and silent. She began, "Now your daddy was the worst of them all. He knew I couldna read, and he fixed it so that I hardly got a nickel off'n all my land. He flat stole it from me!" She said this with disgust, but Davy wasn't registering any of it. "That's why I made you bear witness to your friends bein' kilt. It turned ye idiot I believe. No matter, yer going to suffer the worst, my pretty one. Are ye ready?" Davy did not reply. He was already too far gone. Ruby was thankful for that much. But she feared his death would be so horrid she'd never forget it, and she was right.

The witch tied his hands behind his back, cut off his toes one by one, and tossed them in her pot. Sweet cherub-faced, Davy squealed and kicked till he just slumped over. Then the climax of her atrocity took place. She dragged him off the stump and dunked his head into the boiling water with little toes floating around. He thrashed until he inhaled the brew in his lungs and died with a toe in his mouth, and his once beautiful face became scalded with strips of flesh hanging on his chest. His eyes were open and staring. Ruby cried and cried.

At some point that Ruby wasn't privy to in the vision, the witch had fashioned three nooses from the rope that had bound the kids. She dragged little Davy to his noose, slowly pulled it tight around his neck, and hung him from the tree. He joined his friends in hanging from the Rowan tree. The witch observed her handiwork and decided to see what the other two's innards looked like. So she gutted them like Morgan and thought they made a pretty decoration in her yard. Satisfied, she took her rifle, sat in her rocker, and waited for the fun to begin.

Ruby was suddenly awake and realized where she was and what she held. She dropped the grimoire on the floor as if it had bitten her. Her hands tingled, and her mind was a whirl of images of disgust. Her heart ached for those poor little kids. She felt so sorry for them. And for Baby Annie to use them against their kin was abominable! Ruby was more resolved than ever to defeat the witch. She would pay dearly for what she'd done. It was indeed time for her to pay the Piper!

Ruby realized where she was and glanced around for Mrs. Purdy. . But then she heard the screen door slam as Purdy lumbered back into the house, muttering curses under her breath. Ruby quickly picked up the grimoire and placed it on the table beside her. She had to get out of there fast. So she told a fib and said, "Mrs. Purdy, I'll have to return later. I forgot I have cheerleading practice, and since I'm the captain, I have to set a good example and be there on time." She was nervous, and Purdy picked up on it right away. "Are you feeling okay? Any visions?" she prodded.

"Uh, no." another fib. "I just really have to go. We got three new cheers, and our tournament starts tomorrow, so it might be a while before I can return." She skedaddled out the front door, hopped on her bike, and headed straight to Pappaw. She had to tell the Yarn Spinners what she saw: It was a game changer.

The October Tale

Wilson McKenzie rounded up the 'Spinners and then told Birdie and Ally-Fair to meet on Thursday evening at the old company store. Ruby told the twins, Whitney and Willie Joe, of course. They didn't invite Vera or Mrs. Purdy. Ruby was no longer sure about her allegiance and wasn't taking any chances. This could be life or death for the people in her town.

October 19, 1984, was a chilly but sunny day. By evening, storm clouds had gathered, and the winds had picked up, bringing with it the northern cold. The leaves were at their peak, and it had been a beautiful autumn, but they were falling fast with the strong winds. By the morning, skeletal arms of bare branches would show through on nearly every tree.

Halloween was just around the corner, and nobody felt that pull of magic more than Ruby. Her entire body was like a live wire; she heard the wind whisper; streams babbled to her; fire hypnotized her. Trees and the earth invaded her senses with knowledge. She didn't know what to expect when the veil was the thinnest on Halloween. She just knew it was something big.

Claude had gotten there first and started the fire in the pot-bellied stove; it was roaring and warmly filled the room. The sun wasn't down, but the evening shadows made it look like nighttime. Wilson came in next with Ruby Lee and her mother, Kate, Matthew, and Edgar. Delano was last, claiming he'd had a nightmare that afternoon and didn't know if he could stand any more horror stories.

When Birdie came in, she looked flushed. Her color was high, and she slurred her words. Guess she had more than a two-finger shot tonight; she probably also brought her flask. She would need it after the tale she was about to hear. She took a seat between Claude and Delano and just gave a nod and stared into the stove, watching the flames flicker.

Ally-fair came in, and her appearance floored everyone. For the first time in forever, her hair was down. It fell to her waist and flowed in steely gray waves with white mixed in. She was a true beauty. Something had changed in her, and it was evident by the smile on her face that showed off a dimple in her cheek that no one had ever seen before. The sadness that had always cloaked her was gone.

The kids came in together. Willie Joe went directly over to Ruby and took the seat saved for him. Whitney and the twins sat behind them, and then 'Shiny came strolling in, to everyone's dismay. Wilson got up and went to him. He was saying it was a private meeting, and he pushed him aside,

"See here now, I know I'm the town joke, and you'll laugh at me behind my back, but I've lived here my whole sixty-eight years and seen a lot, brother. Listen up; they's a bad thing coming here. I've seen it. I sit outside every time you've had yer meetings s, and I listen. People say stuff around me because they think I'm too drunk to listen, and mayhap sometimes I am, but you'll ain't the only ones seeing spooks. Half the town has had spooks showing ' up. Edith is scared to death. Her dead husband shows up for supper nearly every night. Super Sally's sister comes to her house. The one that choked on a piece of candy when she was eight. When she shows up, that candy makes a bulge in her neck, she reaches her hand down her throat, pulls it out, and hands it to Sally. If I'm a lyin', I'm a dyin'," he says with his hand raised to God.

"And Birdie, I've seen your boy Butchie cruising around town in that car that got him kilt. He picks up little Vera, and they take off squealing tires blastin' that devil music he always liked." Birdie puts her head in her hands and then admits she sees him regularly. She has to lock her door and turn up the sound on her TV so she can't hear him knocking or the engine revving. "It kills my soul to turn him away. He looks like my son, but I know it's not him."

Birdie wipes the tears from her eyes and takes a nip from her flask.

'Shiny seemed to wind down. His last words were, "I think we should have a town meeting after tonight. No outsiders, just the original folk." Wilson offers him his chair, and he grabs another one from the back room.

When he returns, he says, "What do you all think? Everyone in favor says, 'Aye.'"

It was unanimous.

He turns to Ruby and says, "My granddaughter has a tale for us this evening that she thinks will shed light on what's coming for us. Ruby Lee, you have the floor."

Ruby stands, letting go of Willie's hand. She makes her way to the center of the room, where the metal folding chair awaits her. When she's settled, she relates the vision she had. She cries through most of it, as does nearly everyone in the room. However, Allie-Fair remains unmoved, but by the end of the story, there isn't a dry eye in the room. Kate comes to Ruby and holds her as they both cry. When she collects herself, she says, "I'm so sorry I had to tell that story, but I think it's important. There were a few things that made me wonder. The demon thing that came out of the water was supposed to have been the original Pied Piper. Since Baby Annie killed the kids she promised to Piper, wouldn't that be going against her deal with him?"

No one answered until Claude said, "I think you're right. I can't remember that story, but I know the saying, 'You'll have to 'Pay the Piper,' comes from it."

"Yes, Mr. Wells, you're right." Josh offers.

"And who might you be, and what makes you an expert?" asks 'Shiny.

"I'm Josh Baldridge, and that's my twin sister, Josie. He points to her, and blushing, she offers a little wave. Josh continues, "I wasn't born here like you all, but my family was, and I've spent every summer here, and now I live here temporarily. So, anyway, I'm a lover of books. I read all the time. One of my favorite things to read is classic folk tales about Europe. I've read about a dozen of these books, and everyone has the story of the Pied Piper. They all agree the tale is true, but the story varies."

"So the Pied Piper is a real thing that helped that filthy witch kill our kin? I don't know how we'll get rid of her." worries Del. He says this shaky, and Ruby wonders what has upset him. It wasn't just a nightmare: He's had a visit from a spook, and it had rattled him. .

Ruby goes over to Del and takes his hand in hers, and suddenly she sees what has happened to him. She sees it all in a flash. Her simple touch allows her to see his nightmare and sense his emotions.

Delano and the Werecat Saw Blade

Del started swearing as he took out the trash last night, seeing that his garbage cans were strewn all over his backyard. This was more than just raccoons or squirrels could do. Suddenly he got a shiver, and he sensed something was watching him. "Now see here, you hooligans. You can't mess with my property because it's almost Halloween! I'll press charges if I catch you." He says this last with a huff.

He stomps out in his yard, which backs up to a heavily wooded hillside. It's dark, and the moon is covered with clouds, so he can hardly see where all his trash has gotten to. He receives the metal can and picks up what's left of the ripped bags. Garbage falls out as he tries to collect it. He curses under his breath and then says, "Well, shit, a brick." He kicks the can, and it rolls to a stop at the base of the hill.

He is no longer scared or angry; he feels put out. His gait is slow and without energy. When he reaches the can, he bends down to grasp the handle and finds it stuck, or so he thinks. Suddenly it's yanked from his hands, and he comes face to face with Sawblade.

Petrified, Del cannot move. He doesn't dare call out for his wife. Del'd never put her in that much danger. Back in the moment, he's first aware of the assault on his sense of smell. It's the most putrid, animalistic odor imaginable- Like rotted meat mixed with mold and soured milk. Del gags, fear hits him, and his adrenal gland goes overdrive. Finding the strength to break Sawblade's grasp on him, he gets about halfway through his yard when tackled from behind and slammed into the ground.

Del saw his life flash before his eyes. The hands with claws like a cougar held his shoulders in place. And to Del's amazement, the man cat spoke to him. He couldn't understand him, but Ruby could. Through Del's vision, she got Sawblade's message. He said, "Help me; I want to be at peace, not forced to do her bidding. She's the reason I was made a monster. I didn't want to kill that boy. She made me. Please help me. Please help me. Help us all."

Del was released, high-tailed it in his house, and locked all the doors and windows. He was panting and close to tears. Thank God Wilma was taking a Calgon bath and hadn't seen his face. Wilma was his second wife. His first wife, Thelma, died of cancer back in '69. He met Wilma at Church. She'd just moved here from Ohio to teach at the new college up in P-Burg. They've been married since '75. However, Wilma didn't care for superstition or ghosts; she said it was Poppycock. Whatever that is.

Ruby got all of this from a handshake. She leaned down and whispered in his ear that everything would be fine and that Sawblade wouldn't hurt him. He wanted help. His plea was so pitiful. Ruby could feel his pain. Baby Annie had all her spooks doing her bidding through no fault of their own.

Ally-Fair Lets Loose

Ms. Ally stood by the stove warming her hands, and Ruby saw her chance. The flash of the diamond glinting in the firelight was a reason to approach. Her hands were outstretched, so Ruby grasped her left hand and asked to see her diamond ring. It was the one that Jesse had given her. Merely a chip, but she had worn it proudly as if it was the Hope Diamond.

Ruby saw in a flash what was going on. Having been so long a spinster, Ally had fallen prey to Baby Annie's power. The specter of Jesse had re-opened her heart, and all the pain and loss had come flooding back. The day after she visited with Jesse, Ally-Fair couldn't even get out of bed. She felt loneliness like never before. The tease of Jesse being back was the cruelest thing ever happening to her. That hope had dissolved when he changed into a hideous corpse.

With nothing to live for, she lay in bed for two days until hunger drove her to get up and eat. It was the night of her second day of not leaving her bed when she went to the kitchen. And there at the table sat her one true love. She yelped and backed away, tears streaming down her face.

Jesse was once again in his full regimental glory. He stood up and took her shaking hand; his touch was warm and inviting. Ally was putty in his hand from then on. She knew in her heart that he wasn't there, but she didn't care: This was better than nothing, and nothing was what she had felt since the day she got the news that he was missing in action.

With those thoughts in her mind, the energy controlling the spooks overtook her; she was now among the army of Baby Annie. As long as she did her bidding, she could have her Jesse. And while she was alone in her house, her youth also came back. She and Jesse could live together as a man and wife. She could have her life once stolen from her.

Ruby saw them dancing in her living room to *You'll Never Know* by Frank Sinatra. She was swaying together and stealing kisses on the sly. They were a beautiful couple. Seeing Ms. Ally's grief being used against her hurt her so much. Jesse was a puppet for Baby Annie, his essence manipulated: All her spooks were powerless against her. Ruby vowed to set them free when she banished Baby Annie.

Suddenly, she was back in the moment and let go of Ally's hand. She didn't seem to notice. She just went on gazing into the fire. Ruby was worried. Leaving her, she went to find her Pap. He was folding up chairs and tidying the little storeroom.

"Pap, I was right. Ms. Ally is possessed and thinks she is spending every night with Jesse. She looks young with him, and they're reliving their past together. It's so unfair. Using her love and grief against her is pitiful."

"I know, honey! That's why we have to stop that old hag. What else can we do?"

"I'm not sure we can do anything. I could free Mr. Wells from her hold on him, but this is different. Ms. Ally wants to be possessed. She has gone to it of her own free will. Mr. Wells didn't. And Vera got something from the bargain, too. That's why I can't break her spell, either. And I suspect Mrs. Purdy has made some deal, too. The ones who have deals with Baby Annie, I won't be able to help," Ruby says this as she puzzles out what to do next. "I might be able to help Sawblade, though. He doesn't want to be under her spell."

"How do you know that?"

"Del had a visit from him last night. I saw what happened when I held Del's hand. Sawblade was talking. Del couldn't understand him, but I could. Sawblade was begging for help and said he didn't mean to kill that boy that Baby Annie had made him. He isn't in control of his actions. He said he just wanted peace. It was pitiful to listen to him. I'm scared, Pap; that vision of those poor kids has haunted me day and night."

"Darlin', I hate it so much that you had to see that. Children's eyes shouldn't witness that. It has chilled me to the bone." Pap says while shaking his head back and forth. There was a racket in the back room, and Matthew stumbled out, looking white in the face and trembling. He'd knocked over several folding chairs and gotten tangled in some cobwebs. He dusted them out of his hair and off his clothes. When he turned and saw us looking at him, he tried to play it off with a smile that didn't reach his eyes.

"What's the matter, Matt?"

Matthew insisted, "Nothing, nothing just got tangled up. I'm fine." But he looked far from fine. He looked terrified. Ruby walked over, grasped his hand, and led him to a chair. When he sat, she closed her eyes, and she saw everything.

Matthew and the Miner

Matthew's tale had been about the mine collapse he'd been in fifty years ago. He'd had to listen to his friends take their last breaths while screaming and begging for help, and he held Buddy Webb's hand as he died. That experience had scarred him in more ways than one. Directly after it happened, he woke up screaming at night and scared his wife half to death.

It was always the same dream: he was coming out of Tunnel Number Nine and came face to face with Buddy. His face was all slack, and his eyes looked dead. He was poised with a sledgehammer, ready to knock out the support beam.

The look on his face showed an inner struggle. His eyes would clear briefly, and he'd say, "Run!" before swinging his pickaxe. Matthew would run as fast as he could but risked succumbing to rock and dirt. Coal dust would crawl down his throat and settle in his lungs and drown his life from him. Instead of him holding

Buddy's hand, it would be the other way around.

This dream would have him clawing his way back to reality, thrashing and screaming. Until he could calm down, he would have to have his wife satisfy him; he wasn't ashamed and might've gone loony if it wasn't for her. Over the years, the nightmare became less and less, and soon, it was a distant memory. That was until he told the story to the Yarn Spinners.

Matthew returned to an empty house the night after the meeting at the 'Nest and read the documents. He was rattled, to be sure, after hearing about the witch and the curse. He missed his wife something terrible, but he did not want to meet her specter. Seeing her cancer-riddled body as she lay dying was horror enough: he prayed she'd stay in heaven where she belonged.

He would get his wish. He saw- not his wife but Buddy Webb. Matthew was out on his porch calling his dogs when he heard a rustling noise from the old well. He had a little chicken coop with three laying hens inside, and he feared it was a fox or a coyote trying to get at them. He grabbed his .22 from behind the back door to investigate.

When he got there, his hens were okay but in a nervous state. Something was out there. He walked over to the well and peered inside. The moonlight shone down, and a face appeared. Thinking it was his reflection, he wasn't frightened. But then a hand reached out and grabbed him. His heart lurched, and he pulled away and ran back to the house. He slammed the door and locked it. He bent over at the knees and tried to get his breath. He felt foolish after the shock wore off, running like a child. He laughed and brushed the whole thing off as his imagination ran wild after all the haunting talks at the meeting.

Upstairs, getting ready for bed with a shower and shave, he went to get a towel from the hall closet. When he opened it, Buddy

Webb stood before him, covered in coal dust, dressed in his work clothes. Matthew pinwheeled his arms and backed straight into the wall, paralyzed with fear.

The Buddy thing advanced on him, and as he did, his face changed. He asked him, "Why didn't you save me? You ran away, and she made me cause that cave-in. Why didn't you stop me?

"You told me to run," said Matthew shakily.

"Yes, and run you did, like a scared little mouse." His face melted and went to ruin.

The side of his head caved in, and his jaw was askew. Most of his teeth were gone, and one shoulder blade was poking through the skin, giving him a hunch-back look. The longer he stood there, the worse he looked. He was decaying as he spoke. "They just left us down there. Nobody came. Why didn't you save me? You held my hand as I died." He lifted a bony skeletal hand revealing green mold around his wedding band.

Matthew was crying and telling him he was sorry. His tears turned to full-on blubbering with the memory of it all. Buddy got up close to his face and, through wobbling teeth, hissed, "She's going to get you. She's coming, and ain't nobody going to stop her. Get ready, chicken shit. Your day is soon." Matthew shut his eyes and continued crying. When he opened them, Buddy was gone and alone again in the hallway. The closet door stood open, and the only thing left of his visitor was a pile of coal dust on the hardwood floor.

Town Elders Meeting: October 25, 1984

The meeting tonight was for the founding families of Mary Luck. Only the heads of the families attended. All but two were of Scottish descent; the Gobles and the Flannerys were Irish. The town was established in 1798, and the folks from neighboring clans in North Carolina traveled through the Cumberland Gap and eventually migrated to Eastern Kentucky. The land reminded many of the Scots of their beloved homeland, and many areas today have names that include Highlands.

The Wells, McKenzie, and Collins clans were the most prevalent throughout the area and comprised much of the founding families. Over the years into the mid-1800s, the town saw an influx of settlers from other parts of Europe, mainly from the Netherlands and Germany. Ties to the old country were kept alive by staying in one place and passing down the family heritage. Recipes for eating and healing went hand in hand. Mothers and daughters learned mending and quilting, but the art of storytelling kept all of this alive. The ability to spin a yarn and keep the listener enthralled was something that these people knew how to do well.

So, when the founding families arrived, the feeling in the air was somber. There hadn't been a meeting like this in fifty years, mainly because the Depression was in full swing, and many were nearly starving. Along with the Scots and Irish were the Germans, Miller, Webb, and Horn. These families could trace their roots to the first settlement in Mary Luck.

When everyone was seated, Wilson McKenzie stood and faced the assembly of friends, neighbors, and relatives. "We've asked all of you here tonight to discuss what's been happening in town since July. With a show of hands, how many of you have had some supernatural experience?" almost every hand went up around the room. Wilson nodded with a look of grave concern on his face. "That's what I figured. Well, folks, there is a reason for it, and I think most of you probably have a pretty good idea of what that is."

Edith Ward stood up and said, "I've seen my Henry nearly every day since Summer. As you all know, he was kilt by a heart attack almost ten years ago. He comes knocking around my backdoor around suppertime, pawing at it like a stray dog." This caused her to break down in tears, and she sat down with her head in her hands.

"I told ya it was true." 'Shiny said with a smug set of his jaw.

"Nobody doubted ye word, 'Shiny." said Edgar Wilcox. He'd had just about enough of 'Shiny as of late. His boasting and acting like he knew it all wasn't sitting well with many folks. People were on edge, and he seemed hell-bent on adding fuel to the fire.

Beechie stood next and said, "I know how you feel, Edith; I've been seeing my late husband and little brother. At first, I thought I had to be dreaming. They appeared outside my window late one night. I got up to drink water, and there they were. They were standing there, looking at me. Before I could even scream, they were gone. I was shaken up and slept with my lamp on for the rest of the night. The next morning, I'd almost forgotten about it until I went outside and saw my brother Timmy sitting on the back stoop. His back was to me, and I didn't recognize him immediately. He was only seven when he died of smallpox, but when he turned around, I knew him immediately. He looked up at me with an angel's face. But then it changed and became riddled with pox sores; lips were peeling and runny with pus. He giggled, put his hand over his mouth, and started pulling out his teeth!"

This bit of the story was all she could get out. She felt over-whelmed with fright and disgust. Birdie Daniels offered her a nip from her flask, but she declined, so Birdie took a swig for her. The crowd was talking all at once, and it was reaching a fever pitch when Wilson finally climbed up on his folding chair and whistled to get everyone's attention.

"Everybody just calm down. Have a seat, and let's discuss what we will do about these spooks haunting us. My Granddaughter Ruby Lee needs to tell you all a story."

Denny Miller shouted, "Cut the shit, Wilson. This ain't no time for storytelling."

"Oh, pipe down, you old blowhard; let the young'un speak,

for Christ's sake," Edith said, and you could tell she was itching to smack him with her greasy spoon.

"Thank you, Edith. If I may be allowed to finish what I was saying, Ruby will tell you something hard for some of you to believe. But please give her your attention and don't interrupt.

Ruby stepped out from the storeroom where she'd been sitting with Willie Joe. She had been nervous about speaking in front of these people, but now she was calm. She went to the front of the room and faced the assembly of people she'd known her whole life. The seance that started it all was the beginning of her tale. By the time she finished, no one could speak. They all just stared at her with their mouths hanging open, catching flies. It was going to be a long night.

Junior Honeycutt exclaimed, "Now, what in the Sam Hell are we supposed to do against a witch?" "Me and mine ain't seen nary a spook that I've heard of. Maybe if ye kept your young'uns on a tighter leash, they'd not be out treatin' with the devil. It looks like this is a McKenzie problem, not a town problem." He finished with a snort.

"Don't you go pointin' fingers at my family, Junior? Your bunch is in this as much as mine." Stated Wilson. Then Matthew Honeycutt stepped up and told his uncle to quit being a horse's ass. "Maybe you ain't seen no spook 'cause you ain't loved nobody enough to have 'em come back and haunt your hateful ass."

"You better shut your mouth, boy, afore somethin' come out you can't take back." Junior threatened. They were getting ready to come to blows when Ruby climbed up on the chair and yelled with all her heart for the wind to come and rattle the windows. With hands held up, she commanded a gale of wind to whoosh inside, rattle the windows, rifle through hair, and send hats flying off heads. This commandment had the desired effect. Everyone hushed, and all eyes were on her.

"We can't fight amongst ourselves. Our greatest weapon is the kinship we have with one another. We should love our land, way of life, and heritage. This witch has hurt us all. If we were to sit down and talk about it, we would see her shadow behind every tragedy. She has cursed us all, and unless we can be on the same side, she will finish us."

She let her eyes roam the room, and in them, she saw fear. "I can't do this by myself. I need you all to be with me. Please give me your strength so I can send her back to hell, where she belongs. We only have a few more days until Halloween. We have to be ready."

Birdie stood up and said, "I'm with you, Red. I have to see my boy put to rest. Tell me what you need, and I'll get it for ye."

"Thanks, Birdie. I know I'll need something." Ruby says with a lop-sided grin. After that, almost everyone spoke words of support, and it felt different in the room. Ruby could tell that as long as they did this as a team, they'd at least have a fighting chance.

"One last thing: she'll wait until Halloween night to exact her revenge. The veil between the living and the dead is thinnest, so she won't need as much energy to run her spooks. She wants to walk the earth again in the flesh to hurt us all. We can't let that happen. Everyone be at the Halloween carnival and get ready for a fight."

October 30, 1984

The day before Halloween dawned cold and dreary, with a steady rain knocking the last brightly colored leaves from the trees. The landscape outside Ruby's window looked like an Ansel Adams picture- everything in shades of gray. This seemed to mirror how she felt on the inside. Not even the fact that she and Willie had been named Harvest King and Queen could brighten her mood. She felt like someone had sucked all the fun and excitement out of her. Ruby carried with her the secret of the hidden spell in the trunk. Not that she was worried that it wouldn't work; it was the price she'd pay for using it. She knew it would be a very steep price.

At school that day, she noticed Vera seemed off. She wasn't snippy or loud, and her face was broken out. She wore a baggy sweatshirt and jeans and looked like her usual self. This tugged at Ruby's heart. She missed her so much and prayed that she would get her friend back if she defeated Baby Annie. As she walked past her desk, she smiled, but V showed up and stuck her tongue out at her, and deflated her moment of hope.

Josie saw the exchange and rolled her eyes, "Ignore her, Ruby. She's a loser." Ruby sat down and didn't even reply. If she did, she might break down in tears. So instead, a steady rain began and lasted through the morning, the outside once again mirroring her inside.

Willie Joe passed her a note that said, "Smile. I love you!" She raised the corners of her mouth in a semblance of a smile, but it didn't reach her eyes.

By lunchtime, the clouds were thinning, and the sun was peeping out now and again to warm up the breeze to around sixty. Ruby and the rest were outside at the picnic table. They were talking about nothing when a voice said, "Why the long faces?" Whitney joined them, and they all turned to stare at her as if she'd grown a second head.

"What?" she asked.

Josie asked, "Um, aren't you supposed to be at school?"

"I didn't feel like going today. Told my Paps I was sick, in a womanly way, and he didn't say another word." She giggled, and the boys turned red. "So, I ask again, why the long faces?"

"I'm just really nervous about tomorrow. I know it will be bad, and I'm afraid I will let the town down."

"Never going to happen. Ruby, you've never lost anything in

your life," said Willie as he rubbed her shoulders like she was Rocky Balboa headed into the last round. "Y'all, just make sure I get that grimoire. If I get too caught up in the spells, I might forget. I have to see Mrs. Purdy tonight. It's been so hard blocking her out of my thoughts so that she won't know my plan. I'm sure she has a deal to doublecross me. She's been asking too many questions and being extra nice."

This news was more than Ruby had said about Mrs. Purdy in a long time. Willie was so worried about Ruby. He was scared to death, too. What would it be like to face down a witch? He had spent the last few nights with his Pappaw, and they had discussed the plan to get rid of Baby Annie. Claude was nervous and jumpy. He looked ten years older than he did three months ago.

This was something else he had to worry about. Thank God his father was back to normal. He didn't seem to remember all the bad things he had done, but he was trying hard to make up for it. Willie knew that his crucial role tomorrow was to protect Ruby. And he was willing to give his life for hers.

The Evening of October 30, 1984

After school, Ruby headed to the 'Bottom to talk to Mrs. Purdy. She would have to guard her thoughts, and that was hard when Baby Annie was all she thought about. When Ruby knocked on the door, Mrs. Purdy was in her ancient rocker reading the grimoire. Mrs. Purdy seemed engrossed by it. Ruby thought she didn't know how to read Gaelic. It looks like she did now.

Ruby sat down on the footstool and waited for her to start her usual line of questioning. A minute went by, and still only a nod of acknowledgment. Finally, Ruby said, "Mrs. Purdy, shouldn't we go over the plan for tomorrow?"

She seemed to snap out of a trance. She looked at Ruby as if she appeared out of thin air. "When did you get here?" she asked. Ruby was at a loss for words. "Mrs. Purdy, I've been here for five minutes. You were reading the grimoire. I didn't think you knew Gaelic."

"I never said that. I know a lot of those words. My Ma taught me before she died when I was about ten."

"Oh, I didn't know that." Said Ruby.

"There are many things you don't know, miss priss." Said Mrs. Purdy with a huff.

Ruby couldn't believe how much she'd changed. Something was different about her. This worried her so much. She had to have that grimoire to read the banishment spell. So she played nice and acted like she wasn't aware she had been betrayed. She just prayed that Mrs. Purdy hadn't traded her soul for power.

"I'm sorry, Mrs. Purdy, I'm just nervous about tomorrow. I had a vision last night, which was the worst. Want me to tell you about it?"

"No, it's too late to do anything about it now. You need to practice your spells and try to produce some fire. You are a fire witch. Born on Beltane, red-headed and named after a firestone. That is your greatest weapon, but try not to burn down the gym with me in it." She said this with a cackle. "I'll bring the Grimoire just in case we need it and keep it in the Fortune Teller's booth." Said Purdy.

Ruby took this as her cue to leave, so she hurried out the door and down the lane in a whirl of Autumn leaves. Her next stop was her Pap's house. She came in the back door, kissed her mamaw, and slurped down a spoon of vegetable soup bubbling on the stove. Mamaw said, "He's in there watching Gunsmoke. Go wake him up and tell him supper is almost ready."

"Okay, I will."

Ruby entered the living room, and Pap was dozing in his recliner. She shook his shoulder, and he jumped, causing the footrest to close, nearly dumping him on the floor. Ruby giggled, and so did

Pap. He was just as jumpy and nervous as she was. "What's going on? Did something happen?"

"No, I just wanted to see if the plan was ready. I need to get something out of the steamer trunk, too."

"The plan is ready. Everyone knows what to do when she shows up. I've put people we can trust at all the exits. Don't you worry about us? You concentrate on sending her back to hell."

"I can't think of anything else. It has been weighing on me since July." Ruby says this with a faraway look, and her Pap sees for the first time how much she has matured. Her eyes were no longer those of an innocent child. She was wizened now and would never be a child again. The whole town was counting on her to save them all. That was too much for someone her age to endure, but she was doing a great job.

Ruby told Pap his supper was ready, and she kissed his cheek. In the back bedroom, she opened the steamer trunk. She carefully slid back the hidden compartment in the lid and found a scroll. When unrolled, it was blank. Elsbeth had said it would only appear when the time was right.

Ruby hoped she could get the grimoire away from Mrs. Purdy. There wasn't a doubt in her mind that Mrs. Purdy had switched sides. She was sure she was promised something in return. Probably the ability to read the spells and cast them. But if what she knew about Baby Annie was true: she'd never honor her promises.

Scroll in hand, she goes home and eats her supper of pork chops and fried potatoes. When the dishes are washed and put away, she goes to her room and lies on her bed. A light wind blows, and rain follows, pelting on the window, lulling her to sleep.

The first thing in this vision is Henry Ward walking through his house, going to get a beer from the fridge. He looks out the kitchen window, and there is his old pal Frank Jenkins. The only thing was, he died when he was ten years old- he fell out of the tree house they were building and broke his neck. This was made evident by the way his head lolled on his shoulder. There were bluish veins on his forehead. He grinned, and his lower jaw dropped and became unhinged from his face. He pointed at him and said, "Henry, it was your fault I died. You pushed me." Henry was in a state of fright he had never known.

He'd forgotten about Franky, but it was all returning to him now. They were in the treehouse, and he pushed him. They were arguing over a baseball card. Trying each other, Henry pushed too hard, and Franky fell over the edge and was gone. No one saw what happened, so he left Franky dead on the ground. It had been an accident, but he thought no one would believe him. He had never told a soul, not even Edith.

That memory hit him like a locomotive; shame overwhelmed him. But when the thing that had been Franky opened the window and came inside, Henry's heart gave a final pump, and down he went: a heart attack that happened so fast he didn't know what hit him. He lay on the floor, and the Franky thing leaned down in his face, and that was the last thing Henry ever saw.

Ruby saw all of this, even their memories, like a movie. Next, she saw a hillside littered with bodies of soldiers. Ruby could hear gunfire and cannon blasts. Then she saw a U.S. Soldier come over the hill. He looked like he was dazed. Close up, she read his name, "McCoy." This had to be Jessup, but what was he doing? He was walking right into a war zone.

The bullets were whizzing right by him. Then Ruby saw why he was now running towards his doom. There was Miss Ally. She was standing just a little way off, wearing a wedding dress. Jesse was calling to her, but she just kept beckoning him. When the first three bullets hit him, he appeared not even to feel it. He was almost close enough to touch her hand when a gut shot brought him to his knees. She leaned down to him, and her face changed into that of a hag. Baby Annie cackled as a headshot ended his life. His dying seconds were thoughts of his one true love: Ally-Fair.

The following vision was back to Mary Luck. A young girl stood on her porch, and Ruby saw it must be Super Sally. She saw her little sister Polly walking home up the lane, and then she saw a humped-over little woman suddenly appear out of the brush and brambles. "Hello, child. Can I offer you a treat?" Polly was a little scared of this ugly older woman but had a sweet tooth.

During the Depression, no one had money for frivolous things like candy. The older woman pulled a large red sour ball from her pocket. It looked delicious. Polly reached for it instinctively, but the hag pulled it away. "I just need you to do something for me." "I don't have any money, but I can help you do some chores."

The woman leaned down and whispered in her ear, "All you have to do is eat this candy in front of your sister. If she asks for a lick, tell her no. Then I want you to swallow it whole. It will melt in your throat, and she'll be jealous." The woman tittered, and her eyes gleamed. "Golly gee, Ma'am, I can do that lickety-split." Polly's eyes stayed fixed on the candy.

Once it was in her hand, it felt hot and heavy. When she got to the porch, she showed it to Sally and said, "I don't think I'd eat that if I were you. You don't know that woman. Where did she even come from?"

"I don't know, and I don't care; you're just jealous that you didn't get one." She plopped the candy in her mouth, and the sugary goodness filled her senses with delight.

Sally watched as Polly wallowed the giant candy in her mouth. "Can I have a lick?" she asked.

"No way, it's mine, all mine," said Polly.

To prove she wouldn't give her any, Polly swallowed the candy, it lodged in her throat, cutting off her airway. She clawed at her neck as the candy bulged out. Sally started beating her on the back, but nothing was helping. Polly was turning blue, and Sally began to scream. Suddenly, there were people on the porch. Her daddy grabbed Polly and turned her upside down to shake the candy loose. Nothing helped. Polly was dead at seven years old. Sally never knew that the older woman was Baby Annie.

The scene changed again; she was in the garage with Beechie's husband, Bascom. He was working on his 1965 Buick Skylark. The year was now 1973, and Bascom was under the hood, trying to check the timing belt. It was way down in the engine and hard to get to. Bascom wasn't tall, so he had to climb up on the bumper to reach the belt. He had one arm on it when someone grabbed his other hand and pulled him face down into the engine. His eye came a hair from being put out by a piston.

He turned to see who had his hand and was so horrified that he knocked the hood prop loose, and it fell on top of him. His neck twisted, but he could still see the horror. It was his great-grandmother. She was the meanest woman he had ever known. She used to whip him with a belt for no reason at all. She'd jack his jaw for anything he said, insisting he was sassing her. He was ten years old when she died, which was one of his childhood's happiest days. He hated her, and she, him.

So now, seeing her face bloated and rotten, he didn't think as an adult that he could feel so terrified. She reached in and grabbed his nose. He tried to squirm away from her, but her hand had a death grip. The final blow came when she, with superhuman strength, jumped on the hood and mashed his head like a rotten pumpkin. His last thoughts were of total horror.

The last vision was of two car wrecks. The first one she saw was Butchie driving around the lake. It was odd for her to see him as normal . He had a great day, revving his engine and flirting with girls. As he sped up on Devil's Curve, he saw everyone he knew and wanted to show off. In the middle of the curve, he saw a hideous older woman. He turned the wheel to avoid hitting her and slammed straight into another car. He was ejected out of his t-tops and impaled on a tree branch. Once again, the culprit was Baby Annie.

She pulled the same trick on 'Shiny's family. His mother, Gladys, drove his wife, Cheryl, home from church. They were on a straight stretch of highway when, out of nowhere, an older woman ran in front of them. When Gladys swerved to miss her, they plunged over the river bank and into the Big Sandy River. They were trapped in the car and drowned.

Ruby saw these tragedies in an instant. She woke up frightened and weak. Unbeknownst to her, though, she had transferred these visions to the loved ones still alive. They now knew what had happened to their kin. The last of the daylight was melting away, and soon darkness would fall, and in a few hours, the witching hour would bring with it the thinning of the veil. Samhain was almost here, and so was the showdown between good and evil.

Halloween:
The Day of Reckoning

It was finally here! The dreaded day of all days. Ruby awoke feeling refreshed. She had slept for almost ten hours, needing every ounce of her strength to go toe-to-toe with Baby Annie. Looking in the mirror, she appeared changed. Her skin seemed to glow, and her eyes were the greenest they'd ever been. It felt like electricity was running through her veins, like a vibration that emitted energy, causing the air to hum like someone cranked up her elemental power to the highest degree. She felt like she had a fever without the side effects of feeling weak. The water in her body made her movements fluid, and the food she digested made her physically strong. When she left for school, she felt like she was floating in the air. The wind lifted her off her feet and carried her along.

When she walked into the classroom, every eye turned to her, and there were audible gasps as she passed by. Ruby was puzzled by this attention. She knew she felt different, but why was everyone staring at her as if she'd grown a second head?

She turned to Willie, "Why is everybody staring at me?"

"Because you look so beautiful. I can't take my eyes off of you. I feel like I'm hypnotized." He says.

Even Josh seemed captivated, "I don't dole out compliments, so me saying anything should tell you something is up. If I couldn't be around you and look at you, I'd go into a deep depression," states Josh.

Instantly Willie shot him a look, "Yeah, well, you can look but don't touch bud."

Ruby blushed from head to toe and looked down at her feet. Thinking that whatever made her so desirable had to do with her ability to command The Four Elements. Sitting in a classroom all day would be more than she could handle. When Mr. Music came into the room, he was mesmerized. She told him she was going home, and he looked utterly saddened. Ruby quickly left the room and stayed away from everyone as she left. She didn't want any more attention.

The Tree of Knowledge

When Ruby got outside, her soul felt relieved to be out in the open. She knew instinctively where she needed to go. Her favorite tree still had most of its autumn red leaves. It glowed, and the wind ruffled the leaves so that they seemed to shimmer. Ruby sat down and melded into the tree. She closed her eyes, breathed deeply, and opened her mind and spirit. The sensation she felt was indescribable, like every neuron in her body was firing simultaneously.

Cascus spoke, "Hello, Ruby Red. You have heeded all the warnings and are preparing for a battle. I offer you one more word of advice. Deep down at the core of your being, you must believe you can win. When you speak the words, make sure you mean them. That is a powerful spell. It harkens back to ancient times before Christianity reached the Celts and Druids. They learned it from the elves. Only then, use it if you must. But know this: It doesn't come free. There will be a price to pay for using it. The law of nature keeps the scales balanced between good and evil. You can't have one without the other."

Ruby listened and didn't interrupt, even though she had a lot of questions. She tried to commit to memory everything Cascus said. When the tree was finished talking, Ruby asked, "Will I still be able to talk to you after today?"

"That will depend on how much magic you have left. It will take everything you've got to bring down a spirit like her. Misery and grief are what she feeds on. That is why she haunts the townsfolk with their loved ones. Grief was pouring out all over this town, and she used that to grow stronger. Love is the counterpoint to hate. Surround yourself with people you love and who love you, too. Kinship and friendship will boost your magic. You have all the tools you need to defeat her. Now it's up to you. So run along, Ruby Red, and do what you were born to do."

Ruby woke up, and the tree was silent. She wanted to ask more questions, but there was no time. She had to go home, prepare for the Halloween parade, and find a place to hide the secret scroll. It would not be suitable for Mrs. Purdy to get her hands on it. Or even worse, Baby Annie.

Preparations

When Ruby arrived home, her mom had just returned from decorating the gym. Her mother was experiencing her allure. She snapped out of it, though, and started barking orders. "Go in the bathroom, plug the hot rollers, scrub your face, and clean your fingernails. I'm going to steam-iron your dress. So hop to it."

When she was as clean as she could get, her mom came in and used two sets of rollers to curl her hair. Seeing as how this was a special occasion, she could wear mascara and tinted lip gloss. Her dress was emerald green velvet to match her eyes. Tea length with three-quarter sleeves, an empire waist with a satin sash tied on the side with a crinoline underneath that made it fluffy. Ruby had always wanted a poofy and frilly dress, and this was the epitome of girliness.

Once she was ready, except for putting on her dress and taking out her rollers, Ruby sat outside and soaked in the surrounding nature. It was Halloween, the wind crisp and the sky cloudless and blue. Birds were chatting, squirrels were twittering, and Ruby knew what they said: "Run and hide!" She missed the rest of their conversation because a dog howled and broke her concentration. But what she heard was enough to put her on high alert.

Today is the day that the veil between this world and the next is said to be at its thinnest. Since Ruby opened the door in July, all kinds of spooks had resurrected. She suddenly felt a chill. Someone was walking around in the cemetery. Then she heard the unmistakable laughter of Jarvis Spears. He was running around in circles, hooting and hollering. It wasn't even four o'clock, and the game was on. She left the swing in the backyard and was inside before it stopped moving. The look on her face told her mother that things were getting started.

Kate spoke nervously, "Come over here, Ruby, and let's take out those curlers." The curls came out beautifully and hung in waves of scarlet. Next came the putting on of the dress and matching green pumps with a one-inch heel. When it was time for pictures, Ruby looked like a princess. She took pictures with her sisters and her mom and dad. Rosie had been the Harvest Queen, so she gave her some pointers on how to sit and walk in the procession.

Finally, it was time to go, but Ruby just had one more adjustment: Tucked inside her bra strap was the secret scroll- her trump card. She hoped she wouldn't have to use it. Ruby wasn't sure she wanted to pay the heavy price, whatever it may be.

Once all the Collins ladies were in the Jeep and ready to go, Kate took a deep breath and a moment of silence. She looked each of her girls in the eyes and told them how much she loved them. They said in unison, "We love you too, Mommy."

With a forced smile, she started the engine and said, "Here we go."

The Halloween Parade

It was a tradition in Mary Luck to have a Halloween parade so that the kids could show off their costumes. The harvest king and queen rode in Victor Sturgill's horse-drawn carriage and were the parade's leaders. The fire truck, driven by Richard Collins, brought up the rear carrying the little kids. All the other kids walked behind the carriage in costumes while people came to their gates to hand out candy. Until last year, Denver O'Connor would follow along playing the bagpipes. He wasn't excellent, but everyone appreciated the effort. But sadly, he fell and broke his hip, so he sat on his porch and watched all the kiddos go by, wishing for his youth to return. He was glad to be alive but thought getting old shouldn't hurt so much.

Before the parade began, the coronation occurred on the park bandstand. When Willie Joe set eyes on Ruby Lee, he was astounded. She was the most beautiful girl he had ever seen. And she was his girlfriend. He wondered how in the world he had gotten so lucky. Ruby took in Willie Joe's attire. He wore black pants, a crisp white button-down shirt, a paisley green tie, and a black sport coat. He was the most handsome she had ever seen him. His eyes sparkled, and his teeth gleamed white against his still-tanned face. He was flawless.

They joined hands and walked up to the stage. Everyone clapped, oohed, and ahhed. It was a moment Ruby had dreamed of for years, and now that it was here, better than she imagined it could be. Principal Ward placed the tiara on her head, a perfect fit. Willie had to bend down to accept his crown. Then Ruby and Willie were draped in the ornamental robes that had been hand quilted with tartans from all the clans of the founding families. They were cherished items only worn by the king and queen once a year and stowed in an airtight trunk for the rest of the year. Some pieces on the robe were two hundred years old, and wearing the priceless heirloom was a true honor.

Crowned and robbed, Willie helped Ruby into the carriage, which, too, was a relic from another time. It was said to be from the Victorian era. It looked shabby now, but Ruby could imagine that, at one time, it was lovely. Black with red plush seats, two ornate lanterns were on either side, but neither had glass. The cloth seats looked tattered, and a spring was poking through. From a distance, though, it cut quite a figure. Ruby had wanted to ride in this carriage since she first saw it.

She vowed she would enjoy this moment and this experience with Willie Joe. Once the parade was en route, Ruby smiled and waved at all the people of her small piece of the world. She felt the love and happiness flowing from every house. The kids were giving off so much positive energy it was hard to handle it. Ruby soaked it all in because the crisp air became cold as they neared the gym, and the sun crept slowly behind the mountains. And with that temperature change, the whole vibe of the town went instantly from happiness to fear. Halloween was here, and so was Baby Annie. Ruby could feel her, even though she couldn't see her yet.

When they arrived and exited the carriage, someone ushered them into the gym for more applause and pomp. Principal Ward immediately returned the robes, folded them perfectly, and slipped them into zippered plastic bags. Ruby was glad to be rid of it; it reminded her of her vision when she was Baby Annie as a child, and everyone was wearing stinky kilts.

Ruby and Willie went to find friends, now that their duties as harvest king and queen were over. Josh wasn't hard to find; he stood a head taller than most people there and dressed as Frankenstein's monster. The carnival was in full swing. Screams were coming from the spook house, and music from the cakewalk. Popping balloons from the dart game, kids squealing at the fishpond, and basketballs bouncing at the ball toss. There was a line to get in to see the fortune teller, which was Mrs. Purdy, of course. Ruby passed by, stuck her head in the door, and got her attention. All she said was, "Did you bring it?" She nodded yes.

With all the sounds and scents and her senses on high alert, Ruby was getting dizzy and needed fresh air. She grabbed Whitney and Josie, dressed as scarecrows, and dragged them outside. Ruby was shaking but calm. It was more like a vibration. She seemed energized. Her friends looked at her worriedly, then Whitney spoke up as if a light bulb had just gone off in her head, "So, like, I scoped out old Purdy. I followed her here and saw her put the grim thing in this old gnarly-looking satchel. She put it on like a crossbody purse, but I still think we could get it from her if need be. I went to the school and swiped a pair of scissors to cut through that cloth strap so Josie could sneak over and snatch it up." They high-fived each other and giggled.

Suddenly, Ruby got cold. Despite the laughter, she had to ensure they knew how serious tonight was. They could die! Josh and Willie joined them outside, and Ruby gave her warning. "I have to tell you all something. I'm not sure how things will go tonight, but there is a good chance someone could get hurt or even killed. I love each of you, so if you want to bow out, now is the time. Once Baby Annie shows herself, we could get trapped inside, and I don't know if I can beat her." She looked at them, searching their eyes.

Willie took her hand, "Ruby, I won't leave your side."

"I know; I just don't want you to get hurt because of me."

"Not gonna happen, 'cause you're gonna beat her raggedy ass!" Ruby started to smile but froze as she heard the cackle: She was here. The witch had come for her revenge.

Ruby's senses went into overdrive. A swirl of leaves was around her feet; the wind lifted her hair away from her face. Her eyes brightened, and her whole body was humming with vibration. She looked at her friends one last time and led them into the gym with her head held high.

Samhain: The Showdown

When Ruby walked through the door, the sounds of the carnival stopped. The tang of magic in the air was sour. It was like someone had pushed pause, but still, people could move. The original families' descendants were the only ones still mobile. The yarn spinners, Birdie, Ally-fair, Beechie, Edith, 'Shiney, Super Sally and Vera. In short, everyone who had taken part in the burning of Baby Annie.

Ruby nearly floated to the center of the gym. Oddly, no one approached her, not even her mother. Her body was shimmering with vibration. S he had turned into someone else. Baby Annie came out of the fortune-telling room with Mrs. Purdy. Ruby expected as much and didn't let her disappointment show. Purdy met her eyes and shrugged as if to say sorry about your luck. Being a traitor or wels her was in the family's genes.

Claude and Wilson took one look at Baby Annie and Mrs. Purdy and stood shaking their heads with dismay. Willie Joe headed toward them, spewing a string of swears, but Ruby stopped him with a wrist flip. "Not yet, Willie Joe."

Baby Annie crowed, "So you showed up. I wasn't sure if you would or not."

"I'm here, alright. I'm going to send you back to hell, where you belong. Your reign of terror is over!" Ruby said with pride.

Baby Annie threw back her head and cackled.

"You think you can stop me?" I'm almost two hundred years old, little girl. I'll eat you for breakfast."

Suddenly, there was a movement in the crowd. The spooks were coming: Butchie, Rebecca Jo, Jesse, Mrs. Phillips, Sawblade, Jarvis, Bascom, Polly, Buddy, and the green lady. They all came shambling through, decayed and horrid. Each went to their respective loved ones and guarded them so they couldn't help Ruby.

The three little kids, Davey, Morgan, and Zeke, came into view, and they were the worst thing anyone had ever seen. Purple and putrid, intestines dragging the floor. Davey tripped over his own innards , and when he stood back up, his liver fell out, and he picked it up and ate it. This atrocity made Super Sally and Kate vomit up their dinner.

Beechie bawled, but Bascom laughed his head off. Everyone was living their hell, but their misery and fear were feeding Baby Annie, and she was getting stronger by the minute. Ruby decided to try something. Approaching Butchie, she put her hand on his arm. He recoiled as if she had bit him, but she held on and said, "Be free of the hold on you. Remember the love you have for your mother." Suddenly a light appeared in his eyes; he looked at Birdie and said, "Momma, I've missed you so much." Birdie broke down completely. Butchie looked as he did in life; it was him, not some puppet mastered by a vengeful witch. Next, she went to Rebecca Jo, and the same thing happened. Claude was beaming and crying. Then it was Vera's turn. Before she could pull away, Ruby held l onto her and released the spell. Vera instantly went back to her old self. She hugged Ruby so tight and couldn't stop apologizing. They were both crying and hugging each other. Ruby was so grateful to have Vera back. She then went to each of the spooks and changed them back.

Last was Sawblade. He was snarling and gnashing his teeth, but Ruby went right on up to him. He grabbed her throat, but touching her brought him out of his possession. She held onto both his arms with her hands. Suddenly a man stood where once was a beast. Sawblade hadn't been human in more than a century. He looked withered but whole. Ruby still had a hold of him, and she said, "I release you from your curse. Be at peace." The relief of being free had never been more apparent to anyone's face. He turned his face heavenward and closed his eyes. "Bless you, child. I will forever be in your debt." He then lifted off his feet, became a vapor, and vanished.

All the while, Baby Annie was searching the grimoire. Mrs. Purdy had brought it, but not for Ruby. With all the joyful reunions, feelings of love were everywhere. Ruby felt all-powerful and believed that her actions embodied what the tree meant by using good to defeat evil. Then all hell broke loose. Baby Annie started chanting, and a hole opened in the ceiling. The moon was shining, and the stars were out. Her voice got louder, and everyone in the gym except for the originals suddenly turned into monstrosities. Faces that were runny with one eye in their forehead, unhinged jaws, humped back with bleeding sores, missing appendages: A horror show that just kept getting worse. Mrs. Perry's false teeth fell out when her jaw let loose, and Delmer Jennings picked them up and crammed them down his throat, where they became lodged in his esophagus and were visible on the outside.

Everyone Ruby freed was back to being monsters, and she felt defeated. Then she saw the grimoire and knew it was her chance. She looked at Whitney and gave her the cue. She and Josie crept up behind Purdy. How she did it, Ruby would never know. She had eyes in the back of her head, which was all she could figure. When Whitney pulled out the scissors, Purdy snatched her up like a rattlesnake on a squirrel. Whitney screamed as Purdy dug her filthy fingernails into her skin.

Remembering she had the scissors, she brought them around, but Purdy was again expecting her move and managed to pry them from her hand. Josie finally snapped awake and grabbed Purdy around the neck, choking her. She released Whitney to claw at Josie. Willie Joe came in quickly, wrestled the book away from her, and brought it to Ruby.

Baby Annie was gaining strength but using a lot of power, keeping the monstrosities going and the ceiling open. Ruby opened the book, and the pages turned on their own to lead her to the one she needed. Before Ruby could read it, magic snatched the book away and flew to Mrs. Purdy. She, in turn, sent it flying to Baby Annie, but Josh stepped in and intercepted it. He tossed it to Willie, and he threw it frisbee style to Ruby, who caught it and quickly opened it up. She pulled out the scroll, and there was no time to waste. She had to open up a portal.

She unrolled the scroll, and the spell appeared in shiny gold writing.

Fuscus proferet. et vocem ejus erit reddere pretium ejus.

Ruby memorized it and said it as loud as she could. The wind rose with her words, and a hole ringed with blackness and fiery brimstone appeared on the gym floor. The base became a flaming death pit. The witch was surprised that Ruby could perform a spell of that magnitude. "Just how do you know how to do this? Petunia, did you teach her this?"

"No, no. I didn't know she could do this either. She tricked me into letting her see the grimoire. I'd never go against my kin."

"Sure you would. I know I would if it helped me. It's just in our blood. And to prove it, I'll be taking back that power I give ye. I got what I needed from you, so be gone with ye." Baby Annie made a shooing motion with her hand, and Purdy seemed to shrivel up like a wilted flower.

"All of you worthless sniveling fools never knew I was the Grim Reaper. Every misery and grief you've had has been because of me." She spoke triumphantly.

Ruby pulled from her pocket a plastic baggie that held a viscous-looking membrane. "That's where you're wrong. I have been given the gift of sight." The caul was her ace in the hole, and she prayed it would give her the power she needed.

Mrs. Purdy suddenly jerked to attention, "Ruby Lee, you have to eat it." Ruby was so in her element that she didn't even flinch. She opened the bag and drank down her birthright. Light shone from her eyes as she glowed.

She told the witch, "I've had visions of all of your wrongdoings and shared them with everyone here. They now know what you did, and it's time for you to pay the piper." Her eyes flicked around, and for the first time, there was fear on her face. She didn't know that Ruby knew about the piper.

Ruby opened up the grimoire and began the spell. The language was foreign to her, but she rattled it off like it was her native tongue. The pit spewed, globs of molten lava splattering all around. Baby Annie turned and raised her hands skyward and called on the water to put out the flames. It rained in torrents, and the pit went out. Ruby immediately called on the wind to drive the rain away. The wind fed the fire, and Ruby used her enthusiasm to ramp up the fire. She repeated the spell, and suddenly, a familiar shape emerged from the pit. It was solid black and shimmered as it moved. It had no mouth but spoke just the same.

"Who is the caller of my name?" It asked.

"Me," Ruby said cautiously.

"Why?"

"I was told to read that spell to send this witch back to hell."

"Witch? Where would she be?"

Ruby pointed her finger at Baby Annie, and she cringed.

"Aw. Yes, it's been a while, hag. I believe you owe me three children. You killed the ones you promised me. I wanted them alive."

"I didn't think you'd mind if I took their lives. You got their souls."

"Hold thy tongue. It spews nothing but lies."

He struck out with a hand made of steel and clenched her throat. He lifted her off the floor and shook her like a ragdoll. He seemed to grow more significant by the second.

"Now, fire child, I'll rid you of this plague!"

"But, there's the price. I require three souls for my help. Since you summoned me, you choose who goes."

Ruby felt her stomach churn. She immediately started shaking her head no, but remembered Elsbeth's warning. His blank face loomed over her, and she couldn't, for the life of her, make this decision. Then Mrs. Purdy stood up and volunteered, "I'll go so that maybe, in time, Ruby and the town can forgive me." Ruby gasped. As bad as she'd been to her, she didn't want to send her to hell.

"I require one more!"

Then, to her horror, Vera Sue Wilcox stepped forward and said, "I'll go. I love you, Ruby." And just like that, they were absorbed into the black mass and sank to the floor. Ruby and Vera's uncle and parents screamed an unearthly cry. Ruby ran to the spot where the hole had been and beat on the floor. It all happened so fast that she didn't have time to stop it. Ruby grabbed the grimoire, but every single page was blank.

Her heart broke into a million pieces. Her mother tried and tried to console her, but nothing helped. Everyone was in tears. The spell broke, and the gym returned to normal. All the spooks were gone. And so was Vera. Later that night, after she had calmed down, she realized Elsbeth showed her the vision of The Piper so she would know how to get him to get rid of Baby Annie. The spell that she read was the one that summoned him. Elsbeth's warning was so very correct. It was a steep, steep price to pay. Too steep.

The End

Epilogue

Mary Luck, KY
Two Weeks Later

It's been two weeks since Halloween when Vera and Mrs. Purdy disappeared. The town has banded together to cover up the truth of what happened. The townspeople decided that it was a community tragedy that should be handled by the original families, seeing as how they all witnessed it. Vera's parents were distraught but saw reason knowing no one outside the town would understand. Vera was reported as a teenage runaway when all was said and done. They initially sent out a search party, but now, two weeks later, the town has decided she may return. Ruby isn't so sure.

As for Mrs. Purdy, out of her ten living children, only one showed up looking for her. Someone told her Mrs. Purdy had run off with an old flame. Shirley tried to make a fuss, but then she saw the advantage of her mother being gone. She took up residence at the house in the 'Bottom and claimed to have the gift of sight and was going to hang out her shingle as a fortune teller. The older people rolled their eyes and let it be. The truth would surely open up a can of worms that would never close again, just like Pandora's box.

If you could associate that word with Mary Luck, things had returned to normal. Thanksgiving was just around the corner, and colored pictures of turkeys replaced the grinning orange pumpkins in the windows of the elementary school. Birdie announced she was back on the wagon and try to straighten herself up. Knowing that Butchie was at rest had spurred her to be a better person, and who knows? She might once again darken the doorway of the Freewill Baptist Church. Heaven, help us!

Again, Miss Ally wore a severe bun and glasses perched on her nose. She had a faraway look in her eyes as if she were going through the motions. Ruby went to see her at the store, but it was closed. According to 'Shiny, she hadn't been in that day. Ruby got an icy chill down her spine. She hopped on her bike and rode by Ms. Ally's house. Maybe she was sick or needed help. Her house was shuttered and locked, and no sound came from inside.

Ruby crossed the street to Claude's house and knocked on the door in a rat-a-tat cadence that shook the door in its frame. Claude opened the door and took in the vision of Ruby Lee. Her face was as pale as milk, and the fervent look in her eyes told Claude to grab his coat and ask her while putting it on, "What's the matter, child?"

"Mr. Wells, have you seen Ms. Ally lately? She didn't open the store today, and her house is closed up tight as the bark on a tree."

"I don't believe I have seen her in a day or two. Just calm down; maybe she's taken ill."

He says this without believing his own words. He is suddenly shaking and none too steady on his feet. Ruby senses this, and she takes his arm as they cross the road. Walking up on her porch, it's as though they are crossing a barrier. One thick with foreboding and sorrow.

They knocked on her door and looked in all the windows but couldn't see inside. Claude pulled out his ring of keys, thumbed through them, and inserted the front door key. Ruby was astonished that he had a key. He just shrugged and turned the knob. Gertrude and Dennis from next door had come over, and 'Shiny was leaning against the Chevy parked on the street, all eager to see if there would be any action.

Claude told Ruby to wait outside, but she wasn't having that. "I've seen enough lately, so I can handle this."

"I suppose you're right. Just get behind me."

As they entered the living room, everything was as it should be. They called out to her and got no response. They trod slowly and silently into the kitchen and found it like the living room. Not even a dirty coffee cup in the sink.

The bathroom was next and as they neared the door, Ruby thought she might throw up. But again, it was empty. The last room was the bedroom. Claude turned the knob and there on the bed was Ms. Ally. Dressed in her wedding dress with her hair fanned out around her, she looked like a picture. Claude ran over and shook her, in vain. Ruby knelt down and picked up the empty bottle of Quaaludes laying on the floor by the bed. On the nightstand was a note.

I know you will all think that I took the easy way out, but life without Jessup is not one I want to be a part of. I want to be with him and if that isn't possible here, I'll go and find him elsewhere. Please don't pity me. I'll be with my one true love. Bury me in this dress and don't have a big to do. I hope to see you all one day in the big hereafter.

Ally-fair Wells-McCoy

About the Author

Katherine Hale Stringfield

The Mary Luck Tales

Born and raised in the mountains of Eastern Kentucky in Shotgun Holler, Katherine's love of books began while reading The Little House on the Prairie series. Her love of writing took off in college when she supported herself by writing papers for fellow students. A professed jack of all trades, writing her first novel came later in life and so at the age of fifty it became a reality. Having a captive target audience in the student body at the high school where she was a full time substitute teacher made her dream of publishing a book a reality.

She now lives in Berea, KY with her husband and daughter.

ABOUT THE AUTHOR

Katherine Hahn-Singleton

Made in the USA
Monee, IL
22 October 2023